A Critical Tangent

Moonlight and Murder
Book One

REILY GARRETT

Acknowledgments

To Siobhan Caughey, for reading through my rough drafts and not laughing. Your perceptions are spot on and always appreciated in delving into a character's mind. First drafts are always the roughest, but where changes in a character's direction takes root.

To Dr. Chris Terrell and Jean Coldwell, your insights into character development and plot points helped the story run smoothly. It takes a lot of time to go through an entire manuscript. Time is a most precious commodity of which we never seem to have enough.

To Laurie Sickles for also helping to shape my characters and pointing out things that just don't work. Thank you.

To Rosie Amber for an in-depth assessment of character and plot, thank you for all your help.

To my editor, RE Hargrave, thank you for your tireless work on this project, and for seeing the things that I missed.

To Jim Benoit of Cajun Arms in West Chester, Pennsylvania for conferring and helping differentiate technicalities between law enforcement agencies in PA. Sharing specific details of Cajun Arms tactical training courses. Your level of professionalism and in-depth understanding of human nature is insightful.

WWW.CAJUNARMS.COM
610-399-1188

To my readers, each one of you who selects and reads one of my books, thank you for the opportunity to share my work. If you've enjoyed it, please consider leaving a review. They are the best way to help your author share her work.

Prologue

"Aw, Keiki, if I could find the *fun* button in your brain, I'd switch it to permanent on. You're always working. You should've come hiking with me. Fresh air would do you good." Shelly *tisked* then smiled. "Not that there's anything wrong with loving your work, but you have an old man psyche trapped in a young woman's body."

"Thanks, Shelly, but no." Keiki manipulated her latest drone to perform the simple but intricate task of picking a flower. The outing did sound nice, but Shelly needed private time to mourn the loss of her sister.

"The next time you fall asleep working, I'm going to town with my entire set of permanent markers." Shelly held her hand out to accept the offered blossom pinched from its low-growing stem and giggled. "You'd look good with cat whiskers and exotic pink eyes."

"Test that theory, and I'll replace your scented shampoo with baby oil." The threat of laying waste to makeup or hair products usually ended any debate. "I'm about out of battery life. Can you bring it in?"

"Sure. Turn off the motors."

Damn. The soft whirr from the small rotors altered in pitch as they shut down one by one.

Malevolent shadows crawled along the edges of the surrounding woods, receding with the rising sun. Even from miles away, Keiki's skin crawled.

"I hear something." Shelly rested a palm beside her woodland flower plot to lean forward.

Through remote viewing, Keiki watched her doppelganger freeze then tilt her head to the side, wrinkles of concern marring her forehead.

"What?" Thanks to the hilly terrain, two-way communication crackled off and on.

4

"Huh, must be a rabbit or squirrel. Anyway, as I was saying. Become a spinster with hundreds of drones instead of cats. I'll keep you in contact with the outside world." Again, Shelly paused and tilted her head as if listening to something off in the distance.

"Hey, why don't you come back now and we'll have breakfast?"

"Yeah, okay. I'm coming. Can you extend the range on this thing's transmission ability? The video feed isn't so great." Lips nibbled between her teeth marked Shelly's worry when she leaned forward to whisper.

"I'm working on it. What's wrong?

"I'm kinda spooked. Something doesn't feel right." Her fingers' wobble shook the drone's body. It listed sideways with a squeak.

"Shelly?"

"I'm fine. It's just my clumsiness in challenging gravity... Oh, about the frat party tonight, wanna go?"

The viewing angle changed again as Shelly stood.

"No. And before you start, I do have fun. I just don't have time to party with you and Gabby. *Some* people stay focused on their future," Keiki grumbled as she monitored her prototype's efficiency on her laptop and sipped a caramel latte.

A distinctive metallic snap coincided with her device's struggle to function.

"Oops. Sorry, Keeks. An arm broke off above your tracker thingy. I'll stick it in my pocket, and you can glue it back on, or whatever. Do we still have audio and visual feed?"

"Yeah, just bring the rest of it back in one piece, okay?" Keiki groaned, predicting the hour it would take to fix. "Careful. That thing is one of two prototypes, but that one gets the best reception." Keiki set her coffee down, the cup tilting when settling on her friend's access card. "Oops, your work ID now has a brown ring on it. You really should be more careful with it."

"How rude of me to leave it where you'd drink your coffee."

"That's why we get along so well. We think alike. I'll stick it on my dresser. It'll be safer there."

"If you'd stop losing yours, you wouldn't have to borrow mine... shit. Something is coming." Fear coiled through Shelly's voice. "Sounded like a branch snapping down the trail. Something big and heavy."

"Is it a black bear? You know what to do."

A silent moment passed.

On screen, the image shook.

"Uh... who are you? What do you want?" Shelly's wrist rotated, tilting the angle of the drone's camera to the trampled weeds.

Through the odd angle, booted feet shuffled backward to leave two furrowed tracks. No one had ever intruded on her friend's private sanctuary.

"I'm a messenger, here to show your boss what happens when he refuses to work with us. We tried being nice. Now it's my way."

Miles downgrading the audio quality to mediocre didn't soften the cruel bite of a temper coming unhinged.

Metal clinking preceded the thud of her drone landing in the meadow's weeds. Its lens picked up nothing but decaying fall foliage.

There was a slight pause, as if warring factions sized up the competition before a fight. Keiki's imagination conjured worst possible scenarios. "What's going on, Shelly?"

"This is private property. My father—" Her words drifted off under deep gravelly laughter.

Shuffling leaf litter and the erratic thump of flesh striking flesh detailed unseen events. Interrupted grunts and thin cries signaled the attack in progress.

The higher octave and tremble in her friend's cries caused Keiki's fingers to fumble in activating and hovering the small drone in order to see the assailant. "Shelly? Who's there with you? What the fuck is going on?"

Private property signposts didn't prevent poachers and others from wandering around the secluded, wooded area. It wasn't feasible any of their college friends knew about the private and sacred place Shelly honored her departed sibling.

Although the sounds of skirmish lessened, Keiki's pulse kicked into overdrive. Her shaking fingers couldn't tap the right keyboard commands to clarify her friend's circumstances. Decreasing sounds of the struggle magnified the fear filling her mind.

"Huh. Are you wearing contacts? Looks like I may have made a mistake. There was a bunch of foliage blocking my binocular's view.

No matter, I wanted a two-for-one deal today, anyway." A deep chortle resonated with sadistic pleasure and tinged with uncertainty.

Instinct motivated Keiki to record video and audio while the sour taste of fear rose in her throat. "Shelly, what's happening?"

"Y-you filthy motherfucker. Get away from me!" Shelly's choked epithet echoed fear and rage amid sputtering and scuffling sounds.

Jabbing the laptop's keys ordered the drone's pivot. It stopped with a snap and thud. Her computer screen transformed to various shades of black and brown.

"Fuck. Shelly, what's going on?"

"Hmm, never had a voyeur before. As much as I'd like to show you what's in store for you, I think your girlfriend would prefer this to be a private time just between us."

"Feisty bitch." A male voice, deep and guttural, groaned and cursed, then promised retribution.

Still, Keiki saw nothing, her imagination filling in the gaps during the assault. Terror filled her mind but froze her body in place. Inside, it felt like a dozen razors shredded her gut.

"Oh, God. Please help her."

The distinctive crack of bones breaking resembled nothing like celery or carrots snapping. Muffled cries and panted breaths amid dull thumping registered during defensive moves chilled Keiki to the bone.

"Shelly!"

A sucking noise, like something pulled from soft flesh, jettisoned bile up Keiki's throat. Her friend's scream cut short, right before a thin mewl which ended in ominous silence.

Panic scattered her focus until the absolute stillness in both the woods and apartment infused her with energy.

"I'm calling the cops, you prick. I've already got your picture. The police will figure out your identity."

Lies poured forth in an effort to scare away the unknown assailant. The minicam had picked up Shelly's face and jean-clad legs, along with a glimpse of a masked assailant.

A dark chuckle supplied a grim answer.

"Shelly?" Keiki picked up her cell to call 911 but the device slipped through her trembling and sweaty fingers to crash on the tile floor.

The phone bounced off the edge of the power adapter and sent spider web cracks radiating outward to cover the screen.

When secured with two hands, her mobile lifeline still had power, but the keyboard failed to light up. Two fingernails broke when she stabbed the touchscreen display where the numbers should have been. Menacing silence supplied her imagination with everything she couldn't face and nothing she could identify to help her friend.

"Well, little chickie-chickie. Now I know who you are, but not where you're hiding. I bet it won't take me long to find you."

Keiki froze with her hand in midair.

The shape coming into focus on her screen presented no clarity of the current nightmare. Gray as the coming thunderstorm and cold as her numb fingers, a pair of beady eyes assessed her through small holes in a black skullcap.

The silence proved more unnerving than the implied threat and froze her to the chair.

Slamming the laptop's lid shut prevented his further evaluation of her features and environment. He would hear the thin whine crawling through her chest. Without video confirmation, her mind conjured the worst scenario of the ongoing audible recording.

Soft rustling of material indicated the killer—for in her mind, Keiki knew her friend was dead—was rummaging through Shelly's clothes.

Vomit catapulted up her throat, most of which landed in the trashcan by the counter. Her vision swam and her balance wavered. She couldn't think what to do, how to help.

Audio from her laptop continued in the background to form a white noise, a buzzing in the back of her mind.

A simple tune hummed through the speakers gave no indication to the horror having taken place.

"Oh, hell, I *did* start with the wrong one. Boss is gonna be pissed. He warned me about you two looking alike."

Like Keiki, Shelly wore her hair in a braid when she hiked. Today had been no exception.

The two girls had been friends since kindergarten and on more than one occasion, one mistaken for the other.

Keiki looked around to see what the killer would've gleaned from her backdrop. White drywall with pictures of dolphins, beaches, and dogs. Generic and simplistic, they wouldn't help define her location.

She wiped her mouth and tried to clear her head. As a senior in one of the smaller colleges, she knew most of the students and was well known in return.

When beady eyes came looking, it wouldn't take long to find her.

Words dried in her mouth while her vision swam. An explosive exhalation arrived with the realization she'd held her breath, concluding with tears and dry heaves.

"Aw, now don't be like that, cutie pie. We're gonna get to know each other real well after I find the little corner where you're hiding. Real soon. Count on it. I'll be sure to remember my cuffs. Hope you won't care they're not fur lined."

Her computer's settings ensured nothing changed with the lid's closing except lack of visual access. Two-way audio remained intact. If she lifted the lid, the camera would reveal another glimpse of her backdrop.

Delayed thinking brought self-recriminations. The bastard could no longer see her or her surroundings. He *did* hear the sounds of her dry heaving and would understand the mind-numbing terror he instilled.

Her mind conjured the sadistic violence embedded in his tone. He was a beast who enjoyed his sick pastime.

"The question foremost in my mind chickie-chickie is this. Are you going to feel as good as you look? Should I describe all the things we're gonna do? Hmm... Tell me, did you build this mini ornithopter?"

The fact he defined her work and used the term appropriately doubled her alarm. Due to its location, the attack was specifically planned. The bastard was educated, to a point.

"It seems I have some decisions to make."

The slight *clink* of metal on metal made her wonder what he was doing.

Why would he break the drone?

"I could leave this little piece of evidence for the police to find and trace back to your door. That might be fun."

Keiki squeezed her eyes shut, breathing through the burning in her throat.

"Or, better yet, I could use it to find you *before* the cops do. Decisions, decisions."

For someone with mechanical knack, it took her far too long to remove the battery from her laptop and shut the prick out.

Tears flowed as she booted up her tower to contact 911. In her heart, she knew her best friend lay dead amid a pile of woodland detritus. In making the call anonymous, she hoped to avoid the police and having her personal information on an official report. Anything to make it more difficult for the killer to learn her location.

The facial recognition program installed by her other part-time employer wouldn't do much good considering the killer wore a mask. If her luck held, she'd finish the semester and head for a different locale before he tracked her down. She was too close to graduating and didn't have enough money for a fresh start.

With so many schools in the area, she should have time if she kept a low profile.

On the other hand, dead girls didn't need educating.

Chapter One

"Step lightly, Detectives, or I'll surround your front yards with yellow tape and chalk an outline of a body on the sidewalk." Covered head to toe in white disposable coveralls, the CSI technician speared Nolan with a persuasive grin while placing some broken leaves in the bag held open by a co-worker.

The young woman who resembled a snow bunny from the neck down had a longstanding crush on his partner, Coyote.

"My home doesn't have a sidewalk. I live in the country," Nolan challenged as he mentally catalogued the crime scene from a distance to take in the big picture before zeroing in on the victim.

The lead tech chuckled then added a glare in Coyote's direction. "I know damn well no one would approach your house without an AR 15 and gator noose handy. Must be how you stay so skinny— outrunning the cousins you call porch puppies."

"Gators don't visit the mountains. They don't like it this far north. 'Sides, they can hit thirty miles an hour for short distances on land. If you're directly in front or ninety degrees from either side, you'd be a tasty snack. Well, *you* might be a little on the tart side." Coyote winked at the tech then grunted when Nolan elbowed him in the ribs.

"And to think you didn't bring some friends up from Florida? How rude." The CSI's hair net swung to the left with the weight of her ponytail when following the southerner's line of sight.

"Careful not to trip over your third leg, partner," Nolan taunted.

Coyote pointed to something specific on the periphery of the scene. "What's that shiny thing poking up through the dead branches?"

Blowing out a breath, the tech shuffled back and squatted near several broken limbs. "Ah, I've no idea. Almost looks like a tiny mechanical arm." Turning to her assistant, she instructed, "Bag it along with the leaves and debris nestled around it."

"Where's Doc?" Nolan shaded his eyes against the rising sun

topping the trees and firing up the valley in beautiful shades of red, orange, and yellow.

Returning to his hometown as part of the small force was worth it. The quiet county offered year-round beauty and a peacefulness he couldn't enjoy in the city.

The area's average crime rate was tame enough that the chief didn't micromanage their hours. The resulting comradery between partners felt more like family.

"Pictures are done. Doc is en route but not happy about the early morning call." Their part-time photographer recapped her lens.

"Who is she?" Coyote stood several yards away on the opposite side of a well-tended, fifteen-foot square woodland flowerbed. "And what's she doing tending a flowerbed in this clearing?"

"Found her wallet. Two IDs. One license said Shelly Harock, age twenty. The other declared her Shelly Harold, age twenty-one. Both are local addresses. She also had a dorm keycard. It doesn't name the college that issued it."

The tech repeated the home address as Nolan took notes.

"College kid. Damn." Coyote, the younger of the two detectives, used his cell to snap pics of the IDs. "They're always in such a damn hurry to grow up."

"Problem is, last I checked, we have twenty-eight colleges within a fifty-mile radius." Snow bunny bagged the victim's hands to preserve trace evidence.

"Right up Nolan's alley. He's the graduate destined for greater things." Coyote hiked his eyebrows up and shrugged a shoulder when Nolan flipped him off.

"I have a business degree, swamp donk. No big deal." Nolan approached the victim and sunk into a crouch. Three years partnered with the southerner had fathered an easy and familiar relationship. "It appears she, or someone, tended this patch of flowers on a regular basis. It'd be nice to know its significance."

"Out here in the middle of the woods? I find that a little strange." Coyote scrutinized the plants tended with loving care.

"Think it's symbolic to another place?" Nolan pointed to foam around the girl's lips. "Is that what I think it is?"

"Could be. I collected samples. If it is Fentanyl, that would put her death within the last few hours. Lab analysis will give us specifics, but either way, she hasn't been gone long. She's still warm."

"Results won't come back for four to six weeks, unless we get lucky."

"Why stab *and* strangle her if he wanted to kill her with Fentanyl-laced smack?"

The tech glanced from one detective to the other. "God only knows. Looks to me like you've got a killer with a whole lot of crazy sending a strong message."

"Message to whom? Her party friends who like to get high, a jealous ex-boyfriend settling a score, or an escapee from Bedlam trying to quiet the voices in his head?" Coyote murmured as he studied the scene before him.

"Could be a message to her family. If her father is Franklin Harock, then she's the local heiress. I was called to her sister's scene—a climbing accident three years ago."

"Which might explain a flower garden along the hillside. We'll have to see who owns this property." Coyote shook his head. "Such a waste."

Nolan froze, then jutted his chin toward the southern ridge. "You guys hear that?"

His partner stilled. "What?"

"Sounds like someone using a weed eater off in the distance."

"In the woods? I don't think so." Coyote stood and strode to the edge of the small clearing.

"Look, it's a drone."

It wasn't uncommon for criminals to want to watch the results of their handiwork with the police present. It *was* the first time Nolan ever witnessed a drone doing the spying.

Against the sky's azure backdrop, the black and silver collection of propellers and parts stood out, but not as much as the round lens suspended several inches below the main body. Its slow approach indicated caution more than morbid curiosity.

"Our voyeur is getting closer but doesn't want his technology identified." Nolan studied the electronic snooper.

"Damn drone has a camera attached. I wonder if it's a zoom." Coyote slid his hand slowly to his back waist.

"Have the news stations started using these damn things?" Nolan looked from his partner to the tech for clarification.

Each shrugged.

Coyote unholstered his Glock and took aim at the incoming device, his expression transforming from curiosity to determination.

"What the hell are you doing, Coyote? You can't shoot down a drone." Nolan reached for the gun hand slowly rising. "It's not a gator in the sky, it's someone's tech. If you shoot it and it lands in a tree, we'll never find it in these hills."

"I won't pull the trigger. I'm just proving a theory," Coyote defended.

"Hey, how about a picture?" Nolan turned to the photographer who'd already pulled the cap from its lens and hoisted her camera into position.

"It's too far away for much detail, but I'll do what I can," she replied.

In rapid succession, the mechanized spy arced in a tight curve and ducked amid the treetops for cover.

"Damn, swamp goblin," Nolan muttered under his breath. "We do things a little differently here up north. I'm surprised you didn't learn better during your military stint."

"It wasn't going to get close enough to see specific markings anyway." Coyote returned his service weapon to its holster.

"Shit. What could a college kid do to deserve this?" The southern accent deepened when his attention returned to the victim, his index finger hovering above the girl's throat. "What a strange way to kill someone."

"It's possible the killer's sending a specific kind of message," Nolan suggested. "We need to figure out what it is and for whom it's intended."

"The sooner we get back to civilization, the sooner we find out." Coyote nodded to the tech. "Can you ask Doc to give us a call? Here's my card."

"No need, detective. I've got your number." Snow bunny smiled. "And you know how grumpy he gets when anyone tries to rush him. This may be a small borough, but he's from the city."

"I wasn't dinging his competency, just his timing." Coyote grinned,

14

his affection for the crime scene investigator increasing the crinkles about his eyes and mouth.

Nolan nudged his partner toward the deer trail leading down the mountainside. "Reel in your eyes, Romeo."

When they left the small plateau, the steep grade required attention to footing. He'd hiked in the area on several occasions, never crossing anything more dangerous than a sunbathing rattler or frightened black bear.

Once out of earshot, Nolan egged his partner. "Why don't you ask her out? She wouldn't turn you down."

"She thinks of me on the same level as a hibernating alligator, not a southern gentleman."

"Alligators don't hibernate. Do they?"

"Mm-hmm, there's some in North Carolina that do. You can see their snouts frozen in the ice during freezing snaps. It's how the cold-blooded buggers breathe."

"You are a storage barn of useless facts." Nolan stared at his partner, unable to reconcile the varied facets of his personality.

"What can I say? I like 'em."

"You would. You're an endless reservoir of data on gators. Did you moonlight in wildlife management in the glades or grow up hunting them?" Nolan stepped over a log and slipped, scrambling to avoid landing on his butt. As in the hike uphill, branches snatched at his suit pants and jacket while sprawling vines conspired to trip him into face-planting. He loved hiking, but not in Dockers and loafers.

"Or something. I'll tell you about it someday, but I've never wrestled a gator. And yes, I know that in this neck of the woods, wrestling the alligator is a euphemism for eating at the Y. You northerners and your sexual innuendos..."

Nolan grinned, ever amazed at his partner's viewpoints. Over the course of their partnership, the younger detective seldom spoke of himself or his past, leaving Nolan to piece together a haphazard sketch of the man's life. A range of scattered clues left him guessing most of the time.

"Stop thinking so much, Nolan. You'll start a forest fire."

"You need a date, and a muzzle. Maybe at the same time. How is it you made it through the military intact?"

"Easy. There weren't many of my type women on base, so I found other outlets to expend energy and vowed to make up for it after discharge." Appraisal and calculation softened his tone. "I was lucky to be assigned near home after being overseas."

"Three years must have felt like an eternity. At least you were near family after..." It was a rare occasion when fishing for information produced results.

Defining where his partner had been stationed or what horrors he'd endured remained off limits.

Nolan blew out a breath as they reached the base of the mountain. They'd parked in the lot where a local news van now waited. Turning to his partner, he groused. "Time to put those southern dimples to good use."

"Gee, thanks." Despite the sour tone, Coyote turned up the amperage on his megawatt smile.

No doubt, easy charm still held sway with the inexperienced reporter who directed her questions to the younger partner. The realization he never took advantage defined his moral aptitude.

Chapter Two

"Did you make any headway while I was working?" Coyote dropped into the passenger seat and slammed his door, waving to the reporter who lingered after her camera man turned to pack up his gear.

"Yeah, according to his assistant, Franklin Harock is home with his wife. I pulled up the information and ran Shelly through LEJIS. No hits." Nolan hated this aspect of investigating. "No one should outlive their child."

"Agreed. Hey, speaking of family, did your sister finish her paper on first responders and stress? I could help if she needs it."

"Ah, how'd you know about Jenna's assignment? I don't recall that conversation over the family dinner last week." Nolan flicked a glance at his partner before cranking the engine.

"That's because I helped the women do dishes while *you* sat on your ass watching the game." Coyote turned to observe the passing mountainside blazing with fall color.

"I like you. I do. But if you fool around with my sister, no one will ever find all the pieces of Coyote Waylin. She's nineteen."

Whenever his partner joined the family gatherings, sparks flew between his youngest sibling and his partner. His mom had made note of it, going so far as to admonish Nolan for warning the man about romantic entanglements.

"Is it because I'm a southern boy or because you think I'm poor?" A new challenge existed in the smooth accent local women loved.

"I don't give a damn how much money you do or don't make. She's in college and needs to focus, to figure things out for herself."

"Your family loves me."

"Yeah, more so than me. Even my dad accepts you, which is kinda rare. He hasn't liked many guys where his daughters are concerned. I think the fact you help out at mealtimes has earned you a few extra points. However, with four sisters and my mother in the kitchen, it's not big enough for two men."

It was a well-known fact the sun rose and set on Coyote's shoulders where young Jenna Garnett was concerned.

"She's too young for you, Coyote. You'd do well to keep that in mind."

"How can I forget, given your calculating glare every time she grinned at me? I felt like you were sizing me up for a homemade coffin. And by the way, she does it to piss you off."

"Whatever."

"Since you're a local, tell me about Shelly Harock's father and his business dealings before we get to his house."

Nolan detailed his sparse knowledge of the tycoon's holdings and current operations. Returning home and wanting to settle down, he'd almost invested in the local tech company himself.

Coyote whistled low as they passed through ornate iron gates with a decorative scroll top. The estate looked like a forbidden fortress. A long winding driveway snaked around well-tended, colorful flowerbeds of the large Harock manor.

"I hear this guy's quite the shark. Keep your eyes open." Nolan estimated the manicured lawn, sculpted hedges, and surrounding specimen trees required an entire team of gardeners to maintain.

When the house came into view, Coyote sucked in a breath. "Now there's a sight you don't see every day. I think I want me one of them."

"Huh. You finally ready to buy a house? Kudos. I didn't know if you were going to put down roots or flee back to the swamps of southern Florida."

"I've been waiting for the right time and the right woman." Coyote smirked as he hopped out of the vehicle. "I look forward to having your family over to *my* place next year for Thanksgiving." A chuckle accompanied the obvious certainty of a man intent on one-upping his partner and enjoying every minute of it.

"Looking forward to soda can wind chimes and alligator fingers." Nolan imagined a cottage surrounded by southern oaks dripping Spanish moss. Though the swamp setting wouldn't fit in Pennsylvania, his partner would somehow make it work. With style.

It took a minute to switch mental gears, his mind circling his sister's penchant for defiance and imagining her sitting on Coyote's front porch with a mint julep in hand.

From the house ahead, a dog barked and restored his focus on their task. Stately columns under the portico of the sprawling brick mansion failed to conceal the video cameras monitoring the home's exterior. All would be scrutinized before entering.

Brick quoins on each corner added detail while the parapet running the length of the home's roof allowed second-story residents access to a beautiful view via the balcony. The home was built to impress.

"You ever going to tell me how you got the nickname Coyote when you're from Florida? They don't even have coyotes, do they?"

"Of course we do. As for the other, I might. Someday."

Marble steps led them to an arched double door entrance under a paladin window. An ornate brass handle situated at chest level offered the only illusion of normalcy.

Before they could knock, the door opened. The manservant greeted them with a pseudo smile. His white mustache, trimmed close, matched bushy eyebrows shadowing his gaze. Time hadn't yet bent the older man's spine nor veiled his eyes with cataracts. Condescension complete with a frown and raised chin declared the visitors not up to par.

"May I help you, gentlemen?" An accent steeped in British formality supported the air of authority and bulky frame. The slight dusting of gray in his hair acknowledged middle age but didn't detract from his air of superiority.

"We're here to see Mr. and Mrs. Harock." Nolan parted his suit to expose his shield the same time his partner swiped aside the flap of his bomber jacket.

"If you'll wait in the parlor, I will let Mr. and Mrs. Harock know of your arrival."

A sweeping gesture ushered them into a well-appointed room with rich jewel-tone rugs anchored by two overstuffed sofas. Various duties had taken the detectives to upscale homes before, but never the likes of such elegance.

Neither he nor his partner sat.

Soft clicks marked the older man's confident strides across marble flooring. The parlor equaled the size of Nolan's kitchen and great room combined.

Two floor-to-ceiling picture windows comprised one wall while a massive stone fireplace divided the room from whatever lay beyond. Built-in bookshelves lined with tomes bearing antique spines took center stage in the back. It bore noting each section of shelf contained books of one hue, making a kaleidoscope of the whole.

Who separates books by spine color?

Coyote cast a dubious glance at the area rug then grumbled a derisive comment after assessing the couch.

Nolan stood at the windows and compiled the list of normal questions he'd ask after the parents' brunt of shock dissipated. He was about to change their worldview forever, and despite the ostentatious surroundings, no one deserved to receive such news.

Franklin Harock's confused mien belied his self-assured stride and outstretched hand. "Good morning, Detectives. What can I do for you?" The suit he wore could pay a cop's salary for a year. "Please, have a seat."

A slim blonde stopped next to him and curved her lips to a semblance of a smile. Shrewd intelligence radiated from her hazel eyes, a mother's analysis which discerned trouble before it was defined. Despite perfect posture, there existed a subtle if longstanding sadness in her demeanor. She didn't speak.

She's already lost one child.

It wasn't difficult to read the worry lines etched in their faces. Concern marked his own father's appearance every time his sisters' lives veered off their chosen path.

The father's stiff shoulders and guarded assessment spoke volumes. He and his wife took a seat and visibly braced themselves.

Both detectives sat on the opposing couch.

The ensuing conversation never got easier. Denials and claims of misunderstanding and misidentification drove each detective to take deep breaths until the finality of the situation sunk in.

Coming face to screen with the picture on Nolan's phone of the girl's ID card silenced their protests and steeped the room in mute apprehension. Long moments later, the beginnings of rage took root in both parents.

"I'll confirm Shelly's identity later today." Grief bore Franklin

Harock's shoulders down.

Despite the husband's protests, his wife insisted on seeing her daughter as soon as possible. A small precinct and the scheduled afternoon autopsy dictated they make arrangements after the detectives left.

Mrs. Harock's vengeful side appeared in spades before the ultimate question. The one Nolan anticipated, yet hated most, for nothing was certain in any investigation until all the facts coalesced to form a complete picture.

Her husband's handkerchief received a fresh round of tears as she blubbered out, "Do you have any idea who would hurt my little girl?"

"As of yet, no. We've just begun our investigation," Nolan replied. "Can you tell me about her close friends?"

The mother appeared to be the teenager's closer bonded parent, judging by the multiple family pictures on the side table and several of the built-in bookshelves. In each, the young girl had slung her arm around her mother's shoulders, pulling her in for a tight hug.

It was the husband who spoke over his wife, consoling her with an arm around her waist. "Yes. Her closest friend is Gabby. Uh, Gabriella Kiernan. The girl's parents are family friends. She's a pre-med student."

Mrs. Harock hiccupped before adding, "We lost our other daughter to a climbing accident. She and Shelly were very close. Gabby had joined them but Shelly backed out once she saw what the climb entailed. She's always blamed herself for not protecting her sister and not been the same since."

"Hon," Franklin rubbed his wife's shoulders, "any child would go through a rough patch after experiencing—that. If not for her friends, she might have traveled a different path."

After jotting down notes of other friendships, Nolan stood and ambled to the bookshelves. Picking up a silver-framed photo, he pointed to the two girls on either side of the now-deceased coed. "Who are these girls?"

Harock narrowed his eyes and thinned his lips. "The one on the left is Gabby. The one on the right is Keiki Tallerman. She's not as close as Shelly's other friends. They've grown apart a bit since entering college. Keiki is a little older."

His declaration drew a confused frown from his wife. "Franklin, those three girls are thick as thieves. Always have been."

The father scraped a hand down his face then rubbed the back of his neck. "Maybe. Since Shelly started college, we've been a bit out of touch. I do know Keiki is a serious student and not one to do the party scene. She'd be the one to go then make friends with the dog."

"Keiki works for us, part-time. I believe you'd call her a mechanical prodigy," the mother added. "She and Shelly wanted to go into the drone business."

"Tell us more about Gabby and Keiki," Coyote requested.

Details spilled from the mother, less so from her husband. When a familiar name popped up in conversation, red flags waved in Nolan's mind. Coyote spoke first.

"Keiki works part-time for Nick Tucker? Two part-time jobs *and* full-time college courses. That must keep her busy."

"Yes. You see, her folks died after she graduated from high school, a carjacking just outside Philly. I don't think she's healing. She's never been able to let it go, insisting police couldn't be bothered to find the killer." A certain wistfulness graced her features. "We knew them well. They were fully invested in their daughter and enjoyed a close relationship."

"Gabriella Kiernan is the same way with her folks," Franklin added.

"Are drones a part of your day-to-day operations?" Nolan asked, observing Harock for variance in mannerisms.

"Not yet, but they will be at some point," he replied without blinking, flinching, or sweating.

Nolan studied the photograph of three girls dressed in ski clothes, smiling for the photographer. Each appeared a carefree teen out for a good time on the slopes. With one viciously murdered, the other two would suffer the ripple effect through time and circumstance.

"Mr. Harock, considering the nature of the attack, do you have any reason to believe it was directed at you or your business? Maybe a rival company?" Nolan met the father's steady regard.

"Possibly. My biggest competitor is Cannon Manufacturing. That bastard has sent several headhunters over the past few years." Fisted hands against his suit pants outlined his anger. "He wants to go international, from what I understand."

"So, he's trying to keep up with you. We'll look into it," Coyote affirmed.

"It's remarkable how much Shelly and this other girl, Keiki, look alike." Nolan's light touch outlined the older girl's face. The eyes had a slight exotic tilt along the outer corners and were lighter. Even among friends, she radiated an intensity older than her years.

"When they were younger, they used to imagine themselves twins, changelings, and all sorts of fanciful things." Mrs. Harock sniffled and wiped another trail of tears from her face.

Further details revealed little pertinent information. Departure of the two detectives left a fast-crumbling relationship in their wake.

"Jesus," Coyote murmured as he descended the elegant steps. "I feel like the bolas spider that sends out sticky globs of silk to catch its prey."

"Crime doesn't happen in a vacuum. It's a matter of asking the right questions to the right people—and sometimes a little luck. If we don't ask, we don't get the necessary information."

Coyote sighed after dropping into his seat and shutting the passenger door. "This isn't going to be easy. And not because I lack your city experience."

"This situation is complicated by many variables. Did you get the sense the father is hiding something? Wealth always brings complications." Nolan grimaced. He'd dealt with a high-profile murder in a larger jurisdiction and endured the foul taste of money-induced interference for his effort. Current small-town politics wouldn't withstand the battering of an enraged millionaire.

"He did seem to prefer the one girl stay out of our crosshairs. You think he's got something going with her? Seemed a little touchy with some of your questions."

"Wouldn't be the first time an impressionable kid got mixed up with a shark. I want to do some background checking before we talk to either of her friends." Nolan guided the SUV back toward the station, his thoughts replaying the conversation and mulling over possible motives.

"He tried to protect Keiki, yet we have no clue why. I was kind of surprised he refused to let us borrow the photo." Harock had started to object, then shut his mouth when Nolan raised a brow.

"Protecting his golden goose?" Coyote suggested.

"It's possible his daughter learned something, somehow, and it made her a target. But, I can't imagine either parent covering for the murder of their own child. There has to be something else to this we're not seeing."

"It doesn't wash."

"Yet." Nolan smiled in humorless anticipation.

"The mother was a lot more forthcoming despite her shock, what with Shelly and Keiki wanting to open up a business. The daughter's other friend sounds like a live wire, type A adrenaline junkie. Jeez. What is the world coming to? The next thing you know, we'll have to investigate midair collisions and theft using mechanical spiders." Coyote retrieved his notepad from his jacket and flipped through the pages.

"Think about it. What PI wouldn't want a licensed drone operator doing surveillance for him? And what better operator than the person who makes the drones?"

The SUV responded to acceleration with a throaty growl, eating up the miles on the near-deserted back roads. Heat from the sun spilling through the windshield thawed some of the dread filling Nolan's gut.

Coyote started a running commentary and review of the interview, which allowed them to bounce ideas and possible scenarios off one another. "Shelly was a business major and Keiki made the drones. Seems like a pretty tight relationship to me, yet the father played it down when you picked up that picture. Did you see him grimace when you used your phone to take a pic?"

"Yeah, but I can't see a motive in there. You?"

"No. One thing I did notice, he doesn't care much for his competition," Nolan suggested.

"We can check out Cannon's background before making an appearance and asking questions. Let's go grab something to eat first."

"Sounds good. I could use some shrimp and sausage stew." Coyote tucked his notes away and twisted toward the onboard computer, digitally entering Pennsylvania's DMV.

"Those two foods don't belong in the same sentence, much less the same pan together. And for the record, there are tons of electronic

24

devices you can use to take notes if you'd care to join the twenty-first century."

"Yeah, but notepads can't be deleted with the push of a button or a virus. 'Sides, it irritates the hell out of you, which makes a minor inconvenience more than worthwhile." Coyote's grin said it all. "You know that's what I live for."

Nolan glared until his partner chuckled. "You are a *complete* douche."

"Nah, there's still some parts missing. I think it has something to do with one of my relatives, a skunk ape from the glades."

"Let me guess, it lives near the Fountain of Youth?" With a sigh, Nolan shook his head.

"Actually, it's rumored that he visits our famous underwater hotel to give guests a scare now and then."

"As long as it doesn't involve my sisters, I don't care," Nolan grumbled as he veered west toward his partner's favorite watering hole. Boundless drive trapped him between the ridiculousness of Coyote's oddities and an eternity of strict, if companionless, self-discipline.

Chapter Three

Nolan opened the door and preceded Coyote into the station. The musty smell of cinderblock and stale coffee never failed to unsettle his stomach. He should've been accustomed to it by now. "It didn't sound to me like Cannon has a clue about Harock's R&D, much less have the stomach for that kind of foul play."

"He did outline the plan to go global. Considering the focus of his expansion, I can't see how drones could fit in. You?"

"No, which means he was either lying or he's simply not involved," Nolan agreed.

Coyote's throat clearing caught Nolan's attention as they entered the open expanse and working area of the squad room. "Crap."

"Incoming, three o'clock." Nolan grinned. The early warning alerted the other detective sitting at his desk. A quick glimpse and smothered smile sparked recognition of entertainment to come.

"Insufficient funds," Coyote grumbled.

Code speak for lack of swear words made Nolan chuckle harder.

"Hi, guys." A long black ponytail swept side to side as the young lady advanced, a determined smile set in place.

Graduating from college with a degree in public relations slotted her into position as the public face of Middleton PD.

Her father being the mayor may have helped create the position, but she'd proven a quick study and near genius at composing news stories, articles, and various periodic and special purpose reports for both their department and the sheriff's office. During quiet times, she supported the office staff with whatever help they needed.

Nolan inwardly chortled but kept his smile rigid. "Hey. How goes it with PR today?"

It had also became apparent during her first weeks of employment she had a thing for a specific senior detective. Nolan had hinted at the reason behind his confirmed bachelor status. The young woman then switched her focus to the younger detective.

Continued pursuit created an awkwardness for Coyote he didn't seem capable of handling.

"All's good." In a theatric whisper she added, "I heard about the woodland murder. I wanted to get some details to start writing up the news release. If you let me know once her identity has been confirmed, I'll contact the press." Her soft inquiry came with a breathy sigh and a light touch to Coyote's arm.

"Thanks, uh, we'll let you know sometime this afternoon." Coyote bit his lower lip as if trapped and looking for a way out of his predicament.

"Are either of you in the 5k Foam Glitter race tomorrow? I was thinking about going but didn't want to run it alone." Her words trailed off with a hopeful smile. "I don't know if my old class mates are gonna be in it."

"No, I'm not. But I think Nolan is gonna run." His partner patted him on the shoulder, a hand off of responsibility.

"Actually, I've got a date." Nolan grimaced. If hard pressed to come up with a name, he'd fail.

Beside him, his co-worker choked out, "Plastic or rubber? We're taking bets on you jogging in flip-flops to remember the sound."

"I'm going to hell, and it's going to be populated with cops." There wasn't enough lye to scour the conversation from Nolan's mind.

"Since there's only a stairway to heaven but a highway to hell, I'm thinking you'll have lots of company. You are planning on going with the flow, the mass exodus, right?" The southern detective had a knack for turning things around.

Nolan took his seat and swiveled away to face his desk. Ignoring taunts frequently came with the bonus of increased effort.

By Monday morning, a variety of printouts from online adult sites would populate his desk with emphasis on bulk and liquidation sales. Unlike others who flaunted every conquest, Nolan preferred to keep his private life just that. Private.

It wasn't the age difference which kept the younger detective from asking the CSI tech or office staff on a date. The former still viewed the world with rose-colored glasses and the latter, well, she didn't have Jenna Garnett's red hair and freckles.

Few memorable events in their moderate-sized town made little things gossip-worthy. Dating the secretary would earn his partner a scheduled dinner with the mayor, his wife, and their three Rottweilers.

Nolan glared at the person whose desk butted lengthwise against his own, daring him to comment on dating or anything sexually related. "I'll take Keiki, you take Gabby."

"Only in your dreams, but I guess there's always hope."

Nolan considered the fastest way to wipe the smirk off his partner's face while his tower booted up. Putting road kill in his bed wouldn't revoke his man card. It would have to be a stellar prank.

"You should never have focused her attention on me." Coyote stifled his grin. "She's young, moldable... right up your alley."

"Shut up, or I'll put chocolate pudding in your whoopee cushion. It's you she's after now." He needed to make his partner see the light. "She works with us every day. That makes her off limits regardless of her parentage." Nolan entered the password to get into the state's database. He preferred to start general and broad, then narrow his search in bits so as not to miss any large informational chunks on his target.

Something about the way Franklin had tried to protect Keiki didn't sit well. If the kid had a romantic involvement with the business mogul, it would muddy a lot of waters and complicate the investigation.

"See, this is the nice thing about college kids. They put their lives on social media." Coyote pulled out his pad and paper to take notes. When farther into the case, he'd add them to their intranet, holding back specific information until they'd either closed the case or declared it unresolved.

Nolan poked and prodded through each database before scrutinizing the girls' social media platforms. The mental picture of Keiki coming into focus formed divergent pathways in his thoughts.

One, the serious student with top grades and workaholic nature. On the other, less public side, she hung out with two partygoers and carved a series of giant S-shaped swoops and tight turns on her snowboard, or—

"Oh, hell."

"What?" Coyote paused his research to look up.

"There's a picture of the three girls with Nick Tucker. Looks like they're socially involved, too."

"Doing?" His partner refocused on his own work.

"Skiing."

"So? The girls hang out with a slightly older guy. I thought you'd found photos of a group orgy."

"He's immature and impulsive." On Nolan's screen, two blondes and a brunette flanked a stocky, dark haired man, all wearing snow gear and holding snowboards or skis.

"Can't say I know much other than rumors."

"He's local, though several years behind me in school. I got the sense he was a bit of a hound dog but harmless just the same. I lost track of him after he graduated from the academy. Once he left the force—he kinda fell off the grid. I don't think he'd be involved with anything underhanded though."

"People don't usually change that much unless there's a significant instigating factor," Coyote reminded him.

"He's got a private investigator's license, and I've got a bad feeling about this. There are too many coincidences to not add up to— something." Nolan flicked through Shelly's social media pictures but found none with just her and Tucker. "I don't think Shelly was the focus of Tucker's intensity."

Not with the way his gaze is fixed on Keiki.

Time passed with a series of "Ums," and "Ahs."

By late afternoon, they'd exhausted online resources and received a call from the ME, the parents having confirmed the victim's identity.

"Next stop—see what we can find on campus. We might have better luck tracking the kids tomorrow morning while they're sleeping off hangovers." Coyote rolled his chair back and stretched his arms over his head.

"Fine, an early Saturday morning it is. I'd like to get in touch with a few of Shelly's professors, too."

Nolan had found and watched the video of a tragedy which would've cleaved any kid's world. Sketching details clued his partner in.

Shelly's friend, Katherine "Keiki" Tallerman had become an orphan just before starting college. When the state's investigator informed her all leads in the investigation had been exhausted, the teenager assaulted him. No charges were filed due to the kid's overwhelming grief and the detective's lack of injury. That scenario would've sideswiped her world in ways not anticipated.

Death of someone you love always changes you.

Nolan Garnett was an expert on the subject.

"I'll drive tomorrow. Your stomach will lead us straight to Chenovy's for some pork and sauerkraut." Nolan could handle a lot of things, but that combination for breakfast didn't cut it. "What'd you find on Gabriella Kiernan?"

"Hey. Don't knock my favorite dish until you've tried it," Coyote quipped as he led the way out of the squad room. "As far as Gabby is concerned. Her father's a spine surgeon at Centerville General and her mother is a retired nurse. Guess the kid's following in her dad's footsteps. She lives in an apartment off campus with her best friend, Katherine Tallerman. Let's check with campus security before we track them down. Might get some insight into the party world."

"You take security. I'll take Admin for schedules and professor's names."

"Trust fund to get Keiki through school, you think?" Coyote asked, pausing with his hand on the door.

"Possible. Her parents owned the hardware store on Chesterfield Ave. So, yeah, probably."

"Any other family? Anything else?"

"One maternal grandmother in a nursing home." Nolan considered his target's life. "The kid is licensed to fly drones. She's buddies with a PI. Her friend is murdered ten ways to Sunday. Stabbed, drugged, and strangled. I don't think there's anything straightforward about this case. I also don't think she's gonna open up to cops."

Nolan considered the emotional monsters that drove an orphan to excel in school and at work. A brief explanation detailed her experiences. Both detectives stepped outside and inhaled a deep breath.

Bottled up emotions erupted at some point, either through acceptable outlets or hidden lives. Keiki's life had taken a macabre turn before her freshman year. The tragedy would remold her, no doubt, but into what?

Coyote paused on the bottom step and sighed. "You think the killer was sending a message to the victim's friends? He targeted Shelly with an awful lot of rage."

"Could be, and you're assuming it was one assailant and a male. We didn't see any sign of restraint, just an all-out brawl. The killer might not have looked at it from a position of total control."

"Thanks for the coffee, partner." Coyote removed the plastic lid and blew across the hot brew. "Decaf?"

"Really? To you, that'd be the equivalent of a hooker who only wanted to cuddle." Nolan snickered. "I'm the one who eats right."

"Hmm, cranky. You need to get laid or rub one out." Coyote shrugged under his colleague's glare. "Sorry, I guess I self-identify as a grief counselor. Just saying..."

"Maybe you should think twice before I self-identify as the tooth fairy."

The campus lay nestled in the valley, the school well known for its strong sense of place and community while preserving local folk culture through extensive outreach programs. Outdoor recreational activities drew nature lovers and adventurers to improve their skills in rock climbing, advance their knowledge in forestry services, or enjoy a vigorous hike.

Nolan parked in front of the admissions office and pointed to a path leading around the two-story columned building. "Follow that downhill and turn left at the bear statue. Campus Police will be the first building to your right."

"Damn, you sure sound like a local when you give directions using landmarks."

"I am a local. I just got my initial police experience elsewhere." Nolan shoved his car door open and retrieved his cell outlining the case notes, not that he needed them. The mystery of Katherine's odd situation had spurred him to dissect her life the prior evening, regardless of whether or not she was involved in the victim's death.

"I'll meet you back here in an hour." Coyote nodded at a passing coed but ignored the student's obvious interest.

Stately brick buildings with manicured lawns offered a quaint and charming, old-fashioned feel. Meandering students and others playing Frisbee on the lawn declared the day free of worry. Snippets of their discussions entailed weekend plans, groaning over homework assignments, and other various sources of teenage angst.

Spotty light filtered through low clouds to shroud the grounds in a sense of gloom despite Halloween cutouts standing sentinel on the front lawn of a nearby dorm. Greek letters marked three fraternity houses to the left, each offered an array of pumpkin lights, mini illuminated skeletons, and windows boasting its own decorations.

Like each of Nolan's sisters, his parents had given him money to start college. Instead, he'd chosen to get a job and fit his schooling in on the side. Saving every cent, he spent his non-working hours studying, learning how to invest his earnings. The result had proven as satisfying as it was fruitful.

Time and experience had forged a path to what he wanted. The results equaled a solid career, a home with a low mortgage, and more time for hobbies and family. He'd not been sidetracked since losing the love of his life.

Again he thought about Keiki, alone and motivated by similar circumstances. He'd soon learn if they'd guided her onto one of life's darker pathways.

Large double doors led him into an expansive lobby with mosaic-tiled flooring and a wide staircase to his left ascending to the second story. The registrar's office lay ahead with orange pumpkin lights in the half window and an animated witch daring anyone to delve into the candy bowl within her grasp.

Inside, it smelled of spices and the forest after a rain, the unusual combination pleasant and comforting.

"Morning." Nolan inwardly grinned when the young woman's interested smile froze as he revealed his badge. Pasting on his friendliest smile, he added, "Appears you all are ready for Halloween. Looks nice."

A tentative grin slid into place while she looked around and tucked a lock of auburn hair behind her ear. "Um, what can I do for you? I'm afraid you just missed my boss. I'm just a student working here part-time."

Her nametag read Sonny.

Getting access to the records he wanted without a warrant entailed one part intuition and two parts luck. If the information was offered, it was fair game. If he had to browbeat or otherwise use coercion, it put him in a sticky situation.

More times than not, he succeeded with charm and developing a rapport, including his subject in a common goal.

"That's okay. I'm not looking for anything earth shattering." He retrieved his cell and pulled up one of the pictures he'd taken at the victim's house.

Leaning on the counter, he offered the coed a view of the screen. "I'm looking to locate a friend of our victim, who deserves to know what happened now that the family's been informed."

The student's jaw dropped as her hand clutched her chest. "Oh my God. That's Gabby, Keiki, and Shelly. Who?"

"You know all three?"

"Well, yes. This is a small school and they frequently hang out together. I'm a senior and pretty much know everybody. I've worked here since my freshman year. What happened?"

"I can't discuss details, but I'm looking to get hold of Katherine Tallerman and Gabriella Kiernan." By not naming Shelly, he answered her question and, with any luck, gained her cooperation. "I'd like to take a look at their records if you don't mind."

"Oh, right. Well, I don't have much personal stuff, but I can pull up what we have. Come around the counter where you can see the screen better."

Within minutes, he had what he needed, using his phone to record information. Specific details about each girl helped form a general picture of their characters he wouldn't have gotten otherwise.

"Should I be scared?" Wide hazel eyes lost all semblance of romantic interest while fear raised her voice an octave.

"Like with any situation, you should always be aware of your immediate environment, know who's around you. Does this school have a buddy system?"

"For those who drink, yes, otherwise, it's a bit loose. Is there a killer or rapist on campus, as in one of our students?"

"I'm sorry to say we don't have details yet, but I would advise you to take extra precautions. You have one less student now."

Before he left, three girls entered the office, one bearing a plate of chocolate chip cookies. No doubt, word would start spreading like wildfire before the evening news aired.

Various scenarios came to mind involving Franklin, Keiki, Gabby, and Shelly. None formed a reasonable picture. In the parking lot, he found his partner leaning against the SUV, observing the students' meanderings.

"I got pretty much nada. This Gabby likes to party hard, but keeps her nose clean. How'd you do?"

Nolan slid in behind the wheel and waited until his partner shut his door before answering. "Interesting. I got pretty much the same on Gabby, yet Keiki is more of a loner. They don't see her at parties near as much."

Information sharing drowned out the thrum of tire on asphalt and failed to lead to anything conclusive.

"I think Gabby is the wild child of the three, the instigator. Shelly follows. Keiki is the voice of sanity when there is one. From what security said, they've been to Shelly's dorm room to break up parties a few times. They've only sent Keiki packing on a handful of those occasions." Coyote pulled out two sticks of mint gum and offered one to his partner.

"According to the records I saw, Gabby and Keiki have a near perfect average. Sounds like the pre-med student gets bored on weekends, but I can't imagine either of them partying after the news breaks."

"Which might make them easier to find."

"Shelly was a high-value, low-risk target. We have no idea if her death was personal or related to her father's business. We need to find out what type of contracts he has and with whom." Nolan drove off campus, knowing it would be a long day.

"That means added pressure to make an arrest." Coyote snapped his gum, gazing at the passing hills and sporadic homes.

"I'll make a few calls about Harock's business dealings, later. Let's go visit the girls." Keiki would be Nolan's first stop.

"It'd be nice to find them both home, but I kinda doubt it'll happen," Coyote concluded.

"Any word from forensics on the photo of that voyeuristic drone you almost shot down?" Nolan kept a straight face when his partner groaned.

"I did *not* try and shoot it down. I was confirming that we were, in fact, being scrutinized. The photographer said it was too far away to pick up specific markings," Coyote replied. "It didn't belong to any of the news stations. But we do know a certain student who builds them."

"You think she offs her best friend using not one but three different MOs then hangs around for hours to take photos? I'm not quite sure I'd buy that considering my research, but I have seen weirder scenarios."

"I sure as hell hope we're not dealing with a serial killer. Not what this   school   or   town   needs."

Chapter Four

Scratchy, thick masks never improved his mood. While under the cover of night and lurking in the copse of trees, he took it off and stuck it in his back pocket.

The temporary itch in his pants proved worse but would soon have a more enjoyable resolution.

Time fouled his temper the longer he waited for the chem major to leave the frat house. A few smokes and pacing helped pass the time. Every third turn, he checked the screen on his cell.

Minicams perched in pine boughs offered good side views of the building's front and back doors. Since her car was parked in the main lot, she'd most likely take the shortcut through the woods. It would make his job easier.

Self-control would be an issue. His target was young *and* pretty. He'd been young and carefree once, still was, if he didn't consider the outstanding warrants in his alias' name. Unlike his boss, Interpol didn't have his mug shot hanging on their walls, at least not yet.

Finding a specific college kid on campus during a weekend night was like distinguishing each and every honeybee on its comb. The place was crawling with kids.

Whoever designed the campus had set it up with little forethought, leaving plenty of room between buildings and lots of trees for cover. Some days, he loved his job.

Coed dorms covered the southeast corner of the campus near the woodland park while a row of fraternity houses formed a perimeter to the wooded territory beyond.

He could almost define the gender requirements of each floor by the glowing decorations and colored lights in the windows. It seemed that testosterone drained the creative gene from the boys where Halloween was concerned.

No self-respecting college kid should be alone on a Friday night. She had to be with her newest toy.

Impatience lured him out under the cover of cloudy skies and overhanging tree limbs. His thoughts centered on methods to entice the smart-mouth bitch away from prying eyes if fate didn't oblige his quest.

Several couples crossed the campus, one pair trying to perform tonsillectomies with their tongues while walking. It wasn't worth the risk of being remembered by interrupting a moving make-out session, so he waited.

Patience was not one of his virtues.

"Hey, you seen Gabriella Kiernan?" The boy he'd targeted tripped over uneven walkway while shuffling toward the frat houses and might not notice the age of the twenty-something stranger in his midst wearing faded jeans and sporting shaggy hair and a ball cap. A light windbreaker covered his piece.

"Gabby? She's probably screwing her boyfriend's brains out about now." The kid pointed to a brick building at the end of the row. "Lucky bastard."

He'd known about the boyfriend and where he lived, but couldn't verify her presence inside. If he wasted another night tracking her down, she'd pay the price.

He nodded at the kid and kept walking, assessing the house and best way to approach. Depending on how long she stayed, he might achieve his goal without incident. Foot traffic had started thinning out with the slight drizzle.

Since his prey's car was parked under a bright light, acquiring her there wasn't an option. If she took the shortcut, he'd finish without a lot of fuss. There wasn't a lot of cover to accomplish his goal. Expedience and a little luck would favor success.

The bass beat of the band in the student center thrummed in his chest. It almost made him wish for a different upbringing, one where he went on to higher education instead of following in his older brother's footsteps. Jason had wanted him to join the military instead of the gang.

Thinking back, he had no regrets and no pile of debt. He drove a nice car, when he didn't need to steal one for work. A well-padded bank account and a reputation for getting the job done created comfort and respect. His life was quiet and efficient without complications.

While waiting, he took a new position at the side of the building where he had visual access of those exiting from either door.

The equations in her head carried a hefty price tag. Money earned from this equaled a nice vacation, if he obtained the knowledge by Monday morning. That left time between for *play*. This bitch had the answers to their dilemma and he intended to get them.

The drug business wasn't profitable when your product killed off the clientele. With the chem major's knowledge, they'd have the perfect formula, expand their business, and enjoy the fruits of their subordinates' labors.

Sources depicted the student as smart, sassy, and best of all, a party animal. He didn't quite get the leap from chemistry major to pre-med student, but it wasn't in his wheelhouse and didn't affect her final outcome.

Slipping on gloves and checking the baggie in his pocket, he leaned against a tree and waited. Sloppy seconds wasn't his normal thing, but the girl's picture revealed a nice shape and perfect breasts. He couldn't wait to make a beautiful patchwork quilt of her body. His short blade itched for her crimson essence.

Light mist had turned to drizzle and filtered through the leaves by the time she wobbled down the back steps. *That's the thing about this college campus; kids think they're safe.* Discontent stiffened the set of her body long before he registered her grumbled complaints.

In silent preparation, he circled around with uneven steps to get ahead of her using pines, oaks, and smaller saplings overrun with briars for cover. If the small noises registered in her inebriated mind, she'd think a squirrel scampered about.

No escort meant one less body to deal with. His luck had improved. In counterpoint, it was just as well to knock out the brains of an operation before going for the brawn. His boss wanted information now, so Keiki would have to wait her turn.

His objective turned toward the widened deer trail leading to the parking lot.

Yes!

Edging between two large trees put him in position of to see anyone nearby while the bulk of his body remained hidden. He slowed his breathing and waited for the shuffling steps announcing her approach. With a quiet snap, he opened the baggie and removed the prepared cloth.

"Damn boys anyway. Immature and freaking useless." She didn't look around as if the hair on her nape pricked. Her sightline remained fixed on her feet and the trajectory of the occasional pinecone she sent flying. Either her intelligence didn't range in the realm of self-preservation, or she was too drunk to have any.

Erratic footsteps scuffing through the leaves stopped with an oath and soft thud. She'd face-planted. "Sonofabitch. I wasted a whole evening on someone who wanted to play video games."

Muffled threats against all things male and incompetent slurred as she pushed to her feet and struggled to use her phone's light.

It seemed her greatest challenge lay in avoiding small branches hidden in the leaf litter. She'd tripped again.

He'd soon give her bigger problems to consider.

Mumbled curses and her dispute with nature continued with a low string of curses.

It never failed to surprise him how a person could be numb with frustration and liquor one minute, then wide awake with terror the next. He loved it when his assignments were women. Men weren't near as much fun.

Her sixth sense never warned her of the danger from behind, or that her world would forever change.

He stepped up and covered her mouth and nose with the moist cloth while his arm banded her back against his chest.

She was stronger than anticipated and fought like a demon. Hope of her gasping in the sickly sweet drug died a quick death when she twisted her head to the side.

At the same time, she contorted her body and slammed her fist into his groin.

"Motherfucker. Not gonna happen," she gasped, then stumbled sideways. Shaking her head, she darted toward the head of the trail, back toward the frat house.

The cloth fell to the ground when he doubled over in pain. "Bitch. You'll pay for that."

"Fuck you."

It took him three strides to catch her, dealing with pain and his own adrenaline rush. In any other circumstance, he'd give her a sporting chance, a ten-second head start. However, his boss was adamant about getting the job done with as few witnesses as possible.

She'd just inhaled to scream when he tackled her to the ground and knocked her out the good old-fashioned way. The interrupted cry hadn't drawn any apparent attention. It seemed fate favored him after all.

He couldn't afford to screw the pooch now. Tossing her over his shoulder, Porter backtracked and found the useless cloth while vowing to not underestimate her again.

Replacing the drugged material in his baggie allowed him his first deep breath. He repositioned her for the considerable walk in the opposite direction. His mini flash, once away from the buildings, helped him pick out fallen logs and avoid grabbing late-season briars. Considering her slight stature and his anticipated fun, he didn't mind the extra work.

It wasn't until he'd made it halfway to his truck that he realized he'd forgotten to pick up her phone. *I'll send someone back to get it and the cameras.*

The remote cabin greeted him like a long lost lover. Flashbacks of previous escapades flitted through Porter's mental catalogue and ramped up his heartbeat.

Soon.

His quarry lay tethered on the backseat, not knowing she'd never leave the woods. Perhaps he'd situate her grave looking out over the valley below. After all, brunettes should stick together.

Her soon-to-be grave mates had been a little older, but nonetheless shared a common denominator. They were all beautiful. He'd reserved a section for the crème de la crème.

It'd been too many months since he'd last visited the area and his secluded hideaway. It was his greatest source of pride and home to his masterpieces. Each picture in his treasured scrapbook animated memories and details of a life well lived, and in vivid splashes of reds and creams.

Once inside, he secured her in a comfortable room in the hidden basement. If his handling generated more than a slight concussion, there might be complications. The information his boss expected was sophisticated and specific. After relaying it, he could spend the next several weeks enjoying her screams during both pain and orgasm.

Their initial conversation would set the tone for the convoluted relationship to follow. While she slept, he took great care in preparing comfort food and setting the scene.

The space had to engender the right atmosphere. The bedding was clean and smelled like the fabric softener he remembered as a kid. Thick padding and shag carpet covered the cement floor and complemented the light gray block walls where several posters of popular bands added a bit of personality. A scented air freshener helped negate the slight musty odor from the windowless space. If it mimicked a 70s style horror film, well, that's when he'd first learned his nature.

She'd soon learn to appreciate this room over the two others, each intended for a different purpose.

What kid didn't like ham and cheese sandwiches with a cup of cold milk? Paper plates and plastic cups decreased the likelihood of fashioning a weapon. His groin still throbbed with the echoes of her earlier strike.

Setting the tray on the end table bolted to the floor, he smiled in anticipation. In the armoire, an array of lingerie and form-fitting dresses would give her the option of changing clothes, all caught on tape by his concealed cameras.

Waiting for her to awaken proved a challenge since he was anxious to begin matching wits. When she groaned and her eyelids fluttered, she surveyed the room and sucked in a breath. He hadn't used the bed's attached cuffs yet, wanting to make a good first impression.

"Evening. How's the head feeling? I left you some acetaminophen by the glass of water. It's still in the foil packet."

Let the games begin.

"You kidnap me then give me pain medicine? Why?"

He loved the confusion written in her brow. In a few hours, he'd magnify it ten-fold.

"My goal is to extract information, not hurt you. We're going to be partners."

"If your intent including releasing me, you'd be wearing a mask so I can't identify you later."

"I don't like the way they feel. Sides, we're so far from your school, and I'll drug you before taking you back. You'll never know how many state lines we've crossed, much less find this place again. I'm good at flying under the radar. If you accept my offer of partnership, everybody's happy."

"You don't lack for confidence, do you?"

Porter shrugged. "If I discover you've talked later on, I'll just find you again, but with a more, shall we say, *permanent* outcome. Understand?"

She nodded then sat up in bed. Her voice held none of the tremor shaking her fingers. Gabby was smart, but he didn't know if she was clever.

"You're pre-med. Quite the chemistry student."

"Following in my father's footsteps."

"Wonderful. He must be so proud. Actually, I was referring to your *other* studies. The sideline involving chemistry."

She looked away as she ripped the foil and took the tablets. After setting the water aside, she closed her eyes, the small head shake equal to self-chastisement. Did she wonder if he'd drugged the water?

Too late!

He could see the wheels of her mind forming different scenarios and strategies for her desired outcome. Survival.

To help ease her obvious anxiety, he decided directness might serve his purpose. "I know you've been working on perfecting Serenity. Your version has less side effects, and I want the formula. Give it to me and we're done."

A virtual mask slid over her face to cover parted lips and stiffening spine. Increased pallor of her cheeks remained another testament to her distress.

To add incentive for cooperation, he stood and let his bulk multiply the potential hazards of her situation. Instead of locking the door, he'd left the wooden planked barrier to freedom ajar.

A test.

Her focus swung toward the exit as he ambled around the end of her bed and rested his hand on the ornate, iron-slatted footboard. She wouldn't know all the wonderful uses for those precious bars.

"This doesn't have to be unpleasant. As a matter of fact, for the correct answer, you'll receive a reward. Surely more than your boss would provide. Oh, and I'd like some information on your partner, Keiki."

That snapped her attention upright, before her hands clenched the bedspread.

"All I wanted is a less toxic drug. Kids are going to take them anyway. The least I can do is make it safer for them."

"Exactly. Me too. We both want the same thing." Including her in his goal equaled another step in securing her cooperation. "Hell, you can even supply your friends at no charge."

She bit her lip, indecision written in the drumming of her fingers against her jean-clad thighs. "I don't have the recipe in my head. I've been working with someone."

"Keiki? Your best friend?" He smiled his shark smile. "Yeah, I know something about your buddies."

"No, not Keiki. She's got nothing to do with this."

"Oh, but I beg to differ. As a matter of fact, I'm just learning how valuable she can be. She doesn't know it yet, nor does she know her future role in our company."

"You murdered Shelly."

"That wasn't personal. It was a message to her father for dealing drugs in a territory he doesn't own. On the flip side, his use of technology is innovative and kinda cute. I can, however, offer protection for your help." This had all the markings of one of his best games.

"It felt personal to me." She again visually inspected the room before her gaze settled on one of the cuffs peeking out from the foot of the bed. A silent moment allowed her to formulate false assumptions and possible outcomes.

"All right. But I work in tandem with a professor. He's the intermediary and keeps my notes."

"Well, that does sound enticing. Who's the professor?" He should have known the matter would get complicated.

"His name is Bayler. He has a lab in the basement of his house."

"I'll bet it's not as nice as what you have here..."

"It has exits that aren't blocked."

"Tell you what. I'm going to bring down enough food for a late dinner and all day tomorrow. I'll be back before breakfast Monday morning." Porter offered his most benign smile.

"Are you going to kill him?"

"Why bother? All I want is the formula. I don't care if he shares it with the world."

Wariness and suspicion radiated from every pore of her body. In the end, hope won over both. She shrugged a faked indifference.

"Before I go, however..." It was time to sample the goods and see how many orgasms he could force from her body.

Video setup in the corner provided a subtle future threat and would remind her to keep her mouth shut.

Back on campus, he smiled at the memory of her shocked expression. It'd taken longer than expected to coerce her arousal but worth it in the end. No doubt the drugged water helped ease the way.

A quick search for the lost cell phone yielded no result, but he did retrieve the small cameras near the frat house.

The memories warmed him inside. His latest acquisition had been exquisite in her righteous anger, which gave way to screams of release before tears of humiliation had taken hold.

A bit of research provided background on his next prey, Professor Bayler. His newest plaything had divulged the whereabouts of specific records in hopes of sparing her mentor's life.

How sweet. She would've made a compassionate doctor.

Karma was a fickle bitch, giving with one hand while taking away with the other. Bayler hadn't been home when he arrived to retrieve the prized data, which was great. On the flip side, hope for an easy recovery was dashed after scrutinizing the isolated home.

It would have been preferable to collect the research without leaving evidence of his visit. The boss' planned takeover involved minimal violence after the shock of the Harock kid's death. Instead, he'd missed collecting the tech kid and now couldn't pick a lock.

Figures the man would have bars over his basement window but not those on the first floor. Real genius here.

Careful study of the surrounding area revealed no other homes close by to hear the breaking glass.

He hoped Bayler was smart enough to not have an alarm system. It wouldn't do to have cops rummaging through his basement.

Once inside, he smiled. The inhabitant enjoyed a modest home with a few nice creature comforts. If there'd been more time, he would've relaxed and enjoyed the gigantic TV and a beer from the fridge.

Limited moonlight filtered through the home's surrounding trees, yet he didn't need to switch on any fixtures. The bungalow had an open floor plan with a doorway leading downstairs off the kitchen.

Initial efforts to locate specific notes ended in curses and dire threats. This was supposed to be an easy assignment. Expectations crumbled under current observations. *The bitch lied.* He'd suspected she had, but hadn't wanted to take out his anger without proof.

The basement consisted of concrete walls and floor, two tables of various beakers, a grocery list, notes without formulae, and a half-eaten sandwich.

Nothing resembled the typed document containing his prize. It was possible the professor decided to double cross his partner. The amateurs had no clue of the scope or significance of their product.

A thorough search of the home from basement to attic revealed no safe or secret nook with hidden material. In anger, he snatched several pictures off the living room wall and smashed their frames against the TV.

He understood impulse control issues, but having to confront the professor face to face meant another body. His boss would not be happy.

In hopes of appeasing whatever forces set against him, he returned to the basement and tucked the sheath of notes in his waistband. He'd never been called a genius, but knew they didn't contain his sought-after prize.

The man was a chem professor, which meant he maintained a lab at school. That would be the focus of his next search.

The crunch of tires on gravel alerted him to a vehicle's approach. Confronting the professor here was not optimal. No, the best scenario entailed catching him at work and carrying out a quick snatch and grab.

With his head filled with thoughts of malice, he exited the back as a key turned the front door lock.

Simple deception would buy him some time with his boss. After his return trip through the woods, he took snapshots of the stolen papers and sent a text to his boss while his car warmed up.

If by some miracle it was useful, so much the better. Otherwise, he'd at least bought an extension. Luck would see Bayler accusing the student for ransacking his home. The slightest paranoia should force the man to check on the formula. The task now became a matter of follow and observe.

The return text complimented him on a job well done and notice of a hefty bonus. Paper records delivered the next day would allow for another potential pat on the back.

His cell buzzed halfway back to the school, the smile on his face falling away with his boss's text.

"Just examined the formula. This is not complete!" Theo maintained a zero tolerance for incompetence.

Failure didn't bode well for his future. *"I've still got the girl. I'll question her again and get back to you tonight."*

Sudden silence left Porter with no doubts, he would soon follow Shelly Harock in death if he failed again.

It was feasible the professor had moved things after Shelly's death, or his prisoner liked games. So be it, he'd show her how much fun they could be.

First, he'd sit on the professor's office and hope paranoia overrode a working relationship.

Chapter Five

Keiki put one hand on her hip and grumbled when the stout, bald detective refused to sit and talk, instead standing as if expecting a barrage of insults.

"I know you don't want to hear this, but we have no new leads to follow. It doesn't mean we're closing the case, but until something pops up on our radar, we have no direction. You're gonna have to be patient."

Keiki launched herself at the taller man, pounding his chest then aiming for his face. "You promised to find who killed my parents! You're a useless pig!"

Tears choked her words and her thoughts. Her mom and dad would never cross the threshold again and lend their wisdom to her ventures, never offer a smile when she needed it most, and never hug her like she was their world.

The combination of hate and disparity knocked her legs from beneath her, sending her crumbling to the floor.

Keiki opened one eye at a time in hopes of dampening the force of morning light spearing her brain. The room lurched sideways and her head felt heavy until reality crawled inside with a dull ache.

Hunched over the kitchen table, she straightened and rubbed her eyes. The same nightmare haunted her dreams and waking moments.

The project she'd worked on last night lay in pieces across the rustic wood she and her dad had lovingly restored and finished to a fine sheen. She'd reclaimed the planks from an old barn and worked while her father instructed and watched. Her dad's shop was gone, but his skill would live through her forever.

At times when grief overwhelmed her, she remembered the odor of freshly cut boards and the brief smell of alcohol before the shellac dried on a finished stool or cabinet. Her mother often brought out a cup of tea or cocoa and sit to watch, suggesting possibilities for future projects.

Stuck to her left forearm was a piece of a drone's undercarriage she'd been working on late into the night—before falling asleep.

Her roommate still hadn't returned, nor did she answer her phone now. Last night's text stating she'd stay overnight at the frat house meant sleeping in and dragging herself home around lunchtime.

It made no sense that the evening news hadn't detailed Shelly's murder. The cops had been at the scene and had to know Shelly's identity.

She didn't know what to do and had nobody else in which to confide. Her voice would choke if she spoke with either of Shelly's parents, people who considered her family.

Despite the nausea churning her stomach, she snagged a few pieces of colored candy from the baggie kept on the table. Shelly said chocolate made everything better.

The second drone she'd used to spy on the police had given her a grainy glimpse of her best friend's body lying on the patch of ground tended with loving care along with the detective aiming his gun at her mechanical child.

Without a hint of why anyone would target her friend, she had nothing to offer the cops in the way of motive or suspects. Her short piece of video included a man wearing a mask and speaking with a thick accent.

A recorded snippet sent to her second part-time employer, Nick Tucker, produced no match yet from the biometric database including voiceprints. By not sending more than a few sentences, she intended to keep Nick out of the investigation.

She didn't understand sound spectrographs or how they differentiated samples, but then, she didn't understand Gabby's obsessiveness over formulae either. Some mysteries were better left to experts.

Sooner or later, either cops or the killer would show up at her door.

Their town was too small to have experienced competent officers, which meant she had a little time and could do her own snooping. When she found something worthwhile, they could have the evidence.

A knock on her apartment door triggered the evolutionary response of shoving back in her chair and raising her hands to the unknown threat. The small gasp wouldn't travel into the apartment's hallway, but fear clutched her heart and filled her throat with bile.

Keiki swallowed hard. She lived in a small complex with nine other tenants. Maybe someone needed a cup of sugar.

Gabby wouldn't knock, but Shelly's parents would. Her conscience dictated she call the Harock's as soon as the news broke.

If the killer stood on the door's other side, he wouldn't knock either. Regardless, she needed to offload the overwhelming fear suffocating her mind and paralyzing her ability to act.

Dressed in yesterday's T-shirt and jeans, she gave a conspicuous sniff and deemed her level of cleanliness acceptable.

A few wary steps forward and a stumble over thin air allowed her to grasp the door handle. She froze, couldn't make herself move.

Through the peephole, she saw a tall man with hair darker than sin, and a solid build. The laser-type stare, direct and confident, marked the alpha presence as nemesis. His silver-blue gaze could penetrate anything in its path. If adult wolves had blue eyes, he'd fit the bill.

His face could have been rendered by a Renaissance painter with defined cheekbones, straight nose, and a jaw that conveyed strength and masculinity. Confidence and a radiated irritation rounded out the package.

Another man stood close by, equal in height if not stature, and less threatening. He was near as broad but less intimidating, standing to the side and back. Her first impression fabricated the likeness of a large bear, the cuddly kind that could turn protective in an instant.

Both were dressed in jeans and casual button-downs. Experience pinned them as police.

"Katherine Tallerman?" The voice was gruff and raw, attached to an attitude that didn't understand the word retreat.

"Go away, or I'll call the cops... and I'll scream like a banshee." It was the only thing coming to mind.

"Keiki, we *are* the cops," said a different voice with a warm southern drawl. "We'd like to talk to you for a few minutes. It's about your friend."

The use of her nickname suggested they'd done their homework, which a determined assassin would also do. "Look, here's my badge." The wolf held a gold shield up in front of the spyhole.

A wolf and a bear. One to cuddle and soothe my fears while the other prepares to devour me whole.

Neither voice held the peculiar accent of Shelly's killer.

Instead of opening the door wide, she nudged it a few inches then wedged her stockinged foot near the edge for maximum resistance should they try to shove their way in. There was nothing within reach to chock under the knob.

She'd been so sure it would take more time to find her. Time she could've used to prepare her mind and rehearse what to say.

Stupid. Stupid. Stupid.

"Which friend? I have lots." Keeping the solid door as a barrier between them provided a few minutes to get herself under control. She couldn't wipe the image of the more intense man's eyes from her mind, or the coiled savagery lurking within their depths.

Watch out for the Canis lupus.

"Shelly Harock. We understand you two were close." Southern boy seemed to hold more patience.

"Yes, we are." If she couldn't remove the wobble from her words, she'd stand no chance of deceiving either of them.

At least I remembered to say are instead of were.

Her gaze scanned the area as if she'd find an answer to her dilemma in her apartment. A 12 gauge shotgun in the corner leaned beyond her reach, hidden behind the standing coat rack and Gabby's long duster. Her father had refused to let her bring it when discussing college living options, since it was forbidden in the rental agreement. After her parents' death, she couldn't bear to part with it.

As if on cue, the police badge inched between the door and frame. "Katherine, if you don't want us in your apartment, that's fine. We'd be better suited to go to the station and chat." The wolf's silken voice held enough edge to be a threat.

"All right, you can come in." She relinquished her weight against the door and pulled it open. "But the place is a mess."

Despite their official status, she couldn't abandon her instincts and turn her back on either. With a gesture, she ushered them forward and stood back, waiting for them to sit.

"Hi, I'm Detective Waylin. This is my partner, Detective Garnett. Thank you for seeing us." The bear was trim and cute, but a shrewd intelligence lurked behind the tranquil façade, and like the wolf, he assessed everything.

The pair existed as visible opposites, darkness and light, laid back and focused intensity, each sexy in their own right. Forefront in her mind was the fact that they could both be dangerous.

"You look like a mildewed string bean." Keiki bit the inside of her cheek and shrugged. Snark born of anxiety received more tolerance from the bearish cop.

The wolf coughed behind his fisted hand. "Yeah, he could stand to gain a few pounds."

"Sorry, my mouth gets the better of me when taken by surprise." The bear wasn't thin yet wouldn't have to suck in his shoulders to get through a narrow doorway.

"No problem." Detective Garnett leaned back on the couch in the guise of relaxed alpha male. "You, um, look a bit nervous."

"I'm a college student, and you two are cops. Do the math." It was the dark predator's ongoing assessment that sent alternate chills and heat firing through her nervous system. The freeze-thaw cycles would cause upheaval if not held in check.

She wasn't about to sit beside them, or opposite them in the old, overstuffed recliner. Instead, she strode to the kitchen in the guise of hospitality. "Would either of you care for a glass of water or tea?"

"No, thanks," they both declined.

Plastic cups creaked as she retrieved one and poured some sweet tea for herself then sat at the kitchen table, needing the comfort of familiar things to balance the information barreling her way.

"Is your roommate home?" The wolf looked around as if expecting company. He was the kind of man who'd sleep with one foot over the edge of the bed, undaunted by anything that could go bump in the night, since he was the fiercest, most dangerous creature around.

"No. She's at her boyfriend's place." Keiki skimmed her trembling fingers across the tabletop, a gesture that soothed.

Garnett studied her as if dissecting a bug, figuring the best approach to achieve his goal.

A deep throat clearing accelerated her heart rate. Small talk would not be the wolf's forte. She could get through the impending tragic news if he'd stop delving beneath her virtual armor with bullshit.

Chapter Six

A brief scan of the small apartment revealed a dichotomy in the way it was furnished. The sofa was soft leather with finely stitched pillows and a crocheted afghan lying across the top. In contrast, the faded and worn oversized recliner facing it equaled a cherished haven for a college kid to nestle in while watching a favorite movie.

Nolan formed a mental catalogue of the items in view, then frowned at the upper corner by the door. Except for the small cobweb, everything was neat and clean.

"Yeah, our resident night crawler. We feed him daily and leave the one Halloween decoration up year round. Lends authenticity."

Whether her defense mechanism affected snark as a buffer against present company, expected news, or was a natural part of her personality remained to be seen. Either way, it shielded her vulnerability, to a point.

"Nice apartment. When my sisters went to college, the dorm rooms were concrete blocks with thin carpet and iffy hot water." Nolan tested her reactions to get a baseline feel for her responses.

"I have scholarships for tuition and books."

With arms crossing under her breasts, she radiated irritation and a closed-off persona.

"I also have a job. Not all college kids are airheads."

"Which job are we talking about? You have two, yes?" Nolan took her anger in stride, unable to define its source. "You work for Franklin Harock. Does he pay well and have good... benefits?" He couldn't identify the reasoning for skipping normal protocol and diving in on the offensive. His partner's discreet shifting of position reminded him to tone it down.

"I work for him, yes. How did you know?"

Furrowed brow and thinned lips evidenced increasing stress. Her ability to maintain normal eye contact without unusual widening substantiated his belief she held nothing earth shattering behind the wall of swirling emotions.

He wanted to be the one to inform her of the news. Not to break her down but something else, deeper, something more that allowed him to see true character underneath the anger and bundled nerves.

When he told her, the news hit her like a ton of bricks. She turned away to gather herself, flattening both palms on the kitchen table as if to stave off pain.

On the wood surface sat a clear plastic baggie. The unmarked, unknown pills equaled leverage at the most opportune time. Glancing over at his partner revealed he'd also noticed.

Superficial details of Shelly's death provoked tears and righteous anger, all sincere. Whatever had happened to her friend, Keiki's grief came from the heart.

"I saw her Thursday. She was supposed to come over last night, but I got busy and fell asleep at the table."

"Did Shelly say anything that would lead you to believe she was frightened or having trouble with a jealous ex?" Nolan asked, recalling the conversation with Franklin Harock, who claimed his daughter had no serious romantic entanglements or violent ex-boyfriends.

Keiki tilted her head to the side. "She did say there was a guy sitting outside the quad talking to a few of the KAs the other night. She and Gabby had just left a frat party and neither one recognized him. He must have been young enough to pass for a student, or she would've said something else." This time, she briefly closed her eyes, as if trying to pick out a specific detail from memory.

"Description?" Coyote was pulling his notepad from his jacket pocket.

"No, just said he was creepy. Have you talked with Gabby today by any chance? I can't find her. I've been looking all over campus." Fingers twined and twisted in her lap until cracking knuckles and a pointed look from Coyote forced her to shove her hands in her pockets.

"No, we haven't. We spoke with her boyfriend, said she left his place last night after having too much to drink. He claimed he was too drunk to see her home," Nolan offered while trying to keep disgust out of his tone.

"Are you aware of Shelly frequenting a spot off the interstate near

Gap Hollow?" Coyote took the lead, his expression nonjudgmental.

"Yes. Her family owns land around there. She kept a flower and herb patch in memory of her sister." Keiki swiped a tear from the corner of her eye. "Is that where you found her?"

"Yes," Nolan murmured. Unable to tolerate the pain etched in her face, he stood, needing to keep moving to prevent his arms from offering comfort. Being the oldest of five siblings brought out a softer side which needed squelching at times. He examined the pictures on the opposite wall.

"What'cha working on? Looks like a lot of pieces." The sizable kitchen table doubled as her workspace.

Stepping closer, he picked up a thin piece of metal jointed in the middle with some type of broken connection on one end. The other end divided into four parts. *Like a hand.*

"It's a prototype. I build drones for Harock Industries. He'll sell them for me." Keiki took the piece Nolan picked up, a scowl of disapproval creasing her forehead.

"Please don't touch my stuff."

"Can't anyone put together a drone? Where's the instructions?" His goading was unprofessional, unplanned, and had no basis in the current line of questioning.

"These can't. The method of two-way audio and visual feeds make them unique." Pride for her work strengthened her voice.

"Got a patent on any yet?" Coyote asked.

"Working on it. Do you know how long that process takes? I'll get there, eventually."

"I kind of gathered these are a bit delicate, since it seems to match the piece we found stuck in a woodland flowerbed." Holding up his phone for her to see, Nolan swiped to the picture he'd taken of the bagged CSI evidence.

Her quick inhale and widened eyes declared they'd struck a nerve and jumped on the right track, wherever it led.

"Similar design, but that's not one of mine. Look at the area above the elbow joint." Keiki used two fingers to enlarge the picture on his phone. "What the hell?" Confusion that couldn't be feigned hunched her shoulders and narrowed her eyes.

"What's wrong?" Nolan edged a little closer to see what forced the strong reaction. The proximity added a light tinge of her appealing fragrance. He expected a citrus or flowery scent. Instead, it was clean, maybe earthy, practical, and no-nonsense, just the way she presented herself underneath the nervous tension.

Her awareness zeroed in on his screen to the point she seemed to block out all other stimuli, including his proximity.

And how interesting is that?

"See here? There's no engraving." Picking up the metal spider-like piece in front of her, she repeatedly tapped a like area. "Look close here. I mark my parts." Inquisitive energy infused her voice but failed to stop her fingers from shaking.

"So, this," Coyote pointed to what Keiki held, "matches the part we found inside Shelly's pocket."

"You're saying you found two spare parts? One's mine, the other isn't. Someone's trying to frame me." Keiki set her project down with a little more force than necessary. "I had a drone out there. An arm broke off, and she said she'd bring it back, but..."

"Why would someone frame you?" Nolan watched the transformation in her face from wary uncertainty to principled anger; the student had quite a backbone.

Shaking her head, she hardened her glare. "I don't know. I didn't hurt her, but I'll damn well find out and let you know who did."

"I believe that's our job." Nolan prepared himself for the storm but needed to see the depth of her reaction and self-control.

"Like you found my parents' killer? Fat chance."

"I'm sorry about your folks' death. However, you were at the hillside scene, after a fashion." Needing to push a bit further, Nolan made it a statement, insinuating she'd controlled the spy drone Coyote had threatened to shoot.

She ignored the bait, but looked away. "I was here yesterday morning. I can prove it."

Nolan recognized the look in his partner's eyes. The one declaring they'd reached a fork in the road. They knew Keiki had eyes on the scene, which wasn't crossing legal lines. If either pushed too hard, they'd risk alienating a witness and possible suspect. They needed to back off and further study the situation.

"We know. We also know you made the anonymous 911 call." It

was a gamble, but Nolan took it. He'd let her skate on the spying since they didn't have proof and no laws were broken.

"Yeah." Her shoulders slumped and she dropped back in her chair, either guilt or grief weighing her down.

"How long have you known her?" Coyote murmured. The junior partner had a way of soothing interviewees with one part sincerity and two parts southern gentleman.

"Since grade school. When my parents died in a carjacking, her family kind of took me in. I'd just started college." With her palm on her forehead, she sighed as if gathering her thoughts. "Twice in one lifetime. How can this happen?" Tears trailed down her face, to be cleared away with angry swipes.

Nolan's gut clenched in sympathy. She was first set adrift without viable family support, then again from her best friend. "Walk us through what happened."

Similarities between Nolan and his witness generated a type of kinship, a situation he knew to avoid. He'd questioned beautiful women before without his body succumbing to the unnamed quality drawing him closer. That path was impulsive and irresponsible, a road never traveled.

Keiki's voice remained flat through the telling. Despite that, she held something back and remained terrified of the killer.

"So, he wore a mask. Did you notice any identifying marks on his neck or arms? A tattoo maybe?"

"No, but I'll never forget his eyes or his voice. His accent was some dialect of Spanish, but, well, I can't define it." She accepted, and made use of, a tissue Coyote offered.

When she reached in the baggie to grab one of the vibrant pills, Nolan snatched her wrist. "Ah, you do remember we're cops, yes?"

"And you remember that I'm in the privacy of my own home, and as such am entitled to eat what I choose? I like chocolate."

"Chocolate?" Coyote asked in disbelief.

"Yeah, colored chocolate candies. I'm addicted to them."

"Hmm." Nolan picked up the bag and sniffed.

Keiki snatched it back and snagged a handful, tossing them in her mouth with a glare. "Mine. Get your own." Stepping away, she opened a cupboard and removed a brightly colored package. On it, the name and picture of said candy confirmed her claim. "See? I have to divide them in baggies and hide them from Gabby. She can finish a whole bag in no time."

After watching her world crumble, Nolan couldn't leave her in such an emotionally charged state. Through his own loss, he realized the simple support he could offer entailed directing her energy toward something positive.

"About these drones. What can you do with them?" His interest stemmed in part from innate curiosity and wanting her focus away from death.

"Pretty much anything you can dream up. This one can pick up and carry small objects for a half mile. I'm working to double its distance."

"Ah, for surveillance, like your work with Nick Tucker?" Nolan couldn't scour the image of her in ski gear with Nick's arm slung around her waist. "Work on anything interesting lately?"

"Not in particular. No."

"You and Shelly look a lot alike. You ever get mixed up?" Coyote pocketed his note pad but didn't break eye contact.

"Occasionally." Changing the subject, she added, "I've got a device that's so quiet, you won't know it's there unless someone told you to look. This one here, it delivers a puff of forced air or shoots out a soft spongy ball."

Nolan perked up at that. "Why would someone deliver a puff of air or shoot—?"

Oh, shit. It could deliver chemicals.

"Why not?" Keiki shrugged. Directing her attention to Nolan, she spoke with genuine enthusiasm about her creations. "I used one to wake Shelly up last week, then flew it out of her window before she could swat it down." A bittersweet smile slid into place.

"What kind of payload are we talking about?" The thoughts forming in Nolan's mind—drugs, drones, and delivery—painted a dark scenario.

"Not much considering their size. A few ounces up to a, um, maybe a pound. Keep in mind, there's a correlation between weight and the distance you want it to travel."

"So, this piece here, the one we found at the scene, not in Shelly's pocket. It's not one of yours," Nolan reiterated, hoping to gain further insight.

"No. Mine broke off in Shelly's hand. She must have stuck it in her jacket. I—"

"Can we take a look at Gabby's room?" Nolan urged Keiki toward the short hallway with two doors on one side.

"Sure, the one on the end is hers."

"Some of your drones have cameras. Did the one yesterday record any visual or audio?" Nolan pressed for more information.

"No."

Both detectives turned at her sharp denial to see crimson flooding the coed's cheeks, and Nolan sighed.

She's determined to play investigator in a dangerous game. Is she otherwise involved?

A cursory search of the room yielded nothing to indicate darker dealings. No drugs, no beer bottles, everything in its place, neat and tidy. When finished, Coyote returned to the kitchen with their interviewee while Nolan went into the shared bathroom.

He'd braced himself to find a few prescriptions, something not marked, birth-control pills, or condoms. Either she wasn't sexually active or relied on her partner for protection, which didn't fit his current image of her. He found nothing other than OTC pain reliever and an old, near empty prescription of a strong NSAID.

A minute later, he slipped into the second bedroom. Keiki's room. Anything found couldn't be used against her in a legal sense, but it would round out his mental picture of her character.

Instead of posters of specific bands or movie ads, he found a large family portrait and a wall of framed photos, some depicting tie-dye or mud runs, others of her and an older man with the same eyes holding up a rough plank board with an unusual grain and large knots.

The same wood in the kitchen table.

Woodworking tools in the photo's background showed all the makings of a top-notch hobbyist.

What he didn't see were any photos of boys her own age, bands, or expected teenage memorabilia. She was direct, fairly open, and focused.

The young lady in the photographs radiated an intensity he'd never seen. She wore the kind of smile which came from contentedness. He assumed her mother had held the camera.

Time and experience dictated several short visits, strategically spaced, to acquire more information and create a fuller picture of the respondent. Once gathered, conflicting details would be used to their advantage.

Leaving on a positive note was imperative during this critical phase of the investigation.

"We'll retrieve video footage from the school to see if we can find the stranger." Coyote's assurance seemed to help. "Keep your eyes open for anyone suspicious lurking around school or your apartment complex."

"Thanks for talking to us today. We'll keep you updated." Nolan followed Coyote to the door but stopped when his partner froze.

The man's small gesture toward the coat rack presented another thread for them to pull.

"Katherine, is that yours or your roommate's?" Nolan nudged a long black garment aside to scrutinize the firearm.

Giving name to it aloud meant red tape. Something that would hinder their investigation and create a barrier when they needed the appearance of open communication.

Trust was a tenuous commodity which straddled the letter of the law. Catching a killer held higher priority than enforcing the bylaws of an apartment complex. Other than that, it was legal.

"It was my dad's, and I don't have anywhere else to keep it. It's not like I can store it at the nursing home with Grams. Please, don't take it."

Coyote cleared his throat. "Take what, Keiki? The only thing we're taking is our leave."

Nolan recognized shades of anger built on the backs of anguish, suffering, and loneliness. To her, it probably wasn't considered a weapon, merely a connection to the past. "There's no shortcut through it, kiddo. Pain is part of the process."

"So, either I numb it with alcohol and drugs or bury myself in work?"

"I've seen some mourners make friends with the devil. Others hunker down, avoid numbing agents, and plod on until one day, something changes their worldview."

It was the best Nolan could offer despite what his conscience urged. She needed a shoulder to cry on. A lifetime of dealing with four younger sisters made his strong enough.

"We were gonna do some early Christmas shopping." Soft sniffles filled the apartment.

A will made of iron halted his return to wrap her in his arms. She wasn't faking the grief needing a verbal outlet.

Time was the most precious commodity anyone could offer. He listened until her words dried up and the silence stretched out. He nodded when his partner nudged his shoulder, realizing her well of despair had emptied, for the time being.

Her sorrow struck a nerve he couldn't protect, and it scared the shit out of him. "Stay safe with... Just stay safe, kiddo." Establishing her as a kid in his mind erected the necessary barrier of emotional detachment.

Once back in their vehicle, Coyote gave him the stare, the one that spoke volumes without a sound. "I know that look, Nolan. I've seen it too many times on too many people, even felt it myself."

"I'm not crossing any lines," he argued. However, the frustration of dealing with the grieving young woman was making him straddle one.

"Except the part where she's probably a witness, I don't see a problem, not that I'd complain. I just want you to think about it and get the timing right. She's a rather fetching, if not charming, package of dynamite. Be careful when she detonates."

Nolan waited, knowing his partner had more to say. He sensed the familiar underlying hesitation and wondered what truths lay beneath the calm exterior.

"She doesn't have the killer instinct... I would know." Quiet words indicated a mountain of experience under the tip of the iceberg.

"Because you pulled the trigger in the military?"

"Yeah." Coyote glared out the passenger window but offered no more.

It wasn't worth pushing boundaries. "She's withholding information." Nolan jammed the key in the ignition.

"She knows the killer. Or, at least knows something about him,"

Coyote vocalized what they both felt. "And she doesn't trust us to find him."

"Yeah. I think she saw the attack happen, or at least part of it. A nightmare in progress she couldn't associate with a name or face. I believe she thought her friends fingered the creep outside a frat house. Maybe Shelly's murder has nothing to do with Harock Industries."

"Could be he was trolling for his next victim and didn't like the way the girls looked at him. Ready to go hassle Tucker?" Coyote logged into the onboard computer to locate the PI's address. "He's got confidentiality on his side, and if she's working for him, then she does, too."

"We'll save that conversation for after we've acquired more facts," Nolan advised. "Keiki is mixed up in this, and more weird shit we haven't even deciphered yet."

"Agreed, but I don't like her for the murder or conspiracy."

"You're right. She seems to prefer non-confrontation unless riled," Nolan puzzled over their earlier conversation.

"The dorms have security cameras. We need to check them," said Coyote as he gestured south when they reached the highway.

"Something's going on between Keiki and Franklin. I'd swear my sister's virtue on it. The damn thing is, I get that impression from Harock, not the kid."

"That sure of your siblings, are you?" Coyote's smile appeared to hold knowledge best not vocalized. "And again, I agree about Franklin. However, Keiki's not a kid in case you haven't noticed."

Nolan leveled a stare. "Jenna's not for you, swamp goblin. No offense, but I don't want my nineteen-year-old little sister dating an older man, a cop at that."

"Understood." Coyote scrubbed a hand over his jaw. "I didn't get the sense Keiki is romantically involved with Franklin. Not at all. She didn't even flinch, much less blush, when talking about either of Shelly's parents."

"Harock put off strange vibes, though." Nolan's sixth sense had kicked in the minute the father diverted attention away from the coed. "Which means the connection probably isn't mutual and, as you said, not romantic."

"Do you think she's tossed your card yet? I can't see her calling either of us if the killer targets her."

"Probably." *Why do kids think they're invincible?*

Chapter Seven

The evening air was warm and thick with the excitement and murmur of fellow runners. Each anticipated the *bang* starting the race. They still had fifteen minutes to go.

Keiki secured the numbered bib to her shirt, fighting the tears threatening to fall. She'd felt stronger before leaving her apartment and remembering when she and Shelly had run races together.

Three weeks prior, Shelly had pre-registered them both. Somehow, it seemed right to be here now, in honor of their friendship.

This was to have been her and Shelly's second Foam Glitter run. They'd bought matching white long-sleeved T-shirts and special hair dye. Neon green wasn't her color but would look great under the numerous black lights along the woodsy trail.

Flashbacks of the detectives in her apartment further blunted her pre-race jitters. She'd considered calling the wolf to hand over the video then decided to wait till tomorrow. Tucker hadn't yet matched the voice recording to a name.

Spectators stood on the sidelines, camera and phone flashes lighting up the night. Participants milled around, stretching their legs and backs, activating glow sticks to wear as necklaces and wristbands.

Off and on, she thought she heard the soft hum of a drone. The fact she could hear it over the crowd indicated it had a few large engines rather than multiple small ones. As a result, more sound was produced and the device was capable of bearing more weight.

Given the events were highly publicized with pictures splashed over the local paper, it made sense the sponsors wanted video.

The idea of installing a night-vision lens held merit. She could work on the logistics as she ran. Anything to keep her mind off the death scene stuck on repeat.

Two juniors, better friends with Shelly, talked in excited spurts behind her, discussing how they'd pose for pictures at the finish line.

"Evening."

In her current existence, one man had the power to scrape her nerves raw with a greeting.

The wolf is hunting.

Keiki whirled and stumbled, bumping into a fellow contestant who steadied her by grabbing her upper arm. Her mumbled, "Sorry," blended in with the crowd's increasing frenzy.

With hands on her hips, she glared at the detective and demanded, "What are you doing here?"

A benign smile masked whatever emotion lurked under the surface of his practiced façade.

"Like others here, I came to have my body turned into a work of art." Nolan held his hands out, the increased arm tension accentuating well-defined pecs and abdominals under a snug, white T-shirt.

She didn't mention he'd already attained that goal and wondered if he ever got tired of women staring. He was the type of man every woman wanted on her arm, and in her bed. Multi-hued color covering him from head to toe in the coming hour would only add to his charisma.

"I've haven't seen you at one of these before." She couldn't help the peevishness in her tone.

A nonchalant shrug said he didn't care, but the focused stare declared otherwise. "I thought we agreed you'd keep a low profile."

"I am. There are hundreds of other people here to mask my presence."

He used his index finger to draw an imaginary line from the crown of her head down the length of her hair. It felt like an angel's caress without physical contact. The staggering effect forced a stumble-step back.

He grinned.

"How, in heaven's name, is neon green part of laying low? I could spot you from the space station. Please tell me that's a wig." To further his evaluation, he gave a little tug, glaring harder when realizing the truth.

"Ow. Shelly bought the colors for this event. It's a special shampoo that glows under the black lights they use here."

"Which is how I zeroed in on you so fast. Can you at least wear a ball cap and stuff it up underneath?" The suggestion came with the detective removing his own hat and offering it in silent supplication.

"No, and you can stuff it." Keiki pivoted away, until he spun her back around to stare face to face with him.

It was a moment where he drew his line in the sand. One that further defined the budding chemistry between them. A fine silken thread with the tensile strength to bear all the weight of her grief while tethering their souls in an unexpected web. It would grow stronger with each test of faith.

"You have no sense of self-preservation, woman. You know that? What if *you* were the original intended target? You two look alike."

Raw determination briefly shredded his façade. The minute implacable resolve slid back into place, he sighed.

The cop was up to something. She didn't know what, but the certainty was written in his lowered brow and the hard set of his jaw. Determined blue met defiant blue, each glaring their intent. He would not delve within the depths of her pain again.

"And here I thought you figured I was a suspect."

"I haven't said you weren't, have I?"

The challenge lay thick in the air, an unspoken demand for her to prove her innocence. They would've verified her whereabouts Friday morning.

"Either way, I think you're in over your head and could be a target."

Tension in his frame indicated he had more to say, but he held his tongue. His frustration festered in the tightening of his mouth, but the announcer picked that moment to rev up the crowd.

"You know this is three miles, yes?" While she couldn't resist the taunt, she couldn't picture him with a donut in hand, either.

"Don't worry, I'll slow down for you."

He smiled in the face of her mumbled threat to leave him in the dust, a wolf's rise to challenge.

His moods appeared equally mercurial, vacillating between intimidation tactics and reeling her in close to protect her against any threat. Her body preferred the latter, a will of its own forcing her to lean in slightly.

"Where's your partner? *He* looks like the type to run."

"Only if it's toward a gator," Nolan muttered as he scrutinized the people around them.

"What?"

"Nothing. Private joke."

"How'd you know I'd be here? You obviously came prepared." Her hand's motion indicated his jeans and white T-shirt.

"I'm a detective, remember? Just doing my job."

"I'm a job?" Disappointment added another layer of gloom to her crumbling mood, cooling the molten flow through her veins until bedrock formed an unsteady base from where she perched.

Nolan stepped closer, ignoring the crowd's roar in response to the announcer's pre-race pep talk.

"I didn't say that."

Inches apart, he invaded her space as if realizing why she'd come and needing to drive home his point. "Don't let your grief overshadow everything else. A good friend wouldn't want you to pay that price."

Keiki froze when his finger under her chin lifted her gaze. The underlying attraction to a cop was as pointless as it was unwanted. It contradicted everything in which she believed.

General resentment and lack of confidence toward all law enforcement spilled over to the man challenging her. Just because she believed in right and wrong didn't mean cops were the answer to catching criminals. Hard work ensured she'd one day prove it.

"You have no idea what she'd want. But I do." Despite her attempt to harden her heart, tears gathered at the corners of her eyes. She refused to let them fall. Turning away, she didn't want *him* to see them.

"You think she'd want you to risk your life and track down a vicious killer? I don't think so. Not from her parents' description."

"They didn't know her, not for the past couple years." The cop was fishing for information. He'd find better waters elsewhere.

The countdown began over the loudspeaker, aided by the surrounding spectators who joined in for a deafening and incentive chant.

"C'mon, kid. Let's do this."

Nolan's brief touch of her shoulder was gone before she could shrug him off.

He was taller, hence would have a longer stride. That didn't make him faster. She debated on going slow just to tick him off, except that wasn't her style, and she refused to dishonor Shelly's memory by throwing the race.

Those out in front were the first to experience each foam zone. Black lights placed along the trail would reveal the various colors soaking her white T-shirt and jeans as she ran.

With the bang came an explosion of racers from the starting line. She took off with grief urging her forward. Nolan kept an easy pace beside her.

Their route started in an open meadow but then wound through the woods on a dirt road. Low path lights provided enough illumination to visualize the way. The cleared path allowed five racers to run abreast.

Bright blue froth blasted from the first zone's cannon to coat the runners. Black lights highlighted each racer's clothes and shrieking laughter filled the atmosphere. Keiki's right shoulder and jean-clad thigh sparkled with the thick fluff.

Peals of merriment and giggling behind them was reminiscent of how Shelly would shout and threaten a buzz cut if the colors didn't wash out. Several runners held their arms wide to gather more froth and spread it over their shirts.

The knot in Keiki's throat grew to golf-ball proportions and caused her to stumble, but Nolan's waiting hand at her elbow steadied her step.

In response, she shot forward, needing to outrun the laughter and party atmosphere. It had been a mistake to come. The noise level couldn't drown out her remorse or the memory of the killer's threat.

Her conversation with Shelly's parents earlier added another layer of grief. They'd asked her to come to their home, but she'd refused, needing time and not wanting to bring trouble to their door.

Nolan kept pace without a trace of heavy breathing or clumsy footing. By all appearances, he was in better shape than most of the runners.

Appropriate for his wolf avatar.

The two juniors who on occasion ran with them kept a steady stride behind her. Through several more stations, they each collected their due of color while making fun of each other.

Bright green suds spuming through the air indicated the next color zone to decorate her shirt. It reminded her of the greens Shelly liked to gather for Christmas wreaths. Thinking about the coming holidays brought a fresh lump to her throat. A small burst of speed pushed her ahead, where a small clearing offered the foam cannons particular advantage.

A sudden buzzing of small engines snapped her focus up to distinguish movement against a backdrop of fall leaves. Split-second analysis declared the drone not something an amateur would pilot. The dive-bomb maneuver it performed indicated more threat than curiosity.

Beside her, Nolan's lateral shove sent her tumbling to the ground where a broken branch jammed into her calf and several small rocks embedded in her hip. His body covered hers as one of his hands cupped over her nose and mouth.

From the side, she caught sight of a small cloud of powder floating downward but then taken back with the breeze.

She fought like a demon possessed. "What the hell's wrong with you, cop?"

Nolan quickly recovered, rolling to his side and sitting up while identifying himself as a police officer to those in close proximity.

The gun he'd palmed appeared a reflexive behavior.

"Weaponized drone. Stay on the ground, face the dirt, Keiki." To reinforce his command, he shoved her head down.

In the periphery, she saw him searching out the threat. Nearby runners yelled, some turning to run back the way they'd come, others taking a lateral plunge toward the closest wooded cover.

Screams filled the air.

Gurgling sounds from the fallen junior behind them preceded an ear-splitting wail from the companion. Three yards away, the downed runner lay on her back, one hand at her throat and the other grasping at the air.

Keiki couldn't ignore a friend in trouble. Curling on her side allowed her a view of their immediate vicinity along with being able to shield her face if necessary. When she started to inch toward the injured girl, Nolan shoved her down again, using his greater weight to keep her immobile.

"No, Keiki. We're not clear yet."

Behind them, the victim who'd dropped began stiffening then jerking with seizures.

One of her classmates in grade school had suffered from epilepsy, so Keiki knew what to do *if* she could get to the girl's side.

Approaching runners froze then backed away to create a backlog until several took charge and stopped the forward progress of any others.

The drone with a death wish grew louder.

It's coming for us again.

The thought, *drones aren't weapons,* came unbidden, followed by the epiphany, *they are now and the cop recognized it.*

Intuition turned her face to the ground, her mind trying to piece together various parts of *what the fuck,* and, *please God, don't let anyone else die.*

Beside her, Nolan knelt on one knee and followed his target with the barrel of his gun. He aimed and fired three shots in quick succession almost straight up in the air.

The loud crack made Keiki startle, her body freezing in fight or flight mode. Her fingers clenched in a protective gesture over her head while she lay on the ground panting and shaking in terror.

This was supposed to be a run honoring Shelly, not a mass murder site.

Once others heard shots fired and saw the scene including the seizures, the small meadow cleared with incredible speed. Teens and adults alike shrieked while running for cover, unable to see the threat's origin.

A steady hum of rotors suggested the drone was either making a return trip or hovering nearby while the area evacuated.

Nolan stayed hunkered down beside her, she realized, so he could direct his shots upward and decrease the possibility of injuring bystanders. That he was willing to discharge his weapon near a crowd specified the severity of the threat.

She saw nothing except clouds and tree limbs, but heard the retreating sounds of the drone which had dive-bombed them. "What the fuck is happening?"

The next time she shifted toward the junior who'd stopped seizing, he didn't block her path.

"Didn't you see the way that thing approached?"

"No, I was busy kissing the dirt."

"It dove like a kamikaze pilot. I knew something was off. Then it released a cache of powder." He pivoted toward the victim, now unconscious.

After Nolan returned his pistol to the ankle holster, several young men waiting at the clearing's edge approached with caution.

The victim lay quiet while her panicked companion spoke in clipped words in a useless attempt to help.

Nolan continued to scan the area above them, his body tense and ready.

Keiki edged closer. Glow sticks revealed a deepening blue tinge to the unconscious girl's lips. "Someone call 911! We need an ambulance." Her shrill demand goaded the calmer young man to withdraw his phone from its pouch and make the call.

"Keiki, you all right?" Nolan watched the sky as he retrieved his own cell.

"Yes. What the hell's going on?" Renewed panic set in when she couldn't discern if the girl's chest rose. Her eyes remained closed after her body ceased the random spasms. "I'm not sure she's breathing."

The soft flutter at the base of the girl's throat was fast and thready when Keiki reached closer to see if feeble puffs would warm her fingers. "She's got a pulse, and I feel breath moving."

Nolan grabbed her arm away from the unconscious girl. "Don't touch. She's been poisoned. There's nothing we can do until EMS arrives. Hopefully, distance and the breeze dispersed enough to prevent a lethal dose."

A flurry of "Oh my God" and other expletives replaced the expansive quiet.

The surreal picture unfolded and extended while Nolan's partner arrived and helped take control of the frantic crowd.

Keiki sat in stunned horror, her mind a jumble of images and impressions. "It was the drone. It delivered a puff of—a drug?"

"Yes, and you were the target." The cop helped her to stand and nudged her closer to his side, keeping his arm around her.

"She might die because of me? No, no, no. This can't be happening." Tears flowed unchecked, reviving memories of the juniors always together at the same events as Shelly, Gabby, and herself.

Nolan turned her to face him then nudged her head against his chest as he held her. To the side, she caught Coyote's grim nod of acknowledgment to whatever words Nolan mouthed. Though she wasn't a suspect, the killer had just pulled her deeper into his web.

A cop saved my life, but my presence might cause the death of another.

Since her parents' murder, she'd had little respect for police of any kind. Despite current circumstances, she wouldn't depend on anyone to save her again.

Chapter Eight

Light drizzle formed rivulets on the windshield by the time Detective Garnett returned to the police cruiser where Keiki waited in numb silence. Alone with her thoughts, she'd made no sense of the evening's events.

A mask had prevented her from identifying the killer, so what was the point of tonight's fiasco? In the end, she concluded the attack stemmed from a deranged mind.

The remaining race and scheduled after-party were canceled amid an abundance of discarded paper cups, plates, and other race debris littering the grounds. Event staff dispersed along with the rest of the crowd.

She'd never seen CSI techs in action. Their approach had been professional yet wary following Nolan's briefing. Per his instructions, she now remained in the locked car with the windows closed.

A uniformed officer leaning against the vehicle's hood cast repetitive glances her way as if she'd disappear into the ether. If he popped his chewing gum one more time, she'd hop out to wrestle it away and stick it in his buzz cut.

The evening's horrific events played on a continuous reel in her mind. She'd heard a drone before the race began, but they were common at such events.

Someone wanted her dead. Why? It wasn't as if she embroiled herself in shadowy business dealings. That wasn't her style. Nor was it Shelly's. They were a couple of college kids trying to finish school and start their own business.

She sensed Nolan's presence before he tapped on the window of the passenger-side window. Weariness had settled its mantle about his shoulders long before he'd met the techs and directed them to the scene. They were back and packing their van to leave.

A look of cool determination locked in place when he opened her door. Fresh air blasted drowsy cobwebs away but offered no insight as to the direction of his thoughts.

Her need for normalcy in a world gone mad urged her to wrap her arms around his waist—until seeing his frown slide into place.

"I don't think it's a good idea for you to go home tonight." His close scrutiny flitted around the scrubby field serving as the event's parking lot. Few cars remained, those abandoned as individuals left together and several marked vehicles belonging to other officers.

"You think he'll come at me again?"

"No way to know since we don't have a motive behind all this." His laser-focused gaze asked myriad questions for which no one had an answer.

She didn't object when he took her by the arm and guided her to his SUV. "Coyote will drive your car, if you don't mind."

He obviously considered his *suggestion* a foregone conclusion. She gritted her teeth. *Another instance where he uses charisma and his position to influence my decisions.*

"Where're we going? Is this procedure?" His touch was mild but resolute and created unfamiliar sensations coursing through her chest. Security, recognition of his protectiveness, and a low-level rapport developed a foothold in her mind.

He gave her a look, not that of the wolf, but something different, something she couldn't define, yet trusted all the same.

"Don't worry. He won't search it. He was a kid once."

"Not as long ago as you, I suppose." One ominous barb after another surfed her thoughts. Confusing times and an uncertain future made her strike back.

His half-grin declared he understood.

"Sorry." After the long wait in the patrol car, she was wired and knew there'd be no sleep in her immediate future.

"You want some coffee or a soda? Non-caffeinated? We can stop by your vehicle and get your jacket."

"I'd love a latte. Grumpy's is open all night."

"Grumpy's?"

"College dive."

"How about some place you don't normally frequent?"

"Sure. I could use a burger."

"One burger, coming up."

"How is it my face and hair look like I stepped inside a tie-dye washing machine and yours doesn't?"

"Luck, I suppose."

"I need to wipe this Goth makeup off my face. Glowing in the dark is one thing, but showing my face in public looking like a clown is different."

"Don't worry. I know just the place."

He carried the build and confidence of an athlete. That combination along with his masculine grace proved more seductive that anything she'd ever experienced.

Opening the passenger door of his SUV earned him another notch on the respect-the-man scale. The slight gesture forced her to rethink her stance of lumping all cops in a pile.

He scanned the empty lot as he rounded the hood and dropped into the driver's seat. The cost of maintaining constant vigilance was sure to take an eventual toll. She wondered if detectives burned out from high stress.

The subdued ride to town was comfortable in a strange kind of way, the source derived from not just safety, but something else. This air of protectiveness was a unique entity, something she hadn't experienced even with her parents.

"You okay, kiddo?"

"Yeah. The paramedics said I'd be fine." The few bruises would heal. "Is she gonna be okay?"

"Detective Waylin got an update. She's in the ICU, but she's conscious and aware of what's going on." The tenor of his voice radiated sympathy she didn't deserve.

"Before you ask, I don't know. I have no idea why I'm a target." He'd either believe in her innocence or not. Regardless, she'd give him a copy of the video when they returned to her apartment. He'd earned that much trust.

When he pulled into the lot of an all-night diner, she grimaced. She hadn't eaten here in years.

"What?" His look of concern coincided with a wary scrutiny of her face.

"Nothing. It's just that I haven't been here in like... forever. My dad used to be friends with the owner."

The small restaurant looked more like a converted home on the inside, but the interior beckoned with vibrant-colored tufted seats, scarred wooden tables, and décor indicating a penchant for the 1980s.

"The food is good, the company better."

Whether he referred to the few scattered customers visible through the massive bay windows or the staff, she didn't know. Instead of waiting for him to open her door, she hopped out and matched his stride up the two wooden steps. "I need to wash my face before I feel human again."

It was common enough for her to hang out with guys when they talked shop, the topics safe and comfortable. Nolan represented an enigma—sometimes a wolf, sometimes an open book. Two halves of the whole always alert like the predator he resembled.

His ploy for relaxing held an ulterior motive.

"Ask," he commanded once they'd settled in a corner booth where he could see both the door and everyone seated inside.

"Is this going to be another interrogation?"

"Should it be?" His steady stare gave away nothing.

"No. I told you. I don't know who's responsible. I really don't. Yet you look like you don't believe me."

"I just don't want another life cut short."

His direct intensity remained locked on her face until she squirmed in her seat.

"Tell me about your parents," He said and smiled at the waitress headed in their direction.

"They were good people, hard-working, honest, and devoted to each other. We used to watch scary movies on Friday nights and have breakfast out on Sunday mornings." Keiki sighed, remembering the incentive for eating out. Her father once prepared a big breakfast and burned everything. "Dad had this old Chevy he was restoring. We'd spend a little time in the evenings working on it. I don't think we were like most families. I was an only child, so, I don't know."

Nolan shifted in his seat. "You've not had an easy go of it since starting college. I think—"

"Hey, fella. Haven't seen you in a while." The waitress spared Keiki a quizzical frown before setting her sights on the detective.

"Hi, Tammy. My young friend here needs to try one of your super burgers." Turning to Keiki, he added, "It's a new addition to the menu you'll love."

"It was new several years ago." A disapproving scowl accompanied a pat on the detective's back before turning her full attention to Keiki. "Haven't seen you bring a *friend* since, well, for a long time."

"We ran the Foam Glitter run." Keiki ignored the other woman's smirk. "I'd love a beer and some fries to go with the burger, please."

Nolan's jaw went slack and the waitress snickered.

"I don't buy alcohol for under-aged young women. I realize you probably drink on campus, but you should do so with moderation."

"I don't know who this moderation is, but she sounds like a bitch. So, no, thank you. I'll have soda." She beamed her sweetest smile at the detective, enjoying the hardening of his jaw.

The waitress cocked her hip and took a deep breath, touching a perfectly manicured nail to the notch at her throat. "I bet you Goth kids had fun tonight. I hear the after-party is an all-night blast." Pursed lips betrayed her confusion over his choice of companions before her focus slipped to Keiki's lap, as if expecting to see handcuffs.

Keiki didn't have the energy to correct the misconception, instead letting an eye roll convey her rising ire. Her skin felt too tight to contain the emotions roiling inside. It was a rare occasion she even sipped a glass of wine, but the evening's events forced her to reconsider.

"I'll have the usual, Tammy." Nolan ignored her murmured, "*Sugar,*" endearment and sashay when she left.

"Do you always attract so much attention?" Keiki smirked at his obvious discomfort.

Taken by surprise, he managed a quick recovery. "Not as much as you do, I suppose."

Whether he questioned her need to be the center of focus with the neon-green hair or dark makeup didn't matter. They both washed off. "Neither this," she flicked a long bright lock, "or this," gesturing to the remains of dark lipstick and eye shadow, "is part of my day-to-day routine."

"You don't seem the type to be into that stuff."

"I'm not. The makeup is Gabby's, and the hair glow stuff, Shelly bought."

Instead of challenging or defining her lifestyle choices, he continued to match her question for question, comment for comment through past memories of her parents, hobbies, and woodworking activities, vacations, and the like.

"So, tell me about your four sisters. I always wanted one but my parents said I broke the mold."

"Well, Jenna is the youngest. She's nineteen and a bit of a wild child and prankster. People never forget meeting her, but not because of her red hair and freckles." Nolan nodded to the returning server and accepted the glass of ice water. "Faye is the oldest girl. She's twenty-five and has a toddler and new baby. Maria and Faith are twins, and pretty much inseparable. We're all pretty tight."

Each glimpse into his life presented another layer declaring him a little more human.

"Why a business degree?" Keiki dug for more information.

"I wanted to learn about investing and earn enough so that when I had a family of my own, I'd be able to spend quality time with them."

"You won't be a cop until you retire?" She couldn't reconcile a detective sitting at a desk studying the stock market.

"Haven't decided yet. Once I got some experience under my belt, I wanted a calmer, less hectic life. City cops learn the ropes a lot faster. Coming back to this smaller department, I know how to handle situations and don't take the work home with me."

"Towns like ours don't typically see such violence. I guess that gives you a different kind of working relationship with your colleagues."

"Absolutely. We're flexible with our schedules and have a different sense of comradery. As long as things are quiet and we turn in quality work, the chief is very tolerant."

When the last bit of pie disappeared from their plates, she was reluctant to go. In his presence, she could almost deny the horrors of the past thirty-six hours. "I'd love to take a crack at your version of Hogan's Alley."

"Well, isn't that a non sequitur." He tilted his head to the side and leaned forward. "Why don't you tell me what else is on your mind, like why you think you need target practice?"

He already knows I'm withholding pertinent facts.

"I have my father's pistol. I used to be a good shot but haven't been to a range since he died. It just seemed like a reasonable thing to do after tonight."

"Where do you keep it?"

"Locked in the back of the entertainment center in our living room."

"Okay. I can finagle a trip to the range." The wolf's grin was back in full force, declaring there'd also be a wager or quid pro quo.

"Look, your apartment is an hour's drive away, and you're mentally and physically exhausted. How about if Coyote and I put you up for the night in a local hotel? We can talk in the morning about safety concerns after you've absorbed the evening's shock."

And there it is. He uses whatever circumstances available to his advantage.

He didn't look away, and she wouldn't give him the satisfaction of doing so. He challenged her at every turn, testing her strength, her resolve, as well as her intent.

"That can't be normal protocol."

"Actually, my partner's been on the phone with the captain. Our department is too small to have a safe house. We need time to figure out what to do with you."

"I'm not an inanimate object."

"You will be if the killer gets hold of you."

He made a valid point. Logic was usually her strong suit. "All right. But no funny business with you two."

"Jesus, kid. Do I look like I have trouble getting a date?" The small smile he cast in their server's direction was answered with a wide grin.

"You think this guy is going to come after me again?"

"Don't know, but he now knows you have armed protection and might figure we're cops. We're gonna switch cars when we leave here, just for shits and giggles."

"What about mine?"

"We'll park it at the station."

"Hmm. I'll spend tonight in Gainesville, but I'm going back to my apartment tomorrow." Again, she gestured to her face and the remnants of cosmetics she'd been unable to remove.

"Not the smartest move for a bright kid. We'll park it elsewhere, then retrieve it in the morning." Nolan fished his phone from his pocket and checked messages after explaining the rest of his plan involving an undercover officer.

"She's gonna want to stay at my place? All night?" Keiki had nothing to hide, not that they could find, anyway.

"It can't hurt. It'd be nice to wrap this up."

Keiki didn't have the answers he sought and couldn't speculate as to the bigger picture. "I don't want anyone else hurt in my place."

"Quinlin looks enough like you, and she's a cop with good instincts. When she gets here, you'll exchange clothes. She's about your height and build. My partner will stake out your apartment while we take his truck."

Keiki grimaced at the thought of the killer tracking her to then breaking into her apartment. Even if he had a drone up, it wouldn't be able to keep pace with a vehicle.

"I told you, she won't search your place. Matter of fact, she'll go straight to your couch, park it, and stay there for the rest of the night."

"I have nothing to hide, but I don't want anyone touching my electronics. Some of the pieces aren't soldered."

"I give you my word. 'Kay?"

"All right." Keiki leaned over and added, "Tell her if she gets bored, the drool-worthy reading material and videos are under the couch in the living room."

She smirked at catching him off guard with his quick inhale and jaw dropping open.

The promise of revenge, or at least leveling the playing field, emanated from his every pore.

Chapter Nine

Exchanging clothes with an undercover officer in a restroom had never made Keiki's to-do list. Confidence wavered with the announcement of her intended doppelganger's recent graduation from the academy.

Keiki wouldn't insult anyone who took risks few others would. The woman deserved respect, if not a visit to a psychiatrist.

Nolan frowned after Coyote shot him a solemn grin on arrival. The nonverbal exchange conveyed more than Keiki could define. If they'd done a cursory search of her car, she didn't have any contraband.

The snippet of blind faith had been extended in hopes of earning their trust. She let them guide her to Coyote's truck.

It hadn't occurred to her that the hide-a-key under the tire well could allow any decent thug entrance. Someone could've planted false evidence. Self-chastisement would ensure adherence to a few basic safety rules in the future.

Nolan's frequent glances in the rearview mirror during their drive kept her hands clenched in her lap. The thought of the killer following them kept her in a state of fearful expectation which drained her nerves.

"Your partner's truck needs a little massaging."

"What?" Nolan's focus snapped in her direction, his confusion thick in the air.

Soft blue light from the console cut though the shadows to emphasize deep-set eyes and a strong jaw. A specific raw quality directed her way forced her to gulp her next breath.

"It rides like a lawnmower with doors."

"He's not mechanically inclined."

"He'd get more power if he'd re-plumb the exhaust. Also, the little whirring noise that increases when the speed picks up could be beginning of an SOS."

"Like?"

"Have to look to check the alternator bearings, water pump, and AC compressor to know."

"You can do that stuff?" He relaxed against his seat, shaking his head.

She'd taken him by surprise, again.

"My dad owned a hardware store. We spent our time in the woodworking shop or tinkering with his old Chevy."

"Handy talent. I'll let him know."

"How come you pulled babysitting duty tonight?"

"My partner had a date. Plus, I owe him one."

The lopsided grin he aimed in her direction would've punched through most women's defenses. Keiki's intuition delved beneath the surface and knew when a man was interested. Nolan was. Yet his divided regard wove a web of confusion she couldn't untangle or disengage.

By the time he parked the truck in the motel lot, she'd formed a vision of his odd partner around the swamp including dripping moss, scummy water, and rotting vegetation to go along with the sound of mud slurped by night predators and croaking frogs.

Nocturnal animals hunting and being hunted in return rounded out the picture. Coyote seemed the type at home wherever he landed, with a preference for the bayou.

She waited while Nolan strode into the office of the one-story structure. A long breezeway might have added to the quaintness decades prior, however, the isolated location and lack of cars on the heaved pavement added a macabre flavor she couldn't shed.

When he returned bearing a single keycard, her thoughts stuttered. Instead of hopping out, she waited for him to slip back into the driver's seat, as if expecting her ire.

"You got two, yes?"

"No." He offered another you've-got-to-be-kidding look again before explaining, "You get the room. I'll be outside."

"Oh." Anxiety jettisoned a questionable scenario from her mind. "Have you worked many homicides?"

"Enough to get the job done and keep you safe." That said, he hopped out.

Before rounding the hood to act the part of a gentleman, he retrieved a small, black canvas bag from the truck bed.

She paused in opening her door. He'd halted to listen and survey his surroundings.

Notching her chin up to proclaim her confidence restored, she concluded, "I don't hear anything, and nothing I know of could travel that speed and distance *and* track us at night, unless it was military grade."

Cool, crisp air spiced with the scent of early fall and damp earth filled her chest. Dead leaves matted by the earlier drizzle formed a patchwork cover and necessitated careful navigation on wobbly legs. "I'm not usually this tired after a race."

"You've had a tough couple of days."

"I am *not* fragile." She wanted to round on him, take out all the frustration, loss, and pain building in her chest. But the minute he took her elbow, the bubble of fear and anger dispersed.

Nolan shook his head and sighed. "Sorry. I realize that. I do."

A pointed look at his carryall leveled part question and part accusation.

"I didn't know how tired I'd be after the run, so I packed an overnight bag. I assume you'll want to shampoo the goop out of your hair." As if testing his theory, he reached out to finger several locks on her shoulder. "Huh, it's so soft. Not what I thought."

A shiver at his light caress startled them both. The benign gesture flipped a switch on her libido, which she determinedly shut down. "You're out of touch."

He grinned.

She scowled, never one to accept pampering. Regardless, it felt so good to know someone cared, even if it was his job.

"Just want you to reach your twenty-first birthday. It's coming up soon, if I remember correctly."

"Yeah, thanks. I appreciate it. My own knight in shining armor."

"Not by a long shot, Keiki. Don't make the mistake of thinking that way."

Her gut instinct suggested him the type whose plans evolved on the fly while adapting to and incorporating any circumstance. He focused with goal-oriented intent, and emphasis on extracting whatever information he deemed necessary.

Which was why she needed to stay alert. Words could be twisted, their meanings dubious at best. She'd done nothing illegal and didn't intend to get duped by charm.

Once in the room with the door locked, he pulled the curtains closed and turned on the light. His bag dropped to the single large bed with a thud.

Standard accommodations included one bed, a small recliner, and a round table with two chairs.

"You gonna be able to ditch the neon green of your hair?" Nolan asked as he poked his head in the small bathroom and turned on the light. "It's not five star, but it's located well and defendable without much risk of collateral damage.

"You've brought... people, here before?"

"No. I stayed here after the triathlon last spring."

"Hmm. This stuff should wash out pretty easily with one shower." She paused in thinking before nodding toward the window. "You're gonna sleep in Coyote's truck?"

"No. I'll snag a blanket and be nearby."

"How are you going to sleep?"

"I'm not. It's called night shift."

"It's going to be cold out there, and it's still drizzling off and on."

"I'll survive." Nolan turned to go, his hand on the door. "Do *not* unlock this for anyone but me. Got it?"

Keiki huffed out a sigh. "Hey, listen. I'm not that much of a bitch. You can have the chair." She nodded toward the worn out lounge by the window.

Nolan hesitated, looked outside, then closed his eyes and shook his head, as if contemplating crossing a line from which he couldn't return.

"This way if someone breaks in, you won't have to race thirty yards to get to my door and find me with a bullet in my brain. You'll be here waiting for them." His hesitation was more than she could bear.

"That's the makings of a bad idea."

"Please?"

He heaved a sigh.

84

"All right. Okay. This way I can hit the ground running in the morning and not have to sleep a few hours first. I'll brace one of these chairs against the door."

The thought of him nearby catapulted her senses to a hyperawareness never experienced around men. Once in the bathroom, she leaned against the door to take calming breaths. The enemy of her enemy was getting under her skin.

The first drops of hot water brought the full impact of near-death experience. A few tears mixed with the green water channeled down her cheeks. Diluted hair dye collected in the grout lines before circling the drain.

Minutes passed in flashbacks with her friends, one dead, one missing. When cold infiltrated every aspect of her body, it was time to get out.

Nolan's sweats and a clean T-shirt made for strange pajamas, but better them than a hospital gown worn in the ICU. In thinking of the bigger picture, she hurried out to find Nolan settled in the chair. He'd changed his clothes.

One look at the bed sent her to the window. She couldn't sleep. En route, she hesitated with her hand over the television's power button until Nolan's, "Um," halted her progress.

"Right. Not a good idea." Vestiges of the adrenaline surge kept her mind ever circling and her body in a constant state of motion.

Because she couldn't turn her back on someone who didn't trust her, because the flashbacks of Shelly's terror wouldn't abate, and because another student was in the hospital, Keiki paced.

Forced concentration couldn't keep her immobile. On her fifth pass between the exit and bathroom doors, Nolan stepped into her path.

"You want to talk?"

"No. You wouldn't understand."

"Because I'm a cop, or because I'm a man?"

"Um, neither. Both. I don't know! Why is this happening?" She'd reached her breaking point, the one that turned her anger inward for going to the race or outward to the detective sworn to protect her.

"We'll figure it out. Until then, we need to keep you safe."

His hand hesitated in reaching out. "Katherine—"

"Keiki. Please call me Keiki. I won't answer to anything else." The edge to her tone developed a decidedly sharp threshold.

"All right, Keiki. But understand this. Tonight wasn't your fault. None of it is. We can't control the actions of others."

He reeled her in and held her loose against his chest, offering comfort mixed with the option to flee. "I talked with Coyote while you were in the shower. Your classmate is talking now."

Relief swept through her like a tidal wave. "Thank God. You don't consider me guilty?"

"Of killing Shelly Harock then trying to deflect suspicion by having someone fly a drone at you? No, I don't believe you had anything to do with either." He rubbed her back, sifting his fingers through her wet hair.

"But you think I'm guilty of... something."

"We're all guilty of something or another. I don't think you have the capacity for killing or creating mass mayhem. I don't see it in your makeup."

It was his compassion, his precise and accurate insight into her world which proved her undoing. One tear trailed another, followed by a broken sob before the floodgates opened.

He didn't pry her away when she wrapped her arms around his waist and poured her heart out through the gush of tears. Just the opposite.

He held her closer, murmuring against her hair and rubbing her back.

Their integrated actions established a pivotal moment, one where she'd look back and say, *"Yeah, that was when everything changed."*

He was no longer a cagey enemy. Harbored suspicions fell away in the light of the ongoing investigation and his determination to keep her safe.

The outcome was anything but certain, and she wasn't sure what transpired now, just that it would define something specific about herself and her character.

He'd earned her trust. In counterpoint, it didn't mean she'd follow his lead, but she would respect his opinion and knew he'd put her life before his own. Something she'd never expect a cop to do. A secret part of her wanted it to be more personal, but her life didn't work that way.

An awkward moment ensued when she pulled back. "Ah, thanks. Sorry I soaked your shirt."

"No problem. You feel like telling me about drones, cars, anything?" He'd known she needed a diversion.

"Nah, thanks. I think I've worn myself out. I'm just gonna go to bed." Rare was the occasion she incurred awkward emotions around men. Despite her one failed relationship, she was self-assured.

When she got into bed, she faced away from the chair but was unable to shut his warmth from her mind. She wasn't some twit enduring her first crush.

"Nolan? Would you..." The words stalled and wouldn't squeeze around the knot in her throat. For the first time in years, she needed arms around her, shelter from memories of death, loneliness, and despair.

The chair's cushion rasped as he stood then settled in bed, on top of the covers. Timeless, wordless, it was a taciturn understanding between a soul ripped in two and another who stitched the tattered ends together with a mere touch on her shoulder. It wasn't sexual, merely comfort offered from one human being to another.

"I know you hurt, Keiki. I promise it will get better. It won't be fast, and it won't be a linear process, but it will happen."

"Because you have experience with four sisters?"

"Because I have experience with a broken heart."

She had no energy to wrangle his tortured past in the quiet darkness. Instead, she let the pain wash over her and took simple comfort in the feel of his presence. It was a long time before sleep granted her peace.

A guttural plea woke her from the nightmare of seeing her parents shot. She thought the hoarse groan came from her throat, but the heartfelt entreaty was decidedly male.

"Nolan?" Keiki turned over to touch Nolan's shoulder, a sliver of moonlight slipping around the curtain's edge to highlight his pain.

He jerked awake and bolted off the bed as if shot out of a cannon. He'd palmed his gun left on the nightstand and searched the room for an enemy. "What?"

"Uh, nothing. I heard you talking in your sleep. It startled me."

"Oh, hell. Sorry." He glanced at his watch. "We've still got a few hours before daybreak. Go back to sleep, kid."

"Okay, if you'll sit here again?"

His uncertainty gave way to resignation as he again sat and rested against the headboard.

Weak morning light outlined the curtain's edge when something hauled her from the depths of a good dream. Vague recollections of rousing to feel Nolan snuggled against her back had given her solace and sent her back to sleep.

Warm comfort dissipated with the loss of heat when he curled up and swung his feet to the side of the bed. With no sexual or hidden agendas, he'd offered security and the chance to rest without fear, in spite of having his own nocturnal demons to fight.

"Morning." Again, without explanation, he stood and checked his weapon as if needing a normal routine to dispel an unpleasant memory. "Feel better rested?"

"Yes... How'd you know what I needed?" Her mouth engaged before her brain could decide on the best way to handle the awkward situation.

Nolan on the other hand, slid into cop mode and typed out a text on his phone. "Four sisters. When the youngest broke up with her boyfriend, I sat with her most of the night. She talked until her voice went hoarse. I think—"

The subtle knock at the door jarred her into motion. "Coyote?" Keiki asked as she bolted from the bed to the bathroom. She didn't want to be found in Nolan's sweats and give the wrong impression.

"Yeah. He's a bit early."

* * * *

Nolan opened the door to see his partner with a corrugated cup holder and snicker. If not for the prior night's sleep, he would've slammed it shut until an apology drifted forth.

"I hope that coffee is hot."

The smell of fresh pastry granted a small leeway and one jibe. A bag dangled precariously below the cups of fragrant brew.

"Because you didn't get any sleep last night and need the caffeine?" Coyote nudged his colleague aside after handing him an insulated cup. His cursory glance took in the bed with the rumpled blankets along with the chair that had none. An arched brow delivered his inquiry.

"No, I didn't. She was having nightmares." Nolan put the extra coffee on the small table and sat. His partner knew him better than that.

"I haven't seen you emotionally invested for, well, in a long time."

"Don't bring Clare into this. It's not the same." Hot liquid spilled over the side when Nolan set his coffee down with a small *thunk*. "Keiki's a college student."

"Plus a whole lot more. Captain wants paper work in ASAP."

"Imagine that. Thanks for filling him in. I owe you."

"Again. Preliminary tests showed the runner last night wasn't exposed to the same combination of drugs as Harock's daughter, but we'll have to wait for a complete analysis."

"Well, shit. What was the game plan? Capture instead of kill?" Nolan listened as the water taps in the bathroom shut off.

"Probably."

Neither needed reminding of Keiki's convoluted involvement in the current case. In attending the race, he'd wanted to establish a rapport on which he could build, then ask tougher questions without running into roadblocks and lawyers. Even so, the web surrounding the young women drew him tighter.

Their platonic time during the night fortified a basic rapport on which he wanted to build into—something greater. The more he learned, the less he believed her capable of underhanded dealings, much less murder. Her grief had been raw and genuine.

Chapter Ten

Keiki inched the bathroom door open to monitor the murmured conversation. Returning Nolan's clothes didn't mean she wanted to endure his partner's false assumptions.

Conversation stopped with the squeak of the door going wide. She nodded to the southern detective in passing, wondering if his cop instincts noted any of the changes she felt. Fate glued bad luck to her back. "What's it like outside, Coyote?"

"Soft sixties." He nodded to the coffee cup on the table and curled his lips between his teeth when she returned Nolan's sweat pants and shirt.

Two wooden chairs offered a place to sit and sip a morning brew. Coyote took one and crossed an ankle over a knee while Nolan sat on the bed.

"Sixty degrees with a northern breeze." She smiled as a fond memory brought a little warmth. "My dad used to describe mornings that way if the wind came from the north."

Nolan nodded. "Feeling better this morning?"

Heat crept up her neck with the memory of holding the detective tight and blubbering on his shoulder. He hadn't seemed to mind, nor had he appeared uncomfortable with sitting on the bed while she cried again.

He had four sisters and had spoken to her as if soothing a frightened child. He never asked which horror had disturbed her sleep.

If Coyote was surprised at seeing Nolan in the room, he was gentleman enough to not show it. A glance flicked between Keiki and his partner had been the single clue of variance to his curiosity.

"How's Quinlin?"

"Fine. All's quiet." Coyote's shortened report came with a shrug. "She went into your apartment, sat on the couch like she said she'd do, then waited. No company, nothing suspicious. It was her first undercover experience and I think she found it quite boring."

"How close were Gabby and Shelly?" Agitated movements revealed underlying anxiety as the more experienced detective removed his cup's lid and blew over the top of the steaming fragrant brew.

He's invested in solving the case. All in.

"You think the killer will go after Gabby next?" Keiki couldn't control her tone's rising pitch.

"Don't know," Nolan answered and gestured toward the door. "We'll look for her today. On the way out, we'll pick up something to eat while you fill us in about her habits, comings and goings, and whatever you think might help us find her."

His tone had softened. Their connection no longer mimicked wolf and prey.

"Home, our apartment, or at school are the places she goes." She couldn't forge the connection between brain and mouth to challenge either man's assessment that she knew more.

The unspoken understanding shared between the two men came through loud and clear. They couldn't find Gabby, and Coyote either suspected her a victim, too, or involved in Shelly's death.

"When was the last time you saw or heard from her?" Coyote paused, waiting for her answer.

"I sent her a message Saturday morning and asked if she was okay. I never got an answer."

Nolan stood and stretched his neck. "Your living arrangements might need a temporary adjustment."

"I *am* going back to my apartment. You said yourself this might not be about me." She knew better, but needed to get to her equipment and hand over a copy of the video.

The possibility of finding a worthy clue was nil, but the longer she waited, the more guilty she'd look. First on her list included finding Gabby. Her drones could cover more area than the police could.

Outside, cool air brushed the hair from her face despite being sandwiched between the two detectives. An eerie quiet allowed her to listen for the telltale hum of a drone. The skies were clear, the atmosphere quiet.

"Have you spoken to any of your other friends?" Coyote, like his partner, cast frequent glances upward. The southern detective's heavy boots scuffed at torn and damp leaf litter blown in from the surrounding forest.

"Not since Thursday. As far as Gabby is concerned, it's not too unusual for her to disappear for several days in a row when studying. Shelly and I got used to it."

"You're going to use your drone to spy?" The teasing quality of Coyote's grin didn't negate his underlying speculation and search for truth.

Keiki let a shrug speak for itself. She allowed Nolan to guide her to the SUV while Coyote headed for his truck.

Her escort put the drive time to good use by explaining his need to know her whereabouts and planned activities. He also reaffirmed there'd be a uniformed officer stationed outside her apartment complex for the near future.

The ongoing monologue entailed the same advice as one of her parents' safety lectures.

Back in the apartment, she took a deep breath and acknowledged the female officer. "Thanks, Quinlin, for swapping places with me last night. I understand it's a risk you take in stride, but I appreciate it."

"No problem. 'S good to get my feet wet." In keeping with her assignment, she'd worn blue jeans and the color-splashed tee from the race. "It's all been quiet since I arrived, Detectives."

Quinlin couldn't be much older, yet she'd put herself in danger in swapping places. Her father's mantra of *"Respect is earned,"* came to mind.

Once alone, Keiki booted up her computer and listened to the horrific recording again. No spark of recognition and no hint of a buried memory lit her path to enlightenment.

It was the nightmare that drew her in with the expectancy of solving the mystery. She was still in the dark as to the killer's identity or how he'd chosen his targets.

If she'd possessed hacking skills, she'd know more about the crime scene. Instead, she had to settle for spying on the police.

Gabby had planned on spending the weekend with her newest

boyfriend, hence should be sleeping off a hangover. It wasn't surprising she didn't answer her cell.

A last check on her quietest device and she maneuvered it out the window toward school. Living close to campus cut down her walk to class yet allowed her the extra privacy she craved.

Familiar landmarks and rooftops passed in quick succession with no one looking up and searching for the quiet hum. After a little look-see, she'd set the device on the roof of fraternity row and call her second part-time employer, Nick Tucker.

This time, *she'd* be asking for *his* help. The private investigator had hired her to fly drones but then became a friend, one who'd taught her some tricks of the trade.

Unlike the detective who forced her heart to beat a staccato rhythm, Nick's easygoing attitude reminded her of the boy next door—the one who put thumbtack-sized holes in his friend's water bottle then backed away when said companion unscrewed the top, or setting his buddy's phone alarm for the middle of the night and hiding the device at the bottom of the laundry basket.

Everyone should enjoy a sense of humor.

The row of frat houses arose like squatting soldiers along a curved road. The two-story on the end was her target. Under ordinary circumstances, respect for privacy would keep her from aiming the lens through the second-story windows. This was not a normal situation. Starting at the back, she checked each room, glad so few bothered to pull their shades.

On the end, she recognized a black-haired boy sleeping in a twin bed. She couldn't remember his name, but Gabby had bragged about his good looks when pulling up his pics on social media.

He was alone.

Please be in the bathroom, Gabby.

Several minutes passed, nothing stirred. Reality drowned hope until another thought occurred. They sometimes went to the *meads* to smoke.

It was the clearing, or meeting place, where small groups could stay off security's radar and not be reported when a distinctive odor permeated the air. Gabby had admitted to the occasional joint, but other than that and the periodic party, the trio held the same values and points of view.

The clearing wasn't a place Keiki went, and if not for traipsing through it while escorting Gabby home after a party, she'd never have known of its existence.

Instead of zipping down the trail just above the treetops, the drone maintained a distance which ensured the little motors wouldn't be heard.

Two men stood in the clearing. Their size first tipped her off to the current oddity. She knew every student and faculty member. None were this large. Strangers were searching for something among the dead leaves.

Hovering her drone at its current height didn't allow their conversation to be heard. If she moved in too close, they'd hear it. It was a gamble, but she lowered it into the crook of a tall oak fifteen feet off the ground and behind the men. Snippets of conversation required intense focus to piece together. Some of it made no sense, something about formulae and rewards.

The larger male, dressed in dark jeans and wearing a black leather jacket gave a small hoot and plucked something from the ground. "Found it. Damn. I win the prize."

Keiki's blood ran cold when he held the device for his partner to see the screen. It looked like Gabby's phone. Due to their stances and the phone's angle, she couldn't be sure. Instead, she picked up her own cell and called her roommate's number.

The phone in the bulkier man's grasp erupted in a familiar tune with Keiki's face lighting the screen.

Bile rose in her throat, her fingers gripping the table until numb.

Where was Gabby?

"Damn. I wouldn't answer that if I were you. Boss said to retrieve it, not use it." Thug number two had long greasy hair tied back in a ponytail. His speech held less of an accent than his companion's guttural rumble. Neither voice matched Shelly's killer. "Looks like I'll have the fun tonight."

"Well, when we find her friend, I get first shot between her legs. And we don't have to tell the boss about it, either."

* * * *

"What was a chem professor doing in his lab on a Sunday night?" Nolan surveyed the office from the door while his partner stepped around the body to examine the second-story window. The parking lot below contained one vehicle—the professor's.

"And why leave the window cracked?" Coyote examined the sill while the CSI tech dusted the frame for prints. "I'll bet that's gonna show a grab bag that'll take months to separate."

The tech rolled his eyes. "I love optimism."

The corpse lay supine with sightless eyes taking in the fiber tile of the suspended ceiling.

"There's powder around his mouth." The ME leaned back to catch the attention of the photographer packing up her camera. "Did you get this, Jansen?"

"Yep. Shot my way in, around, then shot my way out." Attention to detail had never numbered among her shortcomings.

"You say the door was locked. From the inside?" Nolan turned to the campus security officer.

"That's right. We got a call from his girlfriend saying he wasn't home and she couldn't reach him, she asked us to check his office. It's not unusual for these nerdy types to stop in at odd hours to pick up notes or whatever the hell they need. Heaven knows they're always leaving a window open, especially this time of year. It's not like someone's gonna climb in the second story and steal equipment."

"No sign of forced entry. How'd the killer get in? An extra keycard?" Coyote scrutinized the room, dissecting each field of view with a keen eye. Cursory inspection of the bank of windows had him shaking his head.

"No, sir. Our security's tight on access to the science building. It's even layered."

Nolan stepped over to the one window where a small gap appeared to provide the room's only other access. "Hell, this is what, a six inch space? Has someone got a ruler?"

"Looks like it. And yes, I do." Indignation in the tech's voice declared the question beneath contempt.

"Second story. Locked from the inside. No other doors and no escape via the ceiling since the grid isn't strong enough to support anything heavier than fiber tiles." Coyote stared through the dust-streaked glass, then at the one tile on the floor. "Damn."

"One's out and another set askew as if the place was searched," Nolan added. "What the hell were they looking for?"

"Something lightweight and found in a chemistry professor's office... papers? Someone looking for answers to a test in a room that was supposed to be empty?" The ME's skeptical expression closed down after a minute of thought. "Doesn't make sense. Then again, the why isn't my problem, Detectives. It's yours."

Nolan's gut churned with unanswered questions. "Our perp could've been searching for photos or a flash drive."

"It's too early to be thinking about midterms, isn't it?" Coyote directed his question to the campus police officer kneeling opposite the ME performing his cursory examination.

"Midterms are a couple weeks out, and they're scheduled all day and late into the evening." Like many other colleges and universities, this facility had begun arming their security officers. The one in question grew paler with each minute passing.

"Did you have any luck in locating Gabby Kiernan?" Coyote gestured for the campus cop to step out in the hall before he desecrated the crime scene.

"No, but they tend to scatter over the weekend."

Coyote kneeled to get a better look at the victim. "What are the chances that the white powder around his nose is the same makeup found on Shelly Harock?"

"Yeah." The coroner's disgust came with a sigh. "Not a lot there, but then again, many inhaled poisons don't take much to do the job. Helluva lot of death for a quiet area."

"So, we have one student murdered and another attacked at a race. Then, a professor is killed and his place is searched. On top of that, another student is missing," his partner summarized.

"We need to figure out how the professor is connected." Nolan studied the open window again. "When we found Shelly Harock, there was a drone keeping tabs on us."

"Aw, shit." Dawning lit Coyote's expression. "I didn't think her capable of this. I'm usually a good judge of character."

"Damn. The window's gap is enough to slip a drone inside. The MO would connect Harock's murder to this... whatever this is." Nolan didn't want to stain the ME's thoughts with conjecture, the case was already screwy enough.

"Yeah, but we didn't find anything drug related in her apartment. There's always something, even if it's just a vibe. I got nothing when there."

"You shoved her out of the drone's path at the race. Any doubt she could've faked it?"

"No. Absolutely not." Nolan mentally reviewed the events at the race and came to the same conclusion. "No, she'd have been the one in the hospital if I hadn't shoved her. Considering the powder's slight dissipation with space traveled, if it had nailed Keiki, we'd be looking at another body."

"You have good instincts." A sliver of doubt wove its way through the younger detective's words.

"A mechanical arm might be strong enough to disrupt a tile enough to look around..." Nolan grabbed the one straight-backed chair used for visitors and dragged it to sit under the yawning black hole.

He'd been so sure of Keiki's innocence, but new evidence now pointed in her direction.

Coyote shook his head. "We need to expand our search."

"Let's see if combined efforts can help us locate the other girl, Gabriella Kiernan." Nolan took his pen light and scanned the space. "Nothing up here but undisturbed dust."

"Strange that we can't locate the pre-med student and now a chemistry professor is dead. What are the odds?" Coyote stepped back and tucked his notepad in his jacket.

"The other teachers describe Gabby as the type to stay above board," Nolan advised, deep in thought.

"If we can't find her by tonight, let's take another run at our mechanical prodigy tomorrow." Coyote winced, avoiding Nolan's intense stare.

"What's running through your head, now?" Nolan followed his partner down the hall to where a small crowd had gathered, murmured whispers and suppositions turning the late evening into a surreal episode of a popular horror movie.

"Let's suppose Keiki isn't directly involved. Why is the killer targeting her, and with her own type of devices?" Nolan asked.

"Not sure I buy that, now."

"She could be a conduit to something else, in some fashion. With the professor's murder, I'm less inclined to think Harock Industries is involved." Nolan's inward cringe sent a chill up his spine. "Those two girls looked a lot alike."

"Ready to roll?" Coyote didn't wait for an answer to the rhetorical question. "I'll pick you up in the, unless you're planning on having late-night company?"

"No, smartass. She's a witness at best and possibly a suspect, although I can't see how it all fits." Nolan didn't add a comment about having coffee ready, since he preferred to know exactly what was in his cup.

"You two looked pretty cozy in the hotel room from what I could see."

"Coyote, no. Nothing happened. And nothing is going to happen. Trust me." He'd never had a partner question his integrity or ethics. There existed a damn slippery slope and a line he wouldn't cross.

"I do. And, well, we'll see what happens when the dust settles."

Chapter Eleven

Keiki's fingers shook as she sipped her morning coffee while contemplating her dilemma. On the table sat her new phone. It wouldn't be the same without Shelly's numerous texts chewing up the battery life.

The creeps in the woods had talked about a captive and needing information. But where had they taken Gabby?

Regardless, Nolan and Coyote needed to see the footage. She prepared to call them and turn over both videos.

Without sleep and unable to tolerate food, she always had work waiting. It kept her mind occupied while she figured out how to approach the detectives without earning their ire.

Her mechanical spider had *wings* to fly and *hands* to maneuver small objects. By adding more motors, she'd managed to make the drone quieter and increase its strength, but it also meant a larger size that defeated her purpose. She still didn't understand Harock's desire for such a small item, but he paid well and respected her rights to intellectual property.

She needed to design a more effective device while maintaining diminutive dimensions. The narrow gap of her window opening equaled the estimate for which she measured her creations' size.

The drone she normally flew around college kept watch from the top of the Admin building, its video feed capturing the day-to-day activities of life on campus. Desperation to see Gabby strolling to or from class brought reality's darker cousin to whisper in her ear. Deep-seated fear warned she'd never see either of her friends again.

Of note, the two detectives stood out like sore thumbs when ascending the Admin building's steps. One dressed in jeans and bomber jacket, the other wore jeans and windbreaker.

The bear and wolf.

Furtive glances cast their way had to be a normal part of life for them, good looking as they were. The wolf set Keiki's teeth on edge. *What are they looking for and how can I help?*

Her apartment's relative quiet had become a soothing counterpart to her increasing anxiety. Music from the apartment below drifted up as white noise to complete the weekday routine.

Outside, a police cruiser parked at the curb, the officer's head swiveling to inspect his surroundings.

Shelly's killer would strike again. Skilled in the art of assassination, he used familiar technology as a weapon, something she never would've contemplated. If not for the detective, she'd be in the ICU or morgue.

What passed for a sixth sense lured her attention to the door once more.

She waited, her fingers tight on the table's edge.

Faint metallic clicking sounds snapped her focus to the doorknob. Her pulse jumped to a sputtering beat and her breath froze. She didn't see it turn but knew it wasn't her imagination someone was attempting to pick the lock.

The killer was damn ballsy to attempt breaking in with an officer stationed out front.

Keiki stood, her heart pounding in her ears and panic drying her mouth as she thought, *this can't be happening.* She didn't have a viable exit or time to retrieve either gun. Neither was loaded.

The detectives were sincere in wanting to protect her from an unseen and what she'd come to think of as omniscient enemy.

The knob began to turn.

Bile rose in her throat. Terror gnawed at her gut.

In stunned horror, she couldn't move—until the door's hinges creaked and three gloved fingers slipped to the inside of the lock stile just above the lock.

Her breath *whooshed* out all at once in her scramble to pick up her new phone. Shaking fingers dropped the target as the door opened inch by inch, the device's clatter to the floor inviting the intruder to throw the door wide.

Instead of wasting precious time retrieving it, she bolted to her bedroom and slammed the old straight-back chair under the knob after thumbing the weak lock. The second-hand furniture, a rickety piece purchased at a yard sale during her first semester, wouldn't hold for long.

Muffled steps approached the hollow-core door. The handle jiggled, but held.

"Hey chickie-chickie. It's time to party. Come on out and I'll make it fun. Make me break the door down and well, not so much enjoyment. Know what I mean?"

Oh, God. It's him. How'd he find me so quick?

"What do you want?" If he searched for the digital recording of Shelly's death, he'd find her laptop but wouldn't be able to gain access. She'd copied the videos on a flash and hidden it in the bathroom, which he'd probably also find if she couldn't figure a way to scare him off. "There's a cop out front."

"Yeah, probably eating a donut. Turns out, trying to kill you was a mistake. My bad. I didn't realize you had such value as opposed to just being the brawn of the operation. Tell me, did you record your friend's death, perhaps give it to the police? I also want the address of your distribution center. Since my time with the chemistry teacher got cut short, you'll have to answer my other questions."

"What the hell are you talking about? What operation? Distribution center?" Confusion prevented her from prioritizing his other questions.

She considered opening her window and yelling for the officer, but the intruder would reach her long before the cop could. Then the cop would die for interfering.

"You know what I'm looking for. I'll bet it's here somewhere. I'm here to collect."

What could I have that he wants?

Panic filled her chest. Nothing nearby resembled a weapon. Her father's Glock was hidden in the living room cabinet, and her phone was on the kitchen floor. His steps receded, the soft shuffling on tile tracking his location.

His words didn't connect to form sane thoughts, which wouldn't stop him from searching and finding her gun once he left the kitchen. The apartment was small.

The thing about her work, she maintained multiple controllers. Keiki picked up the one on her bedside table and woke the drone on the rooftop of student admissions.

It didn't have a lot of battery left and the audio portion had failed after landing.

Detective Garnett and his partner were exiting the building and heading across campus. If he were half as smart as she thought, he'd understand her message.

The daredevil dive equaled a risk. She swooped the drone low from behind, skimming above the students heading to and from classes. In passing, she tapped the detective on the head in a glancing blow.

His instinctive duck while drawing his weapon startled both his partner, who mimicked his action, and nearby students, who took off running and shouting.

It didn't matter that he pulled out his badge and tried to reassure those hell bent on putting distance between themselves and two gunmen in their midst.

In keeping her device low, she didn't give either detective a chance to shoot without endangering nearby students, which they wouldn't do.

"Chickie-chickie... I know you have what I want. If I can't find it, I'll take you instead, and I promise you'll not enjoy anything I do to you."

Her intruder grew bolder in his search, slamming kitchen cabinets and dumping the drawers' contents on the floor. The clatter of pots and pans came next.

"Let's start with your infrastructure. I want to know who all's slithering in on our territory."

"Territory? What the hell are you talking about?" Her focus riveted back to her bid for the detective's attention.

The next time her device approached him, it did so at a slow pace and at ground level so he could evaluate the situation. At a distance of five feet, she hovered it just above the grass. No audio meant a life-and-death game of charades.

Nolan tilted his head to the side and lowered his gun.

In a like move, she lowered the drone to the ground. To get his attention, she whirled it around, using frantic movements to convey panic.

If he guessed it to be one of hers, he might understand.

He reached for the device.

She moved it a foot away.

Coyote waited, watching.

Nolan moved to grab it again.

Keiki guided her drone toward the adjoining parking lot, praying for a break.

He gestured to himself and Coyote, then toward the vehicle, holding out his hands, palms to the sky. Universal sign language for, *what the hell?*

Another round of wild and furious whirling followed by a steady glide toward the other vehicles carried her message.

In spotting the familiar black SUV, she flew her emissary forward. Since the drone couldn't match the vehicle's speed, she'd need to get it inside.

Once beside the driver's door, Nolan pursed his lips in indecision, then opened it.

She slipped it inside and set it on the dash to conserve energy. There was no way to convey her location.

Another round of whirly, frenetic movement created a sense of urgency, the same flaring in her chest. Her would-be assailant continued to ransack the apartment, the rip of fabric indicating his latest search methods.

As if reading her mind, Nolan picked up the handless mechanical spider and pointed the camera at his face. The words he mouthed resembled, *"Keiki? Is this your idea of a joke?"*

His grip knocked one of the motors askew. She couldn't hover without it.

Directing her avatar to tap repeatedly on the hand which held it was the best she could do to answer.

"I'd call that a no." Coyote had repositioned his partner's hand so the tiny camera lens encompassed his face, then mouthed the words, *"One tap for no, two taps for yes, got it?"*

She used one of the legs to tap twice on Nolan's hand.

"Is something wrong, Keiki?" Coyote mouthed.

Keiki slammed her finger down on the control repeatedly.

The angle changed again until she saw concern written in Nolan's face.

"Shit. She's in some kind of trouble." Nolan cranked the engine and put the vehicle in drive.

It must have lurched forward for the camera's angle to wobble.

Nolan lipped the question, *"Are you in your apartment?"*

Again Keiki rapped out a staccato drumming motion.

"Call dispatch..." Nolan's regard bounced between the road ahead and her drone that Coyote now held.

A lot could happen in a few minutes. Sounds of porcelain lamp shattering and fabric ripping didn't bode well as her party crasher continued to issue vile threats in a singsong voice.

Recognizable, muffled warnings indicated an unbalanced mind. His Spanish accent became stronger with each thud and thump. The voice, the tone, each inflection sent quivers between her shoulder blades.

Images of her apartment in shreds flashed through her thoughts before picturing Shelly's body in the woodland flowerbed.

Sudden pounding on her front door brought a measure of relief.

"Katherine Tallerman? I got a message to check on you."

The officer posted out front for protection was now endangered because of her.

At the top of her lungs she screamed, "Help! He's inside. Be careful."

Quiet ensued.

Calm before the storm which holds its victim in thrall.

The kind that jettisoned vomit to the back of her mouth. Keiki swallowed hard then held her breath.

The explosion of her front door banging against the wall held her rigid. Her fingers on the control clenched as she waited, unable to help and not wanting another person to die.

The blast of a shotgun and the simultaneous crack of a pistol broke the silence. Their combined racket reverberated in her mind. Warning the officer was the best she could do but didn't absolve her guilt.

Silence.

No sound suggested the end result. No telltale noise formed a picture in her mind, nothing to clue her into what transpired in her apartment.

Then, a heavy thud and long squeak as if something slid. Another, heavier thud. Finally, a silence that would haunt her for eternity.

The ensuing deep giggle which followed more so, for it embodied madness and a craving for blood. "Told you so, chickie-chickie. They're gonna blame you for this one."

In the back of her mind, she pictured her parents falling to the cold cement.

"This isn't over, bitch. We're not done until I say so." The Spanish-tinged accent deepened before his rapid tread retreated.

Tears coursed down her cheek, her imagination supplying the image of a police officer lying in his own blood and gasping for breath. He'd been doing his job and trying to help.

She'd altered the course of whatever part of his life remained.

How many people were going to die because of her? If her parents hadn't stopped at the quick mart to pick up ice cream, they'd still be alive. Now, a psycho claimed she had some part in an operation. What type? Where did she fit in?

A solid kick sent the chair from its perch against the door. She jerked it open after grabbing the lamp from the bedside table and yanking the cord from its socket, weak as far as weapons went.

In the living room, she cringed. The thug was gone, but the officer lay on the floor, eyes closed as if taking a nap. His revolver remained gripped in his hand.

Her dad's shotgun lay just beyond his feet.

The police will think I shot him.

She approached on silent steps, each stride adding to the tears brimming her eyes.

Blood covered his left shoulder and pooled on the floor between his arm and chest, soaking his shirtsleeve. This was one of the reasons she'd decided to solve the puzzle herself.

The officer appeared to be her age, but had to be twenty-one to carry a gun. One of her classmates had gone through the police academy at age twenty, the crucial birthday hitting two weeks before graduating.

Behind her, silverware and cooking utensils lay scattered across the tile floor between stainless steel pots and pans. Even the contents of her refrigerator lay strewn across the tile with shattered glass glinting in the sun that streamed through the window. One piece survived intact—her precious table.

Her legs shook as she knelt by the officer's side and reached to feel for a pulse. She'd heard two shots, one from a pistol, the other a shotgun blast. The odds of the officer hitting his target weren't good considering the lack of a blood trail unless the intruder wore body armor.

The officer had a pulse, and it was strong as breath moved in and out of his lungs. His brow furrowed in pain. The nametag read Crowley, the designation forever burned into her brain.

A surge of energy thrust her up to snatch one of her racing T-shirts hung on the wall. Crimson soaked the tie-dyed material pressed to his wound, a reminder of a race where someone else almost died.

Thundering footsteps in the hallway ceased at her doorway. Nolan and Coyote had their guns drawn and aimed toward the floor.

"He's gone," she answered the question in the detectives' eyes, her own blurred with moisture.

Nolan shouldered his weapon and knelt on the other side of Crowley, his grimace convicting her in the court of public opinion despite lack of specific knowledge.

A two-handed grip on the victim's shirt ripped the garment open and sent buttons plinking against the wall to slide to the floor. Underneath, the officer wore his vest, which had caught a portion of the shotgun spray.

"Crowley, EMS is en route." The wolf demeanor slid in place, an unspoken assurance to set things right. A brief scan of her face preceded a deepening frown before turning his attention back to the officer.

Coyote stood guard at the doorway, informing dispatch over his phone of the downed officer.

"I didn't see him," Keiki began in a choked voice. "I heard the doorknob rattle and tried to pick up my phone."

She looked back to the kitchen, not seeing her cell. "I dropped it and didn't have time to pick it up, so I ran into the bedroom and wedged a chair against the door." If the officer died, it would be her fault.

Crimson coated the creases of Crowley's neck and arm, but his eyes snapped open in panic. Nolan placed one hand on the officer's uninjured shoulder to keep him flat when he curled to sit.

Neither remarked on the shotgun lying on her living room floor.

"Not yet, Crowley. EMS will be here in five," Coyote advised from the doorway.

"Was it the same guy who went after Shelly?" Nolan's pitch dropped an octave, continuing his no-nonsense demeanor.

"Yes. The guy had a Spanish accent." Keiki pointed to her father's shotgun in helpless rage. "What does he want?"

"We'll figure it out, kid. We will. What else did he say?"

Keiki couldn't comprehend all that blood, but she couldn't meet Nolan's inquisitive scrutiny either. All the panic, frustration, and fear combined in a soundless scream that rent her thoughts to shreds.

In the next instant, words without meaning spewed forth, broken by sobs and choking noises she couldn't hold back. Nolan reached to touch her shoulder, but she couldn't bear his compassion.

Paramedics arrived and began assessment and treatment, urging the detectives out of their way. Sounds of plastic ripping open and low murmurs signaled emergency work in progress. Two other tenants in the hallway watched the comings and goings of EMS personnel.

Keiki felt numbness creep into her soul as they continued to work in the background. Crimson-stained carpet inside her door marked where the officer had fallen.

Nolan halted the paramedic's progress with an outstretched hand as they wheeled past with their conscious patient. "Did you see his face, Crowley?"

"No. He wore a mask. Spanish dialect. He said *vos* instead of *tú*." The low murmur spoke of pain, almost an apology. "When he held the gun up, he was wearing gloves."

"What about his choice of words?" Nolan canted his head to the side, waiting.

"He was Costa Rican. I recognized the way he talks—same as my aunt."

Nolan sighed. "We're looking for a shooter from Costa Rica who flies drones and wears a mask."

One minute she was sobbing with her face in her hands, the next, strong arms pulled her against a solid chest, familiar, safe, and warm.

"I didn't do anything wrong. I swear it... Well, sometimes I fly my drones too close to buildings, but Tucker set me straight on that." She babbled, with no control over thought or content. Words without meaning hurled out like an erupting volcano.

"Tucker?" The edge was back in the wolf's voice.

She tried to pull back, but he nudged her closer, rubbing her shoulders and back.

"Yeah. I'm beginning to think I'm not cut out for this shit."

"Aw, hell. You shouldn't be mixed up with the likes of him, anyway." Coyote turned away and scrubbed a hand over his jaw.

"Well, he's nice, and I'm earning extra money."

"Is he working on anything concerning Harock Industries?" Nolan asked.

"No. Not that he's told me."

"You can't stay here, now." Nolan's regard catalogued the carnage on the floor and, at last, stopped on the shotgun.

She answered before he could ask. "I know. I told you it belonged to my father. Was the prick trying to frame me?"

"If not for the vest, Crowley would be dead. So, yeah, I'd say yes." His analytic tone turned sharp.

"He's gonna keep coming," Coyote murmured.

"I have friends I can stay with for a while." Keiki assessed both detectives' expressions, calculating their measure of determination.

"And lead a killer to their door? That's not a very smart idea."

"I can't go far, I have school." A quick inhale coincided with a new awareness. "He got my phone. It has my whole life on it. My schedule, appointments, banking, everything. It even has an application for crude control of my drones."

"Dead students don't learn much. The rest—we can deal with." Coyote flinched when his words startled her into stumbling back against the wall. "Sorry, kid."

She sidestepped and stood by the stretcher where paramedics continued to stabilize the officer. The guilt was unbearable. An IV infused clear liquid to replace the crimson fluid soaking the bandage held against his shoulder.

"I'm so sorry. This happened because you tried to help me. I'm so very sorry."

Despite pain fogging his mind, Crowley offered a brief half smile. "If you wanted, you could make it up to me and share a latte with me while I'm recovering."

Another flood of tears threatened to overcome her attempt to offer comfort. "I'll come see you in the hospital. London Fog? Adaptogen?"

"Did she just switch languages?" Nolan looked to his partner for help.

"No, old man. Get with the times. Trendy lattes are up and coming." Coyote grinned then sobered when Nolan glared. Age jokes didn't go over well with the senior detective.

Keiki freed her hand from the young officer's grasp when the paramedics urged her back. Watching them wheel away sent a powerful message to the darkest corners of her soul. *It could've been a body bag.*

Chapter Twelve

Nolan nodded to the two street cops approaching them. Both were off duty but had obviously heard the call go out. They'd seen the stretcher bearing their co-worker to the elevator. Each appeared grim and determined to help.

The apartment's rural setting offered many avenues for a killer to escape. Procedure dictated they scour the area and talk with neighbors to inquire about suspicious sightings.

Gut instinct warned him to keep the girl close. Reality dictated an alternate path. The war within dumped a hefty dose of indigestion and angst to mingle with the stress of a complex investigation. He had a job to do and a missing girl to find.

"What was it you were saying about someone finding your friend's phone?" If Nolan didn't calm her down, she wouldn't be able to function on the most basic level. On the other hand, her impromptu rambling proved she knew more than previously disclosed.

Keiki scrubbed at her face as if able to wipe away the confusion marring her brow. "Um, I was getting ready to call you. I have video of two guys finding it in a clearing near a frat house."

"Do I want to know how you're sure it was hers?" Nolan asked.

"I called her number while I had them on screen. She has a ringtone just for me."

Coyote's disapproving scowl deepened. He'd stood aside while his partner offered comfort, his posture stiffening. "We can't locate her. No one's seen her since she left a party Friday night."

"Let me get my computer. I'll show you." Keiki stepped around Nolan only to have him halt her with an outstretched hand.

"No. This is a crime scene, and you can't go back in until forensics is finished." In a deft move, he pulled his cell from his pocket, wiping it on the cloth to remove his prints and provide a clean slate. He'd have her prints along with her friend's alternate contact information, if it existed.

Keiki took the cell with trembling fingers and dialed, waiting through several rings before voicemail took over. "Hey, Gabby. Haven't heard from you. I, uh, I—lost my phone. Sorry I ditched you for the race. Call me at this number as *soon* as you get the message."

Defeated and exhausted, she handed the phone back. Nolan handled it with care, acknowledging his partner's slight nod. They worked well together, exchanging information with a glance.

"Now what? I can't go to a friend's house. I can't stay here. I have no place to go."

"I know a place, a woman who has an apartment over her garage." Nolan ignored Coyote's sharp look of warning.

"Is she your sometime lover or an axe murderer?"

"Neither. She's a mother hen who takes in strays on occasion." Nolan waited and reminded his subconscious the young woman needed a safe place and someone to listen to her waking nightmares, both old and recent. What was better than an older woman who'd once taken on the world and understood grisly crime scenes and psychotic killers?

Suspicion radiated from Keiki's very essence. One heartbeat, then another while she weighed her options before she nodded her head, then froze.

"Wait. I need to get some things out of my apartment. I can't leave them behind."

Coyote's shifting stance transmitted an unusual tension. "Are they—"

"They're in my bedroom. The guy didn't get his prints, or DNA for that matter, anywhere near them. He never crossed the threshold."

"All right. I'll go with you. You can get some clothes, textbooks, and whatever, from your bedroom. Everything else, including your laptop, stays." Nolan followed her through the debris.

The way her mechanical creations were displayed on bookshelves and side tables rekindled old memories of his first apartment, the tokens of his hobbies and ambitions laid out for the world to see.

After a few minutes in her presence, he'd known before asking which items belonged to her and which were placed by her roommate. They were shadow and light, introvert and extrovert, two sides of a coin one couldn't separate without damaging both.

The pre-chem student enjoyed a bit of opulence in high-end furniture and collectables with a varied selection of expensive jewelry tucked in her bedroom, which told him the killer wasn't interested in precious gems.

Keiki, meanwhile, embodied practicality and focused on projects.

It came as no surprise when she pulled out a duffel bag and began stuffing clothes en masse into its confines. No nonsense, no frills, just straightforward and direct best described his enigma.

She's not mine.

The way she directed her attention elsewhere after specific questions and bit her lip denoted reluctance to elaborate on her earlier ramblings.

His concern didn't include suspicion of her involvement in murder so much as her mistrust of law enforcement mishandling information. He saw through her layers and the desire to A, solve her friend's murder, and B, make sure justice was served by whatever means necessary.

Undeterred by his arms crossed over his chest and deep scowl, she handed him a plastic case of her precious drones.

"I assume you want to make one trip suffice?" She arched a brow and continued.

It seemed she'd collected herself and bolstered her mental reserves. Silence lengthened until she handed him another. When she gestured for him to precede her out the door, he hesitated.

"No. Ladies first." He'd sensed the agitation in her tone and presumed snark would follow, her self-soothing technique.

"Your parents raised a gentleman? I thought those were mythical creatures." Indecision stalled her step, surveying the room as if debating a tactical move.

"Not all men are pigs. While in college, it might be difficult to discern the difference. You're smart and will figure it out."

With a last look around, she shouldered her bag and picked her way through the remnants of her life lying tattered and torn across the open space.

When she stopped at one of the built-in cabinets, he cleared his throat.

"You know I can't leave this here." Shafts of sunlight burnished her golden locks sliding forward when she hunkered down and stretched to reach the back of the lowest space. A sharp snap, then a false wooden panel opened.

"At the diner, I told you this was here. It's legal. It was my dad's. It's mine now."

Before he could object, she continued, "If *he* comes back and finds it then goes on a rampage, you'll have more reason to doubt me."

The unusual and concealed spot made it highly unlikely the killer had found yet left it. It would've ranked a lot higher on the scale of glittery things than the jewels in the other student's bedroom.

Nolan nodded.

In the doorway, Coyote sighed. They'd have a long discussion about it later with his partner's dissertation on the virtues of reasonable law and policies on crime scene handling.

"Do you know how to use that?" Coyote asked, his voice leaking skepticism.

"Sure. Point the end with a hole in it toward the bad guy and pull this little lever that makes it go bang."

At times, Nolan's greatest accomplishment lay in keeping his mouth shut.

Her smile softened the sarcasm. "My dad and I were members of Jensen's Tactical Group. We went to the range a bunch of times. He thought it was important I knew the basics."

Nolan took a deep breath. "We can take it from the apartment, along with the ammo, but you'll have to prove you're proficient before you can keep it. You won't need it where you're going."

He counted to ten as she tucked both in a secure pocket of her duffel amid lingerie. Whether she had lacy, racy items or not was none of his business, yet his brain short-circuited with a peek of black lace. Justification came in the guise of rounding out his mental picture of her character.

When she reached for the keys on a hook beside the door, he blocked her move and explained. "No. Not until we check to make sure there's no tracking devices on the undercarriage. We'll be discreet in searching your car and bring it to you when finished."

Although he felt fairly sure of her character, he didn't know the other two girls from her trio, both of whom had access to the vehicle.

"Why are you looking at me like that?"

"Before we go, is there anything you need from your car? Anything you might not want other officers to—"

"No. Jesus. I'm in school to get my degree then go into business, not fool around with nonsense and shit."

"Sorry. Force of habit and training."

A slice of deviousness took over her face, her chin raised before adding, "Don't worry, it's not where I store the sex toys. I do like to keep them handy, though. If you need to inspect everything I'm taking…"

Coyote smothered a guffaw behind his hand while Nolan shook his head.

"I can't imagine what you're like at a party." Nolan envisioned his life having taken a different turn. The comparisons thrust Keiki in a different light. Picturing her on a level playing field further strengthened their connection.

A recipe for disaster.

"I sure hope you're the fun and intuitive one." Her remark, directed at Coyote, earned a smirk and nod of deference.

Coyote flipped the toothpick in his mouth side to side as Nolan turned onto the highway. "She didn't look like she was gonna sit tight there for long, partner. What are you gonna do to keep her safe?"

"I'm hoping Carolyn's nurturing skills will coax her to stay until we see this through."

"Well, if anyone can, it'll be her. After all, look what she's done with you. I haven't seen you personally invested in another for a long while." Coyote pulled out his pad and consulted his notes.

"I just feel sorry for her, all alone now."

"Uh-huh. That's why you entered the glitter race," Coyote leaned closer and lowered his voice, "and why she's staying within arm's reach."

"Stop inventing. There's nothing there."

"If you say so. But I haven't had a woman mention adult toys in casual conversation unless we were intimate. On the other hand, she did consider *me* the fun one. Maybe I'll ask her out when this is over."

Nolan glared until his partner held his hands up in surrender, the smile lines deepening around his mouth.

"Gabby's parents said they keep their kids on a fairly strict financial leash," Coyote's change of subject saved him a black eye.

"Yeah, I noticed all the expensive trinkets in her room, too. Yet Keiki's space epitomized practicality and functionality."

"The roommate's bedroom at home was a toned-down version," Coyote countered.

"Agreed. So where'd she get the money to buy the stuff?"

Coyote rubbed his jaw and winced. "How well does Keiki know her friend, or," he paused before wading into murkier waters, "and I know you don't want to hear this, but are they partners in *other* endeavors with Keiki's portion stuffed in the mattress?"

"You think Gabby is selling to earn extra cash?" Nolan wasn't sure that scenario fit either. "It's a big leap between smoking a joint now and then, and dealing. Everyone we've talked to said the roommate had her head on straight."

"Then there's something we're missing. Either way, how does Keiki fit in? Her story about her inheritance checks out, as do the unusual hobbies," Coyote flipped through his notes.

"If Gabby or Shelly were dealing, how could the others not know?" Nolan thought of his own sisters, the times when they'd shocked him with some wild adventure. Women were resourceful.

"Our witness was close to her parents. You can identify with that. Speaking of family, how's your dad's recovery coming along?" Coyote's subject change came with a slight frog in his throat.

Nolan jumped to the heart of the matter instead of beating around the bush. "Jenna's fine. Enjoying campus life in Delaware. Lots of sun in the spring and summer, beaches, bikinis, and boys." In reminding his partner how his youngest sister was off limits, he also compared his sister to Keiki. He groaned under the weight of self-recriminations.

"Okay. I can't see Shelly and Gabby getting in over their heads and going for each other's throat. Not from what we've learned so far."

"It would be one explanation if Gabby is laying low. On the other hand, that doesn't feel right to me either." Nolan considered what they knew about the pre-med student. "Let's talk to some of the other friends and classmates."

The sprawling campus encompassed seventy-five acres of beautiful countryside. Manicured grounds attested to the dedication of presenting a serene setting. Nolan wound the SUV through the campus to the periphery where they'd find their objective. "The science building feels like an afterthought, secluded."

"Nah. Being close to the woods gives them easier access to dispose of the bodies," quipped his partner as he replaced his notepad and the car ground to a halt.

"Jesus, you can take the man out of the swamp..."

"You nervous, partner?" Coyote hesitated before popping his door open.

"No. It's just damned frustrating." Nolan considered the disparity in the girls' lifestyles. "Keiki doesn't seem to care about glitz and pomp. Her belongings are basic necessities of her trade."

"A Glock.45 and sex toys?"

Nolan shrugged. "Shelly was poisoned, strangled, and stabbed, not shot. Awful lot of rage there." He couldn't envision Keiki reaching that level of anger. "I'm taking Keiki through a simulation run after visiting the firing range. If she passes muster, she gets the gun back."

"I think she avoids the party scene except when dragged by her friends. She seems to concentrate on what's important to her." If Nolan pegged her right, Keiki's skill with weapons would match those of her woodworking and mechanics. Her focus was incredible.

"Kinda like someone else we know." Coyote worried with his toothpick, a habit when he wanted to emphasize a point. "According to what we've gathered, this girl Gabby is flashy and colorful. We can catch her lab partner coming out of class now if we hurry."

Generalized fear shrouded those on campus as word spread of two deaths and one missing student. Their target, Gabby's chem partner, revealed no wary or cagy signs of deception but had a right to a few nervous gestures.

"The fidgety coed's disclosure of their *smoking now and then* proved her sole admission toward the party scene. Wonder if we'll find anyone at the *meads* now." Coyote's seldom-used uncompromising glare had scored the smokers' meeting place. He pointed to a trail near the building and grounds shed. "There, bet that's it."

Nolan heaved a sigh, no closer to solving the puzzle giving him sleepless nights. "I think every school has a discreet place where kids hang out when they don't want to be seen by the straight-and-narrow crowd."

"Keiki had to have known about Gabby partying with the fast clique." Coyote started down the trampled path bisecting the woods.

"Hold on." Nolan fished his phone from his pocket. "Garnett."

Listening to the CSI's initial findings snaked a trail of ice down his neck. When he hung up, confusion topped the list of fetid sensations swirling in his gut.

"What's up?"

"They found a recording device hidden in the girls' apartment. Markings filed off, along with specific damage to deny identification."

"Placed by the shooter or before?" Coyote paused and glanced over his shoulder toward the science center. "Don't know, but it would explain a lot. Whoever's listening might have heard our conversations with her, thereby knowing who's protecting her, if not where."

"Could be someone else's equipment, too. Harock, his competition, a dealer... Jesus, there are any number of possibilities."

Reality intruded like the screech of a hoot owl with each step along the well-trampled path. Admission to high school and college cliques had never numbered among Nolan's activities. His focus and ambitions had driven him down a different path, which didn't mean he'd been unaware. He'd made the choice to not participate.

Broken limbs, trampled weeds, and the blanket of fallen leaves led them deeper into the woods.

"Something's wrong with this place. It's giving me the creeps." Coyote rested his hand at his back waist under his jacket.

"More cameras, you think?" If so, then the focus would point more to Gabby than Keiki. Nolan's sigh echoed that of his partner. "I don't hear any small engine noise."

The clearing covered twenty yards square with several stumps presenting uncomfortable seats. Small creatures skittered through the surrounding evergreens while birds provided a natural backdrop for a soothing atmosphere.

"This is pointless. Let's—" Nolan's phone chirped a macabre beat.

A grimace replaced his frown as he listened to the coroner. After disconnecting, he knew they were on the right track even if they couldn't put the pieces together. "The ME says he wants to talk to us in person."

A familiar whine forced Nolan to draw his weapon and search the sky for an incoming threat. His partner did the same.

"Drone. If you see it, don't shoot it until we figure out who's at the controls." No sooner had Coyote spoken the words than the glint of metal topped the tree line.

"It doesn't look like anything I saw in Keiki's apartment." Nolan drew a bead and followed the mini robot's progress with his gun barrel.

"No, but it does resemble the one you described at the Foam Glitter race. Look at the length between the body and—what the hell is hanging down from it?"

"Looks like some type of barrel, but not a lens," Nolan murmured, widening his stance.

They watched the device approach.

The sudden diving maneuver sealed its fate.

"The barrel on the underbelly is carrying a payload," Nolan warned.

Simultaneous shots ruptured the silence.

"Freaking thing's hard to knock down." Coyote leapt to the side as a puff of white powder dissipated in the air between them.

"Don't breathe in that shit. It's poison." Nolan pivoted to take advantage of the machine's retreat. His last two shots brought it crashing down in the nearby ravine.

"Hot damn. We finally got something!" Coyote whooped as he stood and dusted off his jeans, replacing his weapon in his shoulder holster. "Never shot a drone before. Wonder if it has audio."

"Not surprised you missed. I'll bet it moves nothing like a gator. Let's find it and get it to forensics."

Resumed quiet brought the bold and curious students to investigate. Coyote warned them away, keeping an eye on his partner's progress in retrieving their prize.

Like the Boy Scout his colleagues claimed him to be, Nolan retrieved two nitrile gloves from his pocket and approached the downed craft with caution. After picking it up, he held the power button until its light went off.

"Why go after cops? We have next to zero information," Coyote asked when Nolan returned with the evidence.

"Our killer might be trying to frame a certain drone operator to flush her out."

"What do you suppose the range is on that one?" Once on the road to county forensics, Nolan listed specific and detailed information remembered from Keiki's lecture.

Coyote inspected the bagged evidence up close. "Shit."

"What?"

"Someone engraved the belly on this thing." A low whistle boded ill to come. Coyote shook his head before continuing. "It reads 'KT'."

"Katherine Tallerman. Double shit. Whoever flew it could have listened to our discussion in her apartment where she pointed out her initials on her work." Nolan's logic dictated Keiki wasn't at the helm.

"Think she's still with Carolyn? Why don't you do the honors?"

With a swipe of his cell, Nolan connected with Carolyn and asked about her new tenant, whom he heard talking in the background. After assurance the student's classes could continue online due to special circumstances and that they'd been chatting about stuff and nonsense for over an hour, he disconnected.

"Okay. Either Keiki has a partner, or someone's setting her up." Nolan went quiet as he considered recent events.

"Could be a partner who wants sole proprietorship?"

"That doesn't wash. It just doesn't fit." Nolan loosened his grip on the steering wheel when his partner tapped his hand.

"Because she's an orphan, a college kid working her way through school, or because she's beautiful and you can't keep your eyes off her?" Coyote snickered after receiving the bird.

The forensics tech grinned like a kid at Christmas when given the evidence. Unusual weapons were sought after, big-ticket items. Without a serial number or any other identifying marks beside the engraved initials, the broken device would prove a challenge.

More bad news awaited them at the county morgue.

The pathologist who'd performed the two autopsies held his tongue until Nolan and Coyote sat across from his desk in the small office.

Stacked files beside the computer constituted unfinished work for someone who stayed abreast of his duties. Violent, suspicious, or deaths involving a drug overdose required autopsy.

Nolan crossed one ankle over his other knee when he couldn't stay still. By the greatest effort, he refrained from bouncing said foot in a show of impatience.

"What's up, Doc?" Coyote grinned in the face of the doctor's scowl.

"I don't know whose mess you boys have stepped in, but it's a big pile." His glasses sat at the tip of a crooked nose, broken in the past and dotted with a few spider veins from age or drink.

"Explain." Nolan demanded.

"I have a friend in the state lab. Since both bodies had white powder around their noses and mouths, I sent samples for testing. Their equipment is more sophisticated, and they have better resources."

"And..." Coyote verbally nudged the older man.

"He confirmed the powder contained a new street drug, one that's mixed with Fentanyl, except in each of these cases, they found poison in much higher concentration. In fact, the opioids amounted to no more than trace amounts."

"Well, hell. That's disturbing. Someone's targeting college kids and their professors." If not for Nolan's intervention, Keiki would've been one of the victims on a slab.

"I suggest you talk to your vice detective. I already gave him the information since he's on your task force."

"Jesus. This gets better and better." Nolan wanted to believe that what he'd seen in the depths of Keiki's blue eyes was real, honest, and most of all, accurate. He didn't believe she'd deal drugs. She didn't have time. In the end, evidence didn't lie. It was difficult to remain stalwart in the face of present evidence.

Outside in the afternoon's cooling breeze, he voiced his opinion. "I don't believe she's dealing and killing her friends, nor mixed up with a partner who wants her out of the way."

Coyote rested his hand on the open passenger door. "We'll figure it out. I just hope it's in time to prevent another death."

Familiar countryside passed, the bucolic scenes worthy of an artist's brush, yet Nolan found no solace.

"Your gut tells you Keiki's not a perp... because she's a young woman who is focused on her objective. I may be a swamp donk, but I believe two plus two equals four."

Nolan couldn't articulate his feelings, hence shrugged it off. "Coyote, I don't... she's not involved. And I will prove it."

"Stashing her at Carolyn's house might not be the smartest or safest option, even if that old bird is tough and smart, not to mention shrewd as hell... Which is why you've done it. Damn, my partner's sly as a fox." Coyote chuckled before adding, "You want to get her opinion on the kid."

Nolan grinned.

"Side benefit. Not many people can hold out against Carolyn's insidious prodding." Nolan's reply came without thought. His instincts urged him to protect the coed and see the case through, no matter the cost. Current knowledge equated the tip of the iceberg. They needed access to whatever Keiki withheld.

"Whether the kid is guilty or not, she's mixed up in something way beyond her ability to handle. If anyone can get her to open up, it'll be Carolyn." Coyote fished his truck keys from his pocket as Nolan cut the engine in front of the station.

"I figure they'd each benefit the other. Look, it's late. Let's talk to vice in the morning, okay?" Nolan needed to verify, at least in his own mind, certain facts before confronting the other detective.

"Fine. Pick me up at eight."

Chapter Thirteen

Keiki snickered at the thought of Carolyn brandishing a gun at an intruder. The lady had to be seventy if she were a day, yet she moved like arthritis could never touch her.

"Why don't you set these scraps on the back deck for the cat?" Dressing in faded jeans and a flannel shirt didn't subtract years from her appearance as much as the long gray braid brushing her lower back.

They'd just finished dinner and Keiki had insisted on washing the dishes. The fact a plate of food remained covered and warming in the oven created concern over the older woman's faculties, but time would tell.

The explanation of Carolyn waiting for *someone* hadn't eased her overall anxiety over whether the specific someone had a pulse or not.

Taking the ceramic bowl, she stepped out on the wooden planks and set the food beside several stacked tires with cutouts for cat's homes.

Back inside, Carolyn finished wiping the table.

"I appreciate you renting me the apartment over the garage. It's quite comfortable, and I love being surrounded by nature. There's something so calming about living in the woods." Keiki retrieved the new phone from her pocket. Her monthly allowance for miscellaneous supplies had vanished with its purchase.

She'd lost her most recent information. Prior uploading of crucial data to a secure source guaranteed her basic details. Hope filled her with the thought no one could unlock her old phone to retrieve the particulars.

"The apartment will be more comfortable once they put the extra heat ducts in the floor. I was hoping to find a tenant like you. It's quiet back here but not everyone can appreciate the setting."

"I love it. And it's not too far from school, which is great."

"Well, don't thank me yet. The pest control company is sending a man out tomorrow morning to treat for termites. When Nolan gets here, I'll get him to help you move the fridge. It seems vermin have found a way up through a space where the water line comes in."

"No problem. Nice to own a home next to a cop. Round the clock security." She wondered about the circumstances bringing the odd couple together.

Keiki took a mental snapshot of her landlady before the crafty expression lapsed to a benign countenance. Buried in the woman's gaze was a perceptiveness that deciphered and plotted. To what agenda, time would tell.

How much trouble can a nice older lady cause?

"Actually, this isn't my home any more. Not really. I grew up within these old walls, but when my daughter died three years ago, well, her illness cleaned out my accounts. If not for Nolan's generosity, I would've lost it to the bank."

"Nolan?" Alarm bells blared in Keiki's head.

"He was engaged to my Clare. Weeks before the wedding, she was diagnosed with an inoperable tumor." Carolyn's hand covered Keiki's while she sat at the island. "He wanted to marry her anyway, despite the unavoidable ending. She refused." A single tear trickled from the corner of one eye, lifted away by a wrinkled, shaking finger. "Tell me about your Grams."

Now, she understood the connection.

"You remind me of her." Keiki waxed nostalgic in recounting past family holidays and events.

A cursory knock at the back door preceded a gust of cool air blowing through the kitchen. No sound of an approaching vehicle gave advance notice of company arriving, which meant the visitor had walked some distance.

"Hey, Carolyn. I thought I'd check to see how you two are making out." Nolan's cursory nod in Keiki's direction was followed with a heartfelt smile at the older woman.

"Food's in the oven. Fried chicken, mashed potatoes, and greens. Help yourself." Carolyn gestured for them all to sit at the kitchen table. Close scrutiny and a tilted head indicated a puzzle solver at work. After a minute, a knowing look spread across her face. "I think she'd look great with a princess neckline."

Nolan stiffened as he padded toward the oven, his warning frown ignored by the older woman.

Opening the door and taking a whiff, he retrieved the plate then poured a glass of tea. "Smells great. Thanks."

"Welcome. By the way, Horace stinks." Carolyn wrinkled her nose. "You need to take better care of your partner. It's not like he's self-sufficient. Well, not entirely."

Wait. Nolan's gay?

Keiki snapped her jaw shut, trying to reconcile Carolyn's harsh tone with earlier perceptions. He didn't wear a ring, yet the death of his fiancée could've flipped a switch.

Keiki had a good sense about people, and if anything, Nolan issued a subdued if carefully controlled interest, so she reassessed. *Maybe he's bi?*

"I'll give him a bath tonight." Weariness tinged his voice and relaxed his posture. He wasted no time in digging into his meal.

At their initial meeting, he broadcast a sense of formal attentiveness, shrewd but respectable. His current attitude didn't track. Relaxed and speaking his mind presented another facet of his character for her to reconcile.

"You should ask Keiki for help." Carolyn smiled and continued, "Besides, there might be times when you're working and need her to help feed him."

Keiki's first impression of Carolyn took on a new aspect. A certain chord in her tone suggested disdain for Nolan's choice of companions. There was still no doubt the toughened exterior harbored a matchmaker underneath.

"Uh, I'm not qualified to be a caretaker. I don't have any experience."

"Ease up, kid. She figured you the type to like dogs. Carolyn's just a little nuts where Horace is concerned." Nolan shook his head but smiled at their host. "You're a sly fox, indeed."

"Dog? Horace is your dog?" It took a minute for the conversation to replay in her head. The heat of mortification and anger drained away after realizing her earlier impressions still held true, with a twist. She'd underestimated the homeowner. It wouldn't happen again.

"And for the record, I'm not a kid." If not for the older woman's presence, Keiki would've placed a palm under each breast to emphasize the difference.

Nolan and Carolyn communicated well, their nonverbal interplay accomplished with a raised brow, head tilt, or slight twitch of a lip. He understood she bated him, which made it easier to keep his calm.

Still, neither had suffered *her* mischievous side...

"Anyone in college is still a kid." Nolan raised a brow but received a non-committal shrug from their host.

"Well, my friend's lab partner is fifty-eight." Keiki smirked at them both.

"Which proves your college has the age spans covered." When finished, he took his plate to the sink and scraped the scraps into the waiting bowl. "I'll be back later to take out your trash, Carolyn."

"Don't bother. I need the exercise."

"C'mon, kiddo. We need to have a chat," said before holding open the back door like a gentleman.

Common sense dictated she not ruffle his feathers. Nervousness ensured she poke him at every turn. It didn't take a genius to realize he'd pick at her earlier ramblings at her apartment. Try as she might, she couldn't recall the specific utterances which could prove her undoing.

No doubt his perceptions were spot on. His intense focus could decipher every secret, regardless of how deep in the dark recesses of her soul they hid.

"Where are we going?" From the front corner of the garage, she saw no cars, which accounted for the detective's silent entry.

"To my house. Don't worry. I don't pervert little girls."

It wasn't his first reference to their age difference. "Not worried at all. I hear the older men get, the more difficult it is for them to... perform."

He kept pace beside her, shrugging off the taunt despite the slight but perceptible tightening of his shoulders.

Interlacing oak and poplar branches overhead enveloped them in a shadowy pocket, creating a secluded world easily mistaken for safety.

To her left, the winding gravel drive bisected the woods concealing the main road. Seclusion from the outside chaos was welcome, nervous tension created by the detective's presence, not so much.

"What did you want to talk about?" Following him on a well-traveled deer trail leading from the property's side, she got the sinking feeling he'd already slipped into cross-examining mode.

"I've brought some of your things from your apartment. I also have your laptop. We'll talk a bit before I bring you back."

Flashbacks of terror swelled within her mind. "When this mess is settled, I'm probably gonna find a new place to stay."

"It seems you get along with Carolyn well enough, and I'm sure she'd enjoy your company. She fixed the garage apartment up nice, too. I understand she's upgrading the HVAC so it will be more comfortable."

"Your garage, you mean."

Nolan gave her a sharp look.

"She said you need to help me move the fridge for the termite man tomorrow."

"Ah, I forgot about that. Okay." Nolan nodded. "I can help you carry some of your stuff upstairs while I'm at it."

Ever the gentleman, he eased off his pace to match her stride once they exited the thicker forest. The path to his home equaled several hundred yards and hadn't been visible through the tangles of briars and trees.

When it appeared, Keiki stopped mid-pace.

"Wow. This is your house? Nice."

The understatement didn't depict the sprawling ranch or the massive screened porch jutting off the back. The brick patio beside it contained a long stone counter with a built-in grill, stain-steel sink and cabinets. Her parents had also enjoyed a fire pit on cool evenings.

Instead of commenting, he held still, studying her like an entomologist examined a butterfly after pinning its wings to a board.

"It's just a house. You expected axes and swords for easy access?"

"No. And I doubt you leave cobwebs up for Halloween decorations, either."

He didn't answer.

"It has a large footprint."

"I have a big family."

"You're what—early to mid-thirties? How many kids can you have?

126

Oh, unless some are twins?" She wasn't fishing.

No, wait. She was.

The sudden, almost imperceptible flash of heat in his gaze confirmed it.

The back yard occupied a clear space of seventy-five square yards and included a swing set, sandbox, and monkey bars. Split-rail fencing lined the space.

"First, I'm not married, second, I'm twenty-eight, and last, I have four sisters who tend to drop in unannounced. We have frequent barbeques in the spring, summer, and fall."

Each step closer raised the hair on her forearms under her denim shirt. It was like stepping into the spider's web, willingly and for reasons unknown.

"How does a split-rail fence keep your dog from wondering off when he goes out?" As if on cue, a deep ferocious growl morphed into all out canine anger from within the house.

"Hold still when he comes close. He'll sniff, but don't move to pet him. Horace is tolerant but doesn't like people." Nolan waited, relaxed, and nonchalant. "Oh, and don't speak to or make eye contact with him, or he'll say hello with his teeth."

His tone generated more fear than the killer who'd broken into her apartment.

The dog wouldn't be a problem.

As if on cue, a large ball of silver and black fur barreled through a doggy door on the porch. Its ground-eating strides consumed the backyard distance. One leap allowed him to vault over the split fence rails, pushing off the top with a small grunt.

Instead of following orders, Keiki knelt and rested one upturned hand on her knee. Immediate cessation of barking and a curious whine burbled in the dog's throat as he skidded to a stop at her feet.

Animals loved her. A fact which had always amused and baffled her parents. It was sad she hadn't enjoyed a companion's presence since starting college, but current events forced her to reconsider.

Soft nuzzling and sniffing combined with the dog's rough tongue testing her fingers elicited a smile. "As long as there's no taste-testing, Horace, we'll be fine." She avoided eye contact but smiled when the dog's snuffling ruffled her hair.

"Damn. Never seen that reaction before. Do you wear a meat-based perfume I didn't detect? I don't keep up with the latest fads... drinks and fragrances included."

His smart mouth would get him in trouble one day, and Keiki decided it was time to lighten her mental load.

She'd been labeled quirky, outlandish, and sometimes eccentric. It'd serve him right to get a taste of unpredictability that would knock him off kilter. Her deviant imagination hatched a plan that would earn his censure and respect.

The shepherd wagged his tail, the force shifting his entire back end. When he advanced to rub his face against her chest, she sifted her fingers through the soft hair on his shoulder.

"Wow, such a soft coat. What do you feed him?"

"BARF diet. We tried the Prey Model Raw, but he tends to like a few fruits and veggies."

"Dogs' digestive systems can't break down a plant's cell wall. You either have to boil vegetables or chop them."

"Which is why I grind and freeze them once a month."

A vague frustration twisted his lips before he turned to stride through the gate. "How is it a college kid knows about raw feeding?"

"Student and stupid are not synonyms." Keiki looked around and released a small sigh. "Ya know... you really do have the perfect setting for parties. No one to complain about loud music, overcrowding, or spy out their windows to see what you're doing."

"Thanks, but I don't do wild."

"See, that's the problem. You need someone to take the starch out of your step, loosen your spine, and maybe plan an orgy."

Nolan paused in opening the door and pivoted to gawk. His expression morphed to the usual mask but heat flared in his eyes. He opened his mouth then closed it and shook his head.

"They have books on orgies, kind of a how to. With all the hands, legs, lips, and ah, other parts, it gets complicated, physically, emotionally, and politically."

"Politically? I didn't know there was etiquette involved. Do you have a manual?"

"Maybe."

His frown turned sly, indicating a deeper understanding. "Did you

128

know people babble when nervous?" The wolf's grin took shape as he ushered her in to sit at the kitchen table. "It's amazing the trash that comes out of their mouths."

"Would you like to hear blond men jokes? I have some good ones."

"Not particularly."

After she sat, he stopped behind her and leaned down, his breath stirring her hair and warming her ear. "I've been in your apartment and know how you live. I've also seen you interact with others and have a good fix on your life. You don't do orgies, don't have a boyfriend, and except for what might amount to a little experimentation, have probably never had a solid relationship... *kid*."

He hadn't touched her, but the subtle difference in his tone caressed her in ways no one ever had. Failing to conceal the noise from her gulp, she closed her eyes tight as a shudder jiggled her shoulders.

When she opened them again, he'd taken a seat across from her, studying her every move.

Unable to meet his close scrutiny, she looked around. "Nice place."

The room was large, the open plan giving a view to a massive shared living and dining space. A definite masculine flavor held sway in the geometric-patterned rug anchoring two leather sofas. Wood floors gleamed in the fading light. One table lamp, consisting of a series of small pipes and a glass shade appeared out of place.

"One of my sisters' idea of a joke." He hadn't needed to ask what absorbed her attention.

"I like it."

"You would."

She ran her hand over the smooth oak grain. The table didn't look homemade, at least not by a hobbyist, but the unusual etching on the top gave her pause. "Did you do this?"

"No. A friend of mine did." His no-nonsense demeanor melted when his dog padded to his side and nudged his knee. "In a minute, Horace. You won't starve."

Whatever he wanted to show her was likely contained in the manila envelope on the lazy Susan. If he intended to arrest her, he wouldn't have brought her to his home. No, he wanted answers, ones she might not give. Despite trusting him, she wouldn't say anything could be misconstrued and incriminate herself.

"Carolyn said you didn't eat much. You hungry? I have some leftover chicken pot pie in the fridge."

Food was a universal icebreaker. "Ah, my three favorite things, all offered by a cop. However, no thanks."

Nolan elevated scowling to an art form.

"You're getting pressure to make an arrest." Her statement was more of a question than fact, a search to see where his priorities lay; closing the case fast versus finding the truth.

"There's always pressure to close a case. Parents want answers, and the public wants to feel safe."

When he moved to the fridge, the clink of metal aroused her curiosity until he set a bowl down and removed the shower cap lid.

Horace sat, the brush of his tail sweeping the floor, warm chocolate eyes imploring his master for the necessary command. Once given, the canine bit into the chicken leg quarter, turning and trotting through his personal door.

"He likes to eat in the yard on nice days." Nolan shrugged as if reading the dog's mind before taking his seat again.

With the flick of the envelope's flap, he retrieved several glossy photos from within. "It's time to tell me what's going on behind the scenes. I'm fairly certain you weren't involved in Shelly's death, but you *are* involved in this mess somehow. Let's have it."

Heat draining from her face wouldn't be missed by the shrewd detective. In his hands, he held a photo of her newest device, a prototype.

"That's mine."

"I know. It has your initials on it. We discussed how you mark them."

"No. Not that *specific* one. Mine is a prototype, not in production yet."

"This looked pretty finished to me when it shot a puff of what I suspect to be the same drug that killed your friend, a Fentanyl-laced narcotic."

"No. I didn't do any of that. I'm not behind this. Really!"

Chapter Fourteen

"Prove it." Nolan monitored her expression.

Disbelief, shock, denial, and then determination surfaced to remain.

She snatched the photo from his hands and held it close for inspection. A sudden inhale preceded her growl. "Hold on. I *can* prove it."

Standing quickly knocked over her chair but didn't slow her rush toward the front door.

"Where're you going?"

"To get my laptop. You said you had it in your car."

"This way." Nolan led her through the side door. "It's in the trunk, along with some of your other stuff."

Once they'd returned and the soft hum of the laptop's fan filled the kitchen, anger and raw determination filled her expression.

Nolan took the seat beside her. The soft glow and flicker from the boot-up process didn't cover her slow and controlled breaths.

"Take a closer look at that photo. Notice the initials, the way they've been engraved." Her fingers flew over the keyboard.

The tremor in her voice matched her hands as she opened one file after another in new windows. Pictures of drones populated the screen.

"Yeah, 'KT' is etched above what looks like the knee joint of your spider drone."

"Spider drone, really? That's the best you can come up with?" Keiki snarled, then enlarged one of the pictures bearing the letters KT.

"Yeah, just like—oh." Nolan squinted, and leaned in to look closer at each of her photos.

Her soft exhale stimulated the fine hairs on his arm. The scent of her shampoo defied definition.

"See? Look closer at each of *my* drones."

Nolan's frown deepened. "None of yours have a period following your initials like the one in the photo."

"It's my signature. I never put a period on my work until it's finished. When I *do* turn it in for production, I put a period after the *T* and only the T. What you found, I haven't turned the final prototype into Harock yet. It has a bit of an issue with the legs I need to fix. You saw it in my apartment when you first came to question me."

"Apparently someone fixed it. What's the range and flight time on your models?"

A detailed explanation ensued specifying other differences between her prototypes and the finished product. Finer distinctions verified her claim.

Relief flooded his mind in the end. Throughout, she'd demonstrated no sweating or nervous gestures to indicate deceit.

"From this location, you could've controlled the one that attacked Coyote and me, but Carolyn confirmed your presence with her." He flicked the photo, sending it to the table to slide toward the center.

Anger and indignation emanated from every pore of her body. She met his stare with one of her own, innocence and determination proving a heady mixture.

"The problem is, who's stealing my designs, and why? What's their end game?"

"Tell me about your boss and his operation. How many engineers does Franklin Harock employ?"

"I—I don't know for sure. I've always worked on the fringes. I have talked with several of his mechanics over the last few months, working out flaws and checking on what specifics they want included, what they want each drone to do."

"Is Harock a hands-on kind of guy? Does he take much interest and micromanage his employees? I don't have enough detail on his background."

"He's not capable of designing or fixing problems that come up during the process. He's strictly a business man."

"So, we might be looking for someone in his company. Or someone who went after Shelly to send him a message."

Delving through one problem spawned several new ones. A cursory check had indicated Harock Industries' payroll included over a hundred employees in the local office alone. Several satellite facilities operating under the regional umbrella were scattered throughout the country.

Further conversation yielded little useful information. She described in detail, other works in progress and her goals for each. Incorporating GPS seemed a logical step for the company in protecting their products. The notion of drones bearing infrared sensors sparked a darker curiosity.

The fact remained someone targeted Keiki after killing one of her friends. The third of their trio was still missing and a professor was dead with the same MO as Harock's daughter. All this while trying to frame the coed for murder.

"I hate multi-tasking thugs." Perhaps a dealer held a vendetta against the company and its employees. The longer he thought about it, the less feasible it seemed.

"I don't want to be framed for something I didn't do."

"You won't be, kid. That's not gonna happen."

Since his daughter's death, Harock had stepped up security both at home and work. Nolan wondered if it would be enough, considering the instruments of death involved.

"C'mon. I'll take you back and help carry your stuff up the steps." Getting her settled seemed a nice thing to do.

Clarification of her working status settled the question of her innocence in his mind, yet he needed hard evidence. En route to her apartment, they were quiet, each guarding their thoughts.

"I'll set this last box on your bed." From the door, he could see her entire space, except for the bathroom. The double bed sported a blanket depicting a mountain scene complete with deer and rabbits.

"Thanks. I still haven't put away my other stuff."

The drones she'd brought from her apartment covered most viable surfaces.

Chapter Fifteen

Heavy cloud cover shielding the morning sun couldn't wipe the grin from Nolan's face when picking up his partner. He'd obtained enough facts, if not concrete evidence, to clear Keiki's status as person of interest.

Once his partner opened the SUV's door and settled in, Nolan handed him a hot coffee.

"Aw, is this bring the teacher an apple day? I seem to have missed that memo."

"No, smartass. Drink your coffee and fuck off."

Coyote sipped his brew but didn't hold back the commentary. "So, you got some last night. Who's the lucky lady?" A light snicker served as advanced warning for future insults. "About time, too."

"If you're referring to particular details about the case, then yes. Yes, I got very lucky." Dawn's gray light had crept into the corners of his bedroom by the time he'd finished his to-do list.

"Damn, and I was wondering if you'd suffer from tennis elbow before rejoining the world of dating. Dare we credit a certain prodigious blonde?"

The reference to Keiki irked him more than it should have. "She's a student. You'd do well to remember that." The darker side of his imagination pictured her on his bed, her hair cascading over the side.

"It's not like I'm the one harboring a potential suspect, buddy."

"She's not staying with me. She's renting Carolyn's apartment over the garage."

"To-*may*-to, to-*mah*-to. Carolyn would be homeless if you hadn't helped."

"It's her name on the deed, not mine. If the captain wants to split hairs, I'm fine."

"We'll see."

"Keiki's no longer a suspect. If you can keep your thoughts above the waistline for a minute, I'll explain how I know."

"Partner, I'm not the one who needs a roll in the hay, but for future reference, I have a friend..."

"No thanks. I hate shots." Nolan disregarded Coyote's derogatory comments and waited until the running flow of verbal abuse dried up.

During the night, he'd thought of the best way to present the facts to the task force. Now, he tossed the folder containing pictures of Keiki's other prototypes to his partner. "Take a look before others weigh in. Study them up close and tell me what you see."

To his credit, it took Coyote less than a minute to notice the difference between the marked photos of Keiki's devices and the one that had carried the fatal poison.

"Okay, I'm listening. Given your smile, I take it this is going to be good."

That was code for his partner having an open mind. Nolan launched into precise details and a working theory. "We both know Harock was holding something back. What we don't know is if he's being framed, blackmailed, or targeted."

"It'd take concrete evidence to get a warrant, and I hear he's got high-class golfing buddies. Gonna be hard to get." Coyote bounced one heel on the floorboard, his agitation contagious.

"That's not the biggest hitch."

"Really? There's more?"

"Keiki's got revenge on her mind. I saw it in her eyes last night."

"Was that before or after?" When no answer came forth, Coyote continued, undaunted, "We can't sit on her without making her feel like a suspect, *and* she'll shut us out regarding anything else she learns. However, she does have access to Harock's inner sanctum..."

"No. We are not asking her to snoop. If she gets caught, they'd kill her before we could intervene."

Coyote grinned. "You know she's gonna poke around anyway."

Yeah, this was the part of the puzzle Nolan couldn't stomach. "She's working part-time for Nick Tucker. We could involve him."

"You've heard as well as I have, he's a man who colors outside the lines on occasion. Would she go to him for help?"

"Doubt it. He wore a badge and that's a deterrent for her. No, she'll take on Harock Industries all by herself." Nolan pictured her scooting out in the dead of night for her own sneak and peek.

"I don't fancy being one step behind her, either, but—"

"No, Coyote. Just no."

"Look. Harock has the drones. Gabby is a chemistry major. The chem professor had some type of—something—hidden, which we can speculate has been found." Coyote pulled out his notepad. "Oh, and by the way, I talked with campus security again. They found nothing of significance in reviewing the videos for the stranger the two girls saw after a party."

"Figures. That doesn't mean footage doesn't exist." Nolan made a sharp turn to enter the highway. "I think Keiki saw the killer's face, which would explain his persistence in targeting her. I don't believe she has any interest in drugs and doesn't feel the need to stockpile cash. Look at the way she lives. No, I think her interests drive her to succeed. It's just the way she's wired."

"Takes like to recognize like, I guess," Coyote replied.

"Either Harock, one of his employees, or even the competition is using drones for whatever current purpose they have in mind."

"Can I have assassinations for one hundred, please? And they're using your kid as cover. I think she or Gabby has something they want. God knows what. Apparently they didn't find it when ransacking the apartment."

Nolan continued his partner's line of thought. "The picture I found in Harock's home showed the resemblance between Shelly and Keiki. It would've been easy enough for the killer to mistake one for the other at a distance, then have to dispose of the body after realizing his mistake. Shelly might have been collateral damage."

"Sounds about right."

"The killer could've been pissed off at the mistaken identity and went into a rage." Nolan's agitation took form as his fingers tapped on the wheel. "We need to go over Harock's employee files again. At least he gave us that much."

"Which he wouldn't have done if he suspected one of them of killing his daughter. He seemed the hands-on type to me."

"Fentanyl-laced opioids could be a red herring." Nolan shook his head, not believing his own words.

"Yeah, me neither. Not after the professor's death."

The soft hum of tire on gravel supplied white noise for the remaining ride to the precinct, each detective delving through their own thoughts, forming their own suspect pool, and finagling a way to prove out their theory.

They would have just enough time to slip in to see the vice detective before the joint task meeting.

Warm air buffeted his thoughts as Nolan shoved the heavy glass door to the station open. He nodded to the duty officer who buzzed him past the bullet-resistant enclosure.

A half-eaten bagel and extra-gulp-sized coffee sitting on the counter accounted for his disgruntlement when the phone rang.

Discreet tapping on Nolan's shoulder interrupted his thought process. "What?"

Coyote pointed toward the captain's office where the man himself stood in the open doorway with a deep scowl. "When you two have finished wool-gathering and can spare a minute, my office please, Detectives."

Nolan nodded but ignored his partner's murmured, "Get your head in the game before he hands the case to the feds."

"Just trying to work out the puzzle." The lie slipped from his lips and avoided rebuttal since Coyote couldn't read it in his face.

Instead of heading to his desk for the ME's final report, Nolan strode down the hallway leading to the smaller vice department. "The information must be noteworthy and highly sensitive to request an urgent face-to-face meeting."

Behind him, Coyote mumbled a greeting in passing a uniformed officer.

Monumental effort focused Nolan's thoughts away from the strong-willed enigma and back to the problem at hand. Someone was determined to bury Keiki, in one fashion or another.

Stale air and burned coffee filled the room dedicated to the dumping ground of all offenses deemed not belonging to the two-man vice squad.

Two desks sat at slight angles to one another, one sitting empty since the senior detective's retirement. Filling slots remained low on the captain's to-do list.

"Hey, Bitner. What'cha got for us?" Coyote rolled a chair over to where the room's lone occupant sat. The older detective's years of experience surpassed anyone else's in the department.

Nolan mimicked his move on the other side for visual access to the computer monitor. "I take it you got something back on the powder? You must've burned the phone lines talking with other departments."

"Got a call from an investigator in Baltimore. He caught wind of our powder deaths and pulled some strings." The plastic of Bitner's mouse cracked under his grip when he jiggled it to wake up his computer.

"Let me guess. The feds are anxiously waiting to *help* us." Coyote leaned forward, resting his elbows on the desk.

"Yeah. There's one in with the captain now, because what we have on the task force isn't enough." Bitner opened several windows to reveal various reports. "This first one is Shelly Harock's drug analysis. As suspected, it was laced with a large dose of Fentanyl. She didn't stand a chance."

"She was raped, too, but I don't know if... before or after. I haven't read the full report." Despite years on the force, Nolan braced himself for what he knew to come.

"According to the ME, the defensive bruising suggests before." The older detective scrubbed a hand through his salt-and-pepper hair. "Shit. It never gets easier."

"What about the professor and the coed at the Foam Glitter race?" Coyote took the lead, as if knowing Nolan needed time to collect his thoughts.

"Identical compound. But that's not the interesting part. It seems the narcotic laced with the Fentanyl is a new designer drug."

"Like something a chemistry professor might cook up with his student's help?" Nolan asked, knowing they'd just waded into deeper waters. "Shit."

"No. Baltimore vice says they're coordinating with various departments around the country along with the DEA. This stuff is coming in from Central America." Bitner pulled up another report with Baltimore's city seal at the top. "They also said this new drug has the highest kill rate they've seen."

"What's this got to do with four college kids and a professor?" Coyote offered Nolan a measured look that denied Keiki's innocence.

Bitner swiveled to Nolan and leaned back in his chair to offer his full attention. "Four? Explain."

"We have a missing student, Gabriella Kiernan. Left a frat party late at night and hasn't been seen since. One of her professors was killed," Nolan explained.

"In a locked room on the second floor of his lab," Coyote added. "And by locked, I mean locked from the inside."

"Someone had a key," the vice detective mused. "The missing student?"

"I don't think so." Nolan couldn't explain why those puzzle pieces didn't fit together in his mind.

"And the fourth student?" Bitner turned to Coyote when Nolan remained mute.

"The student nailed at the Foam Glitter race was not the intended victim. Nolan was at the scene and shoved a friend of Shelly and Gabby aside when a drone dive-bombed them. The victim happened to be in the wrong place at the wrong time."

"Well, shit. That means we have one live... something." With several clicks, the vice detective printed out the reports. "Tell me more about the survivor."

"Katherine Tallerman is a mechanical prodigy who designs drones for Harock Industries," Coyote put the worst of the information out front for the older detective to digest.

"You think drug runners are muscling Harock into cooperating, using his drones as what, a delivery service?" Bitner pushed his chair back and retrieved the printouts, giving them to Nolan, who nodded in thanks.

"Sounds plausible," Nolan confirmed.

"I was thinking about this while waiting on you two. It would explain them going after Harock's family."

"But not the professor," Coyote contradicted. "

"That speaks more of a joint effort. Not sure of the end goal. I'd say the supposed survivor could know a lot more. Where have you two stashed her?"

"Tucked away nice and safe." Nolan firmed his jaw, daring his partner to speak.

"Is that it?" Coyote leaned back and prepared to stand, freezing when Bitner pulled up another screen.

"No. Actually, I have one more question, and better coming from me before you hear it from the captain and task force."

Nolan's chest iced over with the new picture appearing on screen. It was a close up of the drone that attacked him and his partner in the woods. Beside it was a piece from another drone.

"The fragment from the Harock crime scene was checked against what you recovered at the campus. The letters match. Katherine Tallerman."

"No. Well, the initials yes, but that arm didn't come from one of her machines." Nolan retrieved the photos from his envelope and the pictures he'd taken of Keiki's prototypes. Explaining the fine differences kept them on thin ice, instead of freezing in the depths below surface.

"This is a damn intricate scenario, don't you think?" Bitner asked.

Vice support would go a long way in convincing the rest of their group to extend a little leeway. An officer's experience and track record always pulled weight.

"Because the organization behind this lacks funds, imagination, and access?" Nolan countered. "If the drugs are coming from Central America, you're talking cartel. Their resources are near limitless."

The room remained silent while Bitner considered the issues, then nodded. "Okay, you think she's an innocent pawn. Possible. Thin, but possible."

Nolan pulled out one last fact. "Katherine's apartment was searched by forensics after a masked thug broke in. No trace of drugs were found, of *any* kind. However, they did find an audio transmitter."

"In a college kid's private domain," Coyote supplied.

"Someone's been keeping tabs on the occupants," Nolan confirmed.

"I heard the bastard wore a mask and shot a uniform," Bitner added. A quiet moment of commiseration followed.

"If she were working *with* a cartel, in any capacity, they wouldn't have bothered concealing their identity. It wouldn't make sense to kill her or take her down." Nolan breathed a sigh of relief when the vice detective nodded in agreement.

"Devil's advocate," Bitner said and arched a brow, holding his hands out in surrender. "Someone could be trying to muscle in on an ongoing operation."

"Again, no drugs in Keiki's apartment, no priors, and no indication she would delve into that world. It's not the crowd she hangs with, according to her professors."

"What about her friends, Shelly and Gabriella?" Bitner asked.

Coyote fielded that question. "As far as Shelly is concerned, she was a business major being groomed to take the reins of Harock Industries. We believe she was clean."

"And the other girl?"

"She was pre-med, top grades. Her father's a prominent surgeon," Coyote replied.

"And she's still missing? Are you thinking because she's dead, or in hiding? You said the three girls were friends."

"Don't know which. One of her classmates said Gabby and her professor were very close. They shared a special camaraderie." Coyote shrugged off the older detective's speculation.

"All right." Bitner shoved to his feet. "I've got your backs where the task force is concerned. Speaking of which, Captain wants an update."

Further conversation revealed no insight and no corkscrew to insert into the knot of confusing evidence. Nolan's instinct declared Keiki a victim, despite lack of proof to wipe doubt from his colleagues' minds.

Meeting with the captain went as suspected. Both his boss and the Special Agent present wanted Keiki brought in for additional questioning.

The united front presented by three detectives argued with convincing evidence that interests would be better served and more information collected under present circumstances.

By the end of the day, Nolan had made little progress unless one counted the raging headache he sported. One thing he and his partner did agree on—Keiki withheld information, maybe not incriminating, it was something pertinent.

He'd seen the truth in her eyes. She hadn't been involved in the recent deaths, which didn't preclude her from harboring valid suspicions. Gaining her trust became a higher priority, and the means to accomplish that left a sour taste in his mouth.

It's her life on the line.

In the parking lot, Coyote took his thoughts one step further. "Keiki looks up to you. I've seen that spark."

"No, damn it." He drew the line at breaking the coed's heart.

As usual, a plate of food waited for him at Carolyn's house. When he walked in, the smell of garlic and herbs reminded him of years gone by, when his fiancée waited for his return with a glass of wine and a smile promising a night of energetic activities.

Painful memories crashed through his mental shields and filled his soul with bittersweet souvenirs of a life not lived. Three years melted away in the blink of an eye.

"It's time to let go and move on, Nolan. She would want that for you." Decades of social work presented Carolyn with the ability to read people with incredible accuracy. She'd honed her skills and often used them.

"I... I don't know how." Clare had been the other half of his soul.

"Sure you do. You're just resisting because the opportunity isn't perfect. But, remember this, *nothing* in life is perfect just as *no one* is perfect."

"She was." He couldn't bear to say her name.

"No, time has let you idolize her. As much as I loved my daughter, she had her faults. Finding you was the best thing she'd ever done. The tumor," Carolyn wiped a tear from her cheek, "was meant to be. God's will."

Both remained quiet until Nolan finished eating and rinsed his plate before putting it in the dishwasher. "Where is she?"

Carolyn's grin withheld a secret he didn't have the energy to decrypt.

"Probably working. I've only known one other in my time who could remain so focused." Shuffling over to the sink, she patted him on the back before retreating to the living room. "She needs help in moving the fridge back. You mind giving her a hand?"

"Ah, pest control day. Yeah, I got it."

Solemn steps carried him out the door and to the outside stairs leading to the garage apartment. Carolyn's words followed, mocking, taunting him with what he couldn't attempt. A true relationship.

Keiki was a student who didn't know what she wanted.

His conscience counter-argued that becoming an orphan had matured the young woman in ways nothing else could. Like himself at that age, she'd know what she wanted.

After meeting with the captain and hearing doubts voiced by others, he needed to reaffirm his thoughts on her involvement, which meant another round of verbal sparring, close proximity, and inhaling her down-to-earth scent. He had no idea what shampoo she used, but would invest in its stock once discovered.

On an average day, he'd fry his partner for contemplating what he was about to do. Nothing concerning their investigation was normal. Gaining Keiki's trust was the most efficient way to get the inside information she hoarded. It was the best way to keep her safe.

Who was to say they couldn't stay friends? Good friends, without benefits. He'd draw the line at physical contact.

A slight drizzle dampened his hair and chilled the nape of his neck as he knocked on her door. Through the window inset, he saw her startle, so enthralled with her project she'd lost awareness of her surroundings.

When she opened the door, it was like a breath of fresh air, until she frowned and barred his entry. "Hey. What's up?"

"Carolyn asked me to help you replace the refrigerator." She'd used her body to block both his entrance and line of sight, so he couldn't see her current work in progress.

And so it begins.

"No need. I got it all put back. Thanks for the offer, though." Her gaze twitched. A sheen of perspiration lined her forehead.

She was either hiding something or planning something.

Neither was acceptable.

"Wanna talk? I have information." He let the carrot dangle and waited for her to take the bait. Forcing her hand would set his investigation back.

"Not right now. I'm in the middle of something, but I could drop over in the AM?"

Her laptop sat on the table, but the screen faced away from him. Was she doing her own covert surveillance? She'd get herself killed yet. He managed to keep disappointment from furrowing his brow.

The fact her eyes were red rimmed and puffy softened his approach. He couldn't bring himself to bulldoze through her emotional turmoil after she'd been crying. He'd find another way.

She wouldn't accept comfort, given her obvious snooping and determined stance. Opening his arms had been his first option, but he remained still and waited. Extreme and acute stress widened the tiniest cracks in her armor.

"Sure. I'm taking a couple hours comp time in the morning. Breakfast is at seven-thirty." Without giving her time to refuse, he turned and trotted down the steps. Mealtime was something he could use to advantage, and besides, she could stand to gain ten or fifteen pounds.

Once home, he set out sweet sausage, eggs, and cheese, all the makings of a breakfast casserole. *Something other than the packaged noodles seen in her apartment.*

Chapter Sixteen

Keiki heaved a sigh of relief. Indecision had warred with determination in Nolan's stare. For reasons she didn't understand, he was determined to get into her temporary digs, which would've been fine if she hadn't been using her drones to spy. Plus, she didn't want him to see the picture on her bedside table.

The look in the detective's eyes didn't declare mistrust so much as curiosity, and heat. The latter introduced a complication she couldn't afford.

He's a cop.

If Carolyn had spotted her late-morning beeline through the side yard before lunch, she would've passed that along and he would've mentioned it. During lunch, nothing had been said, no sly or knowing looks to call her out. Checking on Horace would've provided a reasonable excuse for her excursion.

The dog personified energy while lifting her spirits, not to mention serving a specific purpose. She'd attached one of her mechanical babies to his collar and gained entrance to Nolan's home.

From there, she'd toured the space and settled the small device to get the best view of his kitchen and main living area. Her fisheye lens distorted the view, but she got the gist of his movements from atop the kitchen soffit.

Afterward, she'd sat in the yard with Horace leaning against her side. Top requirement for her next apartment included a dog-friendly environment.

If Nolan discovered her intrusion, she'd earn a free one room, block-walled apartment complete with iron bars. Without knowing him well, she knew he cherished privacy.

Switching between views on her laptop, she watched him enter his kitchen and greet the shepherd. Their mutual greeting warmed her heart and thawed a little bit of doubt surrounding his motives for helping.

Like many homeowners, he used the space above the cabinets for extra storage. A small spot between two wicker baskets provided a perfect angle. Guilt stabbed her chest for intruding, but she needed to stay a step ahead to identify the killer. Trusting the police to solve problems hadn't worked out so well in the past.

The Harock family had taken her in after tragedy destroyed her world. They would never betray her or be involved with a killer. By comparison, she didn't know the engineers well.

What she needed was access to the company's engineers, a tight-knit group she conferred with on occasion. None stood out as a possible traitor or killer. Although to be fair, she'd never gotten close to them.

Local news carried the story of the professor in a follow up to Shelly's murder. No details were given. Gabby had been close to her mentor, claiming him a friend of the family.

To the best of her knowledge and surveillance, no one had entered their apartment or Shelly's dorm room. In fast forwarding through the footage covering the professor's home, video had caught someone rushing from the back.

The professor wasn't home, nor was he married or have a live-in girlfriend from what she could gather.

Dressed in a heavy coat and wearing a wide brimmed hat didn't change her conviction the runner was a man. Scant moonlight couldn't highlight enough details to suggest an identity. He did have the same build as the prick who'd attacked Shelly.

Dense forest hugged the twenty-yard perimeter on three sides of the professor's home. The dwelling formed a pocket of sorts without close neighbors to make for a concealed entry and exit.

The burglar had huddled in the large coat and scurried through the woods where a path granted access to the county road.

Not once did he look up, instead watching every step he made.

"Cameras." Keiki heaved a breath when the figurative lightbulb flashed over her head. "He's protecting his identity from video footage." She hadn't noticed if the professor's house had external security cameras. A little navigation pointed to one on each corner of the home. The fact the professor lived in her drone's range equaled a bonus.

The time stamp was a little before midnight. In going back, she saw he'd been in the cottage for over two hours. "Doing what? Kicking back and watching a movie?" she wondered aloud.

Nothing made sense. She needed eyes and ears in the police world and knew her detective wouldn't be forthcoming.

He might divulge information in hopes of receiving like in return.

Keiki had his number. He protected his witness to gain trust and insight.

She'd damn well figure it out for herself and then tell the cops. That way, they'd get it right and not draw her further into the quagmire of the investigation.

Sticky notes on the side of the screen held a to-do list. With Halloween a few weeks away, memories of elaborate decorations filled her mind. She missed her family more this time of year. Now, though, she missed her friends and felt adrift in a world which cared nothing for the lonely and desperate.

A cup of hot chocolate and muffin Carolyn insisted she take earlier had failed to settle her nerves. Keiki disguised her tears in the water and suds slipping down her body and mingling in the hot shower. Anything to relax for the long night ahead.

Sleep would not come, not with so much in the air and her life at stake. The killer wouldn't stop, driven by finding something she didn't have. He'd demanded details of an operation and the news reports specified some type of drug involved in Shelly's death.

The thing was, her friends would have nothing to do with drugs or conspiracy to commit murder. No, a large chunk of the puzzle was missing.

With the knock-off drones implicating her in some grander scheme, Nolan and Coyote suspected her involvement despite weak evidence to the contrary. She had to find proof, something to convince.

Her designs were, at least in rough form, duplicated at Harock Industries' research and development section. Any of the engineers could have modified her devices and used them to kill. They made the perfect assassin. Light, mobile, and able to get in and out of small places undetected.

Those and other like thoughts kept her tossing in bed long into the night. Nightmares arrived on the heels of sleep to resurrect remnants of fear and send her to the kitchen workspace. Nothing occupied her mind like work.

Gray shadows gave way to a sunrise painted in a soft palette of pastels but failed to dispel the sense of gloom shrouding her mind.

The near future included fear of mini death machines in strafing runs every time she stepped out of the apartment.

A cool shower completed the wake-up process and cleared her mind. Facing Nolan required sharp focus to avoid falling into the sense of security he obviously hoped to provide. Becoming parentless had forged her into a rock of mental stability once grief had worn the edges off vulnerability.

Pride in her parents for preparing her to face life with all its intricate deceptions and pitfalls lent hope that one day she'd do the same for her children. The idea of having a relationship equal to her parents gave hope that her life would settle down and she'd find love. Until then, she'd muddle through.

If the cop were in a different line of work, she'd like to count him a friend, but he didn't trust her. Not yet. Then again, she hadn't given him significant cause to do so.

Once she'd checked the early morning sky for mechanized traffic, the scenic route took her through the woods, preferred in part because of its serenity, but also because of the camouflage it offered. If luck prevailed, she could get two birds with one stone while at his house. She needed information and the man needed to loosen up.

Instead of approaching through the backyard, she circled to the front, hoping he hadn't parked his car in the garage.

Bingo!

Sometimes fate cast good fortune her way. As in every other aspect of his life, Nolan took care of his front yard. Several bags of leaves leaned against the garage awaiting disposal.

The tiniest squeak betrayed his vehicle's door opening. The hair on her nape rose.

"Looking for something?" Nolan stood in the front door as Horace came barreling out for a proper greeting.

She shut the door and stooped to accept her share of doggy kisses.

"Oh, you know, just the usual. Bloody axes, knives, other evidence a serial killer might have around."

He waited her out as Keiki squirmed.

"Just looking for my box of flash drives. They weren't with the stuff you brought over."

By letting the statement hang, she put him on the defensive, or so she hoped.

"Have you unpacked all your boxes?"

"Yeah. I guess I could've missed them. I'll look again." Without hesitation, she marched into his house and mused over the neatness. Small talk might negate the quasi-interrogation feel of her previous visit.

"Have a seat. Breakfast is ready and we can talk while we eat."

Regardless of her intentions, it was clear he had other plans.

Fluid movements denied the insecurity of a novice cook. Before he'd set milk and juice on the table, the oven beeped and he transferred a baking dish from rack to table with a mitt underneath.

"Smells great. What's in it?"

"Just because I'm a man doesn't mean I can't cook." The shadow of his arrogance could shelter a house.

"Your mom teach you?"

He looked away before taking a deep breath. "No. my fiancée did."

Keiki looked around. He wouldn't know Carolyn shared detailed descriptions of his nonexistent love life. "Oh. Am I intruding?"

"No. She's... not here." His expression belied the statement and revoked the possibility of questions.

"Okay." Instead of waiting for him to get around to it, she decided to jump into the deep end. "How's the investigation coming? Any news?"

"Hmm, we're making progress, but initial steps are usually slow. We still haven't been able to locate Gabby."

He scrutinized every breath, every blink, and every aspect of her being. Doubt tinged with suspicion expanded and surrounded her, burning her to the core.

"If I knew where she was, I'd tell you. I've been looking, too. I want to know what's going on just as much as you do. I'm the one who has one friend dead and another missing." Anger and resentment crept into her voice. She couldn't help it.

"Any ideas where she might go or who she might turn to in times of trouble?"

"As I've said. Me, family, and Shelly. The three of us have always been tight. Though a little less with Gabby since starting college."

His look softened. "Tell me more about your family."

The non sequitur took her off guard, which reverted her to autopilot. "My parents died during a carjacking. You already know that. You probably also know Grams is in a nursing home after a stroke. She's all I have left, but doesn't know who I am anymore."

Nolan sucked in a quiet breath. "Sorry. That must be painful." Solemn steps took him to the counter to pour coffee. Holding up a cup, he arched a brow in offer.

"Sugar, and I'll add milk."

"When did you start designing drones?" The cop settled in as if talking to an old friend.

"Not until I was a teenager. On my thirteenth birthday, Dad taught me how to solder parts together. We fixed little things at first. We progressed from there."

"You made the kitchen table in your apartment?" he asked, pausing his cup halfway to his mouth.

"Yeah, and a bunch of odds and ends. The thing is, neither of my folks seemed disappointed when I turned to electronics. They supported me all the way."

"As any good parent would. I wanted to ask—"

Nolan set his cup down as the sound of crunching gravel outside signaled an approaching car. Panther-like grace reminded her he was a cop first and foremost, regardless of the tempest-blue regard that kept drawing her into his world.

The doorbell rang in a trio burst of tinkling bells.

"I'm not expecting anyone this morning." When he opened the door, his shoulders sagged and a short exhale indicated sources of frustration.

The fact Keiki wore yoga pants and an oversized T-shirt with her hair in a messy bun suggested the status of overnight visitor.

"Hey, Knotty. Carolyn called me last night and said you might need—oh, sorry. I didn't know you had company." The visitor's long ponytail swiveled over her shoulder to land in the grasp of the baby she held.

"Hi, Faye, I'm sure Carolyn didn't mention she had a tenant," Nolan snarked.

She pushed past him ignoring the jibe, and approaching her. "Hey there. I'm Faye." A certain deviousness entered the young mother's expression.

Keiki couldn't help but return the infectious smile. "Knotty? You call him Knotty?"

Nolan growled and looked up as if the ceiling held some long-forgotten answers. The sternness of his expression melted as he approached his guests. "Keiki, this is the eldest and most frustrating of my four sisters." In spite of his words, he leaned over to kiss the baby on the forehead. "Please don't grow up like your mama. Or, actually, it would serve her right."

"Never mind him, let's talk. I'm starved for adult conversation." With assurance born of experience, she deposited her bundle in Nolan's waiting arms then smacked her lips together in an appreciative gesture. "Ah, this smells great. Mind if I join you?" Without waiting for an invite, Faye grabbed a plate and served herself.

He peered out a side window of his living room before remarking. "I'm guessing the other three will take turns visiting now?"

Gentle cooing and a murmured stream of baby talk conveyed both confidence and familiarity. The man was comfortable with kids.

In the kitchen, he froze at seeing the women's expressions. "What? I've spent enough time with your toddler to know what I'm doing, not to mention the fact I was eight when the first of my hellion siblings was born."

His eyes widened when his phone rang. Stepping toward Faye, he held the baby out, but stopped when she pointed to Keiki instead.

Turning a pleading look to the younger woman, Faye urged, "You don't mind do you? Just for a minute...?" Words drifted off with a mouthful of egg and sausage. "I rarely catch a break these days," she said after swallowing.

Keiki held her hands out as if warding off a great evil.

Nolan, deciding this equaled an affirmative, placed the now-sleeping babe in her arms with reverence.

"I—I don't know what to do with this." The act of holding the babe raised the dilemma of whether she'd turn to stone or throw up. Unlike when faced with the intruder's violence, her current threat came from within.

If she had to guess, her landlady's previous elaboration of Nolan's virtues and obvious phone call to Faye had something to do with the devilish gleam in the sister's eyes.

"You're doing fine. If you give her a little bounce now and then, she's more likely to stay asleep and not scream in your ear." Faye mimed the action of patting a baby's bottom.

"What if I drop it?"

Nolan pulled the phone away from his ear. "*She* is fine, and looks more in danger of being suffocated than falling, judging by your grip." His presence beside her offered little fortitude.

Keiki's reflexive jolt when the infant burped almost dislodged the infant from her grasp.

"Ah... um. Okay. I got this." Soft patting stemmed more from involuntary shaking than intentional rocking.

A pleading look to Nolan returned a grin formed from pity and understanding. After cutting his call short, he took the child back, snugging her to his chest with one hand and sitting to continue his breakfast with the other.

"Trouble?" Faye turned innocent eyes to her brother's hawkish glare.

"Nothing I can't handle." Nolan shifted the conversation to the family's current events, including visits to the pediatrician and their youngest sister's newest fascination, Coyote.

When the infant woke and squealed in Nolan's arms, he sighed. "She sounds hungry. I'm not equipped to handle this one, sis. You're on your own."

A wry smile preceded her soft, "Obviously."

Keiki swallowed hard, wondering if the mother's strong sense of self extended to breast-feeding among strangers.

As if reading her mind, Faye smiled as she took the baby. "Don't worry. You'll do fine when the time comes. But here's a tip. Line your bras with panty liners to keep your shirts dry." With that, she turned and disappeared down the hallway toward Nolan's guest bedroom.

Nolan slapped his hand over his forehead then covered his face while chanting, "I love my family. I love my family."

Faye reappeared, then diverted toward the sofa in the living room. Once settled in a chair facing the fireplace, she glared at her brother. "It's not like we're discussing *down-there* care. Although I think this diaper does need changing."

A conspicuous wink and amusement dancing in wide green eyes signified the game afoot.

Of course, Keiki jumped on board. Unseating Nolan's self-assuredness proved a worthy cause. "Did you know there's a national study showing forty-five percent of the people polled wear their underwear more than one day in a row?"

Faye laughed. "I love useless trivia!"

"And... thirteen percent of women surveyed wear their panties a week or more." Keiki laughed at Nolan's horrific expression before clarifying, "I, myself, am not among them."

Nolan mumbled something unintelligible and dropped his phone on the table. Crimson stained his cheeks. "Jesus. It's an epidemic. I'm surrounded by women who stuff their brains with annoying and useless facts."

"Aw, Knotty, you look miserable. Must be the equivalent of your time of the month?"

Keiki couldn't resist. "Wow, it really does suck to be a man. It's not like we can give him a *happy period* with vibrating tampons."

"No! Please stop! No more." Turning to his sister, he added, "Why today? Why now? Did Carolyn put you up to this?"

"Well, no, actually. Although we did talk at length."

This time, Keiki's face heated. Carolyn *had* set them up.

"You." Nolan glared and pointed a finger at Keiki. "You have no business even knowing about such things. And my sister is not a good role model. You do realize she's here at Carolyn's bidding?"

It was a virtual bucket of ice water. Possible retorts flitted through her mind, but embarrassment overrode them all. In her haste to get up and hide, anywhere, Keiki kicked his shins under the table. "Sorry. I've got to use your restroom."

Mumbled curses between siblings followed her down the hall. She didn't think to "ask" which door held her destination, merely rushed to where she'd seen the guest bath during her electronic fly-through.

Cold water soothed the burning in her cheeks even as Nolan and Faye continued to argue back in the kitchen.

The visit both humanized the cop and revealed a vulnerability she'd never thought to see. His armor remained intact except where family delved underneath and flipped his world inside out, uncovering his greatest weakness. His reaction had been reflexive, direct, and severe.

Self-protection.

Minutes later, she returned to see the baby sleeping in Faye's arms.

"I'm gonna get her home for her morning nap. See you this weekend for barbeque, Knotty?"

"Sure. Why not."

A pointed glance in Keiki's direction accompanied the indisputable directive, "You don't need to bring anything."

"Um..."

"Good. It's settled. Carolyn's gonna make pies. You'll love 'em." Grabbing the infant's diaper bag, she smiled. "See you two later." The whirlwind who was Faye departed without another sound, leaving destruction and confusion in her wake. Along with the odor of a dirty diaper.

"That went... well?" Nolan scrubbed a hand over the back of his nape. His expression matched how she felt.

"At least I know how to keep my shirts dry when the time comes." She enjoyed the deep crimson climbing his cheeks again but needed to clarify their non-relationship status. "About this weekend..."

"Don't even think about backing out. My entire family would swarm your apartment. By now, Carolyn has given them the rundown on everything she knows." His pause spoke of a man searching for endurance. "I'm sorry. Maybe this wasn't such a good idea, after all."

Chapter Seventeen

Time never dragged unless she had somewhere to go and something to do. Classwork was finished despite the painful and constant reminders of her missing friends.

Her methods of investigation had bent the law at sharp angles, but with each passing hour, the line between right and wrong became a little dimmer.

That line had disintegrated in the face of her desperation, evidenced when Nolan returned home and found her latest device in the kitchen. Who was she kidding? She'd known it was wrong when she'd hidden it there. How he'd spotted it, she'd never know.

His response sent a chill through her which numbed her mind. His eyes had widened for a split second then narrowed with barely suppressed wrath. The thunderous expression while retrieving her drone sucked the air from her lungs. Though distorted, the view conveyed enough to know she was in deep shit.

Now she'd have to find another way to gather information—if she managed to stay out of jail.

The minute he backed out of his driveway, she searched for a plausible explanation.

Tires on his personal vehicle didn't squeal to a stop in front of her apartment. His door didn't slam with unnecessary force. The wolf was under control, at least outwardly, and that scared her more than if he'd come tearing in.

Tensed muscles hunched her shoulders as he thumped up her wooden stairs.

She'd already unlocked the door so her jellied legs wouldn't betray the trepidation snaking its way through her chest.

Seen through the glass inset of her door, his face was a mask of indifference. She knew better. She'd read the signs.

He's pissed as hell.

At the landing to her apartment, he didn't knock and didn't announce himself, he merely opened the door.

His frame blocked most of the exit, coiled and ready to strike, the thinnest filament of an iron will holding him in check, waiting. The setting sun backlit his form, making him appear like an avenging God.

He accepted her motion to enter without a word.

She wasn't ready for this. Would he arrest her?

Her seat at the kitchen table offered direct access to the other exit but not the time to gain it before he could snatch her up like a rag doll. He was probably mad enough to do it at the moment.

Without preamble, he fished her micro drone from his jacket and set it on the center doily beside her scented candle.

His arched brow declared he could outwait, outmaneuver, and would use any means necessary to acquire the answers he sought.

"So, um, maybe I haven't told you everything," she hedged.

"Really? That thought never crossed my mind."

Instead of clarifying, he took a chair, turned it around, and straddled it to face her. "If we do this here, there's no recording..."

"Okay, okay. I got it. I admit I was spying. I need to know what's going on so I can figure out why the creep is after me."

"You have little demon spies everywhere, don't you? Had you placed one in my bedroom, you'd now be wearing handcuffs."

"Shouldn't we set limits—" Remaining words dried in her mouth when his jaw hardened. He was dead serious, and it wasn't the time for her smart mouth to erupt.

Heat drained from her face and hands to leave her fingers shaking and numb.

"I'm not a pervert and haven't done anything wrong. Well, not with drugs or murder." If she withheld information now, it'd be impossible to untangle the spider web of evidence from behind bars.

His fingers drummed a soft beat on the back of the wooden slat, meanwhile, the mini drone stood sentinel to strengthen his wordless disapproval while the tapping digits declared his patience waning.

Heaving a sigh, she motioned him to sit beside her, opening her laptop to let him see for himself. If she couldn't convince him of her innocence, she'd end up in jail charged with killing her best friend.

"I was talking with Shelly when the bastard attacked her." A quick swipe removed the unbidden tear from her cheek.

This time when he sat, he pulled his chair close. "We knew that. Your grief is so close to the surface."

You would know.

"Did you..." he stopped for a beat, then pressed on, "record it?"

"Yes, but even through voice prints, Tucker's contact can't identify him. We've got nothing."

A flash of uncertainty crossed his face. "How many dozens of times have you watched this?"

"Lost count."

On the laptop, Shelly's image appeared. She sat beside her flowerbed and considered the drone sitting on her hand. Keiki turned up the volume.

"This is where she was trying to fix the front right arm. It broke off." Knowing what came next made it harder to look at the screen. "I've seen it a hundred times yet can't pick out anything that would help.

"You two could've been sisters, you look so much alike, Nolan murmured then leaned in to take a closer look, his shoulder brushing her forearm. "Turn up the audio."

"From the time we hit kindergarten, people thought we were twins. It used to make Gabby jealous." Hoarse words rasped her throat.

When the masked face came into view, Keiki had to turn away.

"I've been through this footage a million times. There's nothing on here that will help. If there had been, I would've already turned it over. I had a copy for you, but then the bastard broke into my apartment and I couldn't get to it. Then, everything kinda went catawampus."

"You intentionally withheld the video."

"It's useless. You already know he planted evidence to frame me. How am I gonna prove it except for the mistake with the engraving? It's pretty weak as far as defenses go."

"Yeah, the periods he put after each letter isn't something you do."

"Like a cop is gonna believe that exonerates me? I don't think so."

"You have a damn low opinion of cops in general, or is it just detectives, or perhaps me?" He reached over and paused the recording.

"My parents were killed by carjackers, caught on tape, yet the shooters were never found."

Nolan shook his head as if feeling a personal loss. "Believe it or not, I know losing someone you love is painful as hell."

"You mean Carolyn's daughter?" She couldn't say the name, couldn't bring the specter of lost love to life. "So... I just accept it as a new portion of my life? Make friends with the devil?"

"No." Nolan rubbed his chin in consideration. "I think of it more like awareness and avoiding the pitfalls of certain reminders." His expression turned introspective for a brief moment. "At least until something opens your eyes and one day you realize you don't feel that stabbing pain every time a reminder cross your path."

With his piece said, he continued the recording while Keiki looked away from the eyes that haunted her dreams.

"That's why you were so sure it was the killer who broke into your apartment. You listened to the recording again."

"Yeah. But I'm missing something. I just can't figure out what."

Nolan's cursing filled the room when the footage ended.

"You're punishing yourself. This has to stop. I think you should..." He left the remainder unsaid.

He wanted to protect her. That much was obvious. Hiding or sticking her head in the sand wouldn't solve her friend's murder.

"I have another clip. Two creeps went to the *meads* looking for Gabby's phone. There's no clear view of either of their faces, so it's pretty much worthless, too."

"Ah, the party place behind fraternity row." Nolan watched the next video in silence until it ended. His fingers continued to drum on the table, his mind piecing together details and deciding on a course of action. "Damn, they disassembled the cell."

"Which is why I didn't turn this over to you right away."

"Hell. It *was* you he wanted first."

"Yeah. Shelly died because she looked like me. I used to go up there with her. Her sister was a sweet kid, and they were close."

"Tell me where your extra cash is coming from. Harock pays you by check, but the cash deposits aren't matching up."

"I—I'm a licensed drone pilot. People pay me to fly them around. It's not like I do anything illegal with them."

A twist of his lips and lifted brow declared he needed more

convincing. Considering her current predicament, it seemed prudent to come clean.

"Tucker Investigations."

A mixture of relief and frustration crossed his face. "Nick Tucker. Okay, it could be worse."

"You know him?"

"Kinda." Nolan's refusal to explain his sudden turn in mood boded ill. "You shouldn't be involved with this kind of work. Tell me exactly what projects you're working on, both present and past."

"I know the law where drones are concerned. I haven't recorded any footage that couldn't be used in a courtroom. Taking pictures from a drone sitting in a tree on a public street is the same as a PI taking it, legally speaking."

"And from what cereal box did you obtain that nugget?"

"I looked into it before I started accepting assignments."

"Tell me about his current cases. And for the record, a closed file doesn't preclude a disgruntled client from retaliating when caught on film."

Keiki hesitated, unsure where her responsibility stood as far as client confidentiality. Since she was hired by the PI and not the client. A fine detail could throw her into a different light in a judge's eyes.

In counterpoint, he could go ahead and arrest her for spying in his home. He'd have no reason to believe her about surveillance for Tucker unless she proved it.

"Okay. Let me open the files." Turning back to her computer, she gave him complete access. At this point, she had nothing to lose and everything to gain.

Most of the clips were short and revolved around a spouse's infidelity. One insurance scam and another involving theft in the workplace also presented opportunity for the detective to make assumptions and see she told the truth.

She didn't object when he took screen shots and recorded notes with his phone. Each case produced a barrage of questions and required an abundance of details.

For reasons she didn't understand, her PI boss preferred to have still shots along with video recordings. She never turned over audio files unless the subjects were located in or near an area of public access. It didn't mean she didn't record information, however; she just told the PI she couldn't get closer because the drones made too much noise.

"Will these clips fit on a flash drive?"

"Yes." She wasn't surprised he'd wanted a copy. "It'll take me a minute to load them."

"I'll wait."

She understood how swirling thoughts forced him to pace the small apartment. The entire space, sans bathroom, was open to his inspection. Suddenly, he flinched, his focus narrowed in the direction of her bedside table.

Damn. The picture.

Soundless steps carried him to her bedside where he picked up the frame by the lamp. Without a word, he turned to face her.

His jaw fell open as he shuffled back a step. A low bark of laughter drifted off as cunning awareness took over his expression.

The photo was a captured moment in time at the college when he'd knelt in a modified shooter's stance. A face-off with her drone with his gun drawn and intense focus mirrored that of an action hero.

"Um, a reminder of how dangerous you are to me?" Heat engulfed her entire body, her thoughts conjuring a deep dark hole that would swallow her without leaving a trace.

"And the small heart on the frame?"

"Is next to my drone. My source of protection."

All types of possible reactions crossed her mind where he lay on her bed and beckoned with a smile to one in which he threw her over his shoulder and carried her to his own bed.

A knowing grin acknowledged the power he'd gained in that simple moment in time. Her only defense was to ignore.

He replaced the photo and returned to the kitchen with a particular lightness in his step.

His heavy sigh brought them back to an ominous reality. "If the uniformed officer had died, you would've been charged with homicide considering no one else saw or heard the intruder."

"I know. I've called the hospital to check on the officer. He's recovering." The catch in her voice broke up the apology. "I'm a walking magnet for death and destruction."

"It wasn't your fault." Nolan lifted his hand but stopped short of her shoulder. "It wasn't."

"Had I been with Shelly that morning—"

"Then we'd have two homicides to solve."

Keiki took a shaky breath. "Maybe."

"Something's still not sitting right with you. Spill."

"What? You've got copies of all the recordings."

"Which doesn't preclude you from knowing or suspecting something or someone else. You can either tell me or—"

"Damn it. All right." The last thing she wanted on her record was an arrest for spying, a definitive end to a career that hadn't yet started.

"The piece of drone you found buried in the flowerbed? I've proven it wasn't mine."

"Yeah, so."

"The way it was jointed, not many people do that. It's an extra step, a corner they could cut in the process to save money. Then there's the lettering. They were mine, true, but not placed by me."

"You're thinking Harock or someone in his employ is setting you up?"

"Harock wouldn't. I come up with new designs and Harock builds them. The killer made a mistake with his drone, the engraving. A stupid oversight, but one that proves my point."

"They're not paying attention to details."

"Exactly. I still think there might be an answer in my boss' building. There has to be a clue somewhere, and I don't know where else to look. I'm thinking a connection between the killer and one of the engineers at Harock Industries."

She waited, giving him time to sift through her logic.

"Since you've proven it's not a drone his company made on your behalf, there's no way we can get a court order to search his files."

"*You* can't go in, but *I* can. No one would think twice of my talking to the R&D guys. I do it often enough," she countered.

"That isn't where you're going to find the evidence. However, you can give us the names of the engineers and technicians with whom you generally confer. That's where I'll start."

"You'll need more information than that and you know it."

"Keiki, you are not going to fly one of your little demons in there.

The risk is too high—among other issues."

She wouldn't think of risking her babies. She could do the job herself. Entering undetected would be a piece of cake. The tough part was fooling the detective who seemed to be omniscient where she was concerned.

He wasn't convinced she'd be content to stay in the background. Confirmation was written in the narrow slits of his focus and the way he raked his fingers through his hair.

In the end, it didn't matter. She had an obligation to find Shelly's killer.

Chapter Eighteen

Nolan waited on his couch and watched the screen on his phone. The camera he'd tucked into a branch behind Keiki's apartment waved in the stiffening breeze. His instincts never misfired when it came to a suspect's behavior.

There's a big difference between suspect and victim.

Youth and circumstance would drive her to a recklessness that endangered her life.

Bingo!

Sometimes he hated being right.

Dressed like a burglar, except for a hat so ridiculous only a college student could wear it, she crept down the wooden stairs not realizing Carolyn slept like a log.

Puzzlement halted his stride to the front door when, instead of heading to her car, she headed for the woods and melted into the shadows. A faint light skimmed back and forth across the branches.

Toward my house? Why?

There were no other homes nearby and no well-traveled roads for miles. If she needed to be outdoors to clear her mind, he could give her that space. She deserved it.

Minutes later, however, his dog's soft whine morphed into audible discontent when a shadow darted toward his SUV. Ambient light caught the strip of red in her cap. If she raised the hood, he'd intervene. Otherwise, he'd wait until action declared intent.

Reason scattered when she got into the passenger's side and bent forward.

What the hell is she doing? Flashbacks of pranks pulled between officers made him grimace. If his assessment was correct, she withheld a whole lot of rage and enjoyed a knack for practical jokes.

The door's closing offered more noise, which set Horace to barking and him to smiling when she bolted toward the woods.

"Well, boy. She wasn't in there long. If she turned on the radio and wipers thinking to startle me when I cranked the engine, she's gonna be disappointed."

Again, he waited for her return to the apartment. Katherine Tallerman was an enigma wrapped in barely restrained anger, driving motivation, impetuousness, fascination, and altogether too alluring.

Judging by the picture at her bedside, she contained equally confusing emotions.

Her steps slowed at the edge of the woods then paused. She waited, watching as if expecting someone to grab her. Nightmares of her friend's death would invade her sleep for months to come. Knowing she'd heard every second of the attack, he understood her paranoia.

Instead of heading back up the steps, she slipped around the side of the garage.

Shit. She's going for a ride.

Snatching up his jacket by the front door, he'd headed out, now wondering what she'd done to his vehicle. It wasn't as if she could've accessed the onboard computer in that time.

Once his door clicked shut, he checked his phone again, the second camera hidden by the driveway letting him know which way she'd gone.

Gotcha.

With a soft throaty rumble, the engine turned over before he shoved the gear in reverse. When time dimmed the memory of Clare's vehicle in the far spot, he'd park in the garage again.

Because the temperature dropped with the front bringing cooler temperatures along with the threat of rain, he didn't wait for the interior to warm up before turning the heater on to full blast.

"Shit!"

He expected cool air. What he got was so much more.

The strong gust of cold brought a cloud of sticky confetti from both driver's vents to cover his face and chest. Tiny bursts of color swirled in the small confines and stuck to his hair, skin, and jacket.

The damn stuff glowed in the moonlight and reminded him of the Foam Glitter race.

"Son of a bitch." He hadn't been pranked since his rookie days.

He'd known after finding her mechanical spy in his home—the kid would continue to snoop, and so, he'd planted the cameras in preparation. Meddling was written in every line of her aura. Grief for her friend and compassion for others was etched in her heart.

Keiki thought she'd seen the rougher sides of life due to her orphan status, but she'd barely scratched the surface. She had no idea what lurked in life's underbelly. *Keiki's not equipped for this shit.*

Undisclosed awareness often surfed below the stormy blue depths of her gaze, her eyes brimming with tears she refused to shed.

In the time they'd spent together, he'd observed her interaction with his dog, her grief over so much loss, and even her panic when holding his niece.

He should've called his partner, but instinct held him in check, instead taking extra caution in remaining out of her sight. He knew the roads well enough and could navigate with ambient light.

* * * *

Keiki had never been the kid who snuck out of the house. Fear magnified the adrenaline surge coursing through her chest. It equaled the thrill of working for Tucker, whom she'd debated calling for backup, the type Nolan couldn't provide.

No honest cop would approve her plan, and Nolan's instincts were sharp. The unfortunate combination warranted extreme caution.

Less than stellar computer skills necessitated finding physical evidence in her sneak and peek. Too bad she wasn't sure if she'd recognize it if and when she saw it.

She was in over her head.

Scant traffic along the isolated road allowed time to review her plan without constant vigilance in the rearview mirror. She could think of only one cop who'd be driving this route at this hour.

Quiet reigned over the industrial parking lot. Lack of working third shift meant it lay empty. Despite that, she still had the feeling of being watched. Both detectives had assured her she couldn't be traced to Carolyn's.

She wasn't so sure.

Why Harock chose such an isolated setting for the business baffled as well as frustrated. In counterpoint, thickly wooded land increased her chances of getting in and out without being detected.

Several faux trails splitting off the main road into the surrounding woods offered a place to leave her car, shrouded in the abundance of bushes and branching pines. Luck and the night's stillness should have engendered a sense of encouragement and relief instead of dread taking hold.

Dark memories surfaced to shake her confidence. Her parents hadn't been sneaking around, and their deaths had no correlation with what she now attempted. Yet, the specter of their disapproval flashed in her mind.

Even if the killer knew Keiki's legal name, he couldn't deduce her whereabouts. There were no blood ties between Carolyn and Nolan, and none between herself and Carolyn.

The initial part of her plan entailed veiling her approach. For that, she used one of her *handed* devices.

A stunted breeze whispering admonitions through the leaves broke the late-night solitude while her drone soared over the structure. The thick swatch of cloth in its tiny metal grip flapped in the air currents.

Once hovered over the employee entrance's video camera, it settled on the rim in a stable perch. Increasing wind buffeted the north side of the building with remnants sifting the cloth back and forth over the lens.

Nothing in life is ideal.

Gaining entrance proved easier. The worst part entailed fifty yards of clear space to the side door.

Shelly's swipe card stuck to her glove. Closer inspection induced a flashback of drinking coffee at her table and her friend's gentle rebuke. *My caramel latte.* If she were still alive, what would her friend think of the night's endeavor?

The keycard slid through the slot and preceded an audible click.

Once inside, she forced bile down and straightened her spine. She knew *where* to go. Defining pertinent evidence remained the mystery. Her thoughts drifted over each known employee.

One young man, Calvin something or other, asked her out every time she called. He was handsome, smart, and enjoyed an abundance of dry wit. In all the conversations they'd had, she never received a spark like the cop had delivered within five minutes of their first meeting.

She didn't have to see the detective to know when he was near. Like the bumble bee with its mechanosensory leg hairs which responded to opposite charges, she felt his presence like a jolt to her nervous system.

Tomb quiet and deathly stillness reigned while she rummaged through the research and development section.

It was a little after one in the morning when she huffed a sigh of defeat. She'd sifted through everything she could find and come up with zilch. All appeared as she suspected it should.

The last space to investigate involved a foray into Harock's office. An ultimate betrayal to someone who'd consoled her when her parents died, continued to support her work, and now grieved the loss of his second child.

Keiki was an absolute heel.

Halved stairwells led to the second floor where administration divided responsibility in running the company into various departments. Passing each door of the wide corridor, she recalled employees' faces and normal greetings.

Harock's office took up the far end of the wing, allowing him to enjoy the view through floor to ceiling windows.

Over the years, sitting with Shelly across from his desk had become a normal pastime. Intervals spent there allowed the heiress to keep her finger on the heartbeat of the company. Various files took up a small footprint of desktop, its polished surface a reminder of the grandeur surrounding the family. None of it would comfort them now.

The longer she remained in the building, the more the hair on her arms and nape stood on end. Her sixth sense rarely failed or proved inaccurate.

In for a penny, in for a pound. She wouldn't have the courage to snoop again. And, the longer she took to unravel the mystery, the greater the likelihood of the killer finding her.

She'd never considered his net worth until sitting in the stylish, velvet-draped seat and felt dwarfed by the workspace.

Franklin's desk formed an L shape which allowed him to work at his computer or survey the countryside. Photos of the family's many vacations demonstrated heartfelt smiles amid various activities on built-in bookshelves lining one wall.

Daylight would offer Harock picturesque, lush autumn colors in early afternoon sun—undulating hills that could soothe the roughest soul. Now, however, she saw darkness, death, and a bleak future.

When Shelly wanted to conceal critical information, she wrote it on the back of one of her calendar pages. That way of thinking might be a family trait.

Keiki turned over the calendar and examined the back of each page. *Nothing.*

The drawers wouldn't open. Special tools hidden in her belt wouldn't be of help against the more sophisticated locksets.

A single, archaic opportunity to collect information sat beside the lamp, a rotating spindle of index cards. Keeping a list of business contacts and friends in such an old-fashioned way dated the man she considered a second father.

Using her phone, she used the light to search the listings.

Some of the people she'd heard of, but their contribution to the company was fuzzy at best. The business end of operations was more Shelly's bailiwick.

Toward the middle of the spindle, one card snagged her attention. It was an address. No name, no identifying information, nothing except a street number and name. Curiosity dictated she take a snapshot of it for future reference. If her memory proved correct, the noted road led to neither an industrial nor residential area.

Outside, a roll of thunder strained the last of her inner Zen. If the wind knocked her drone off its perch, she'd be toast. The unanticipated, late-season storm forced her to realize planning could make the difference between success and failure.

One of Tucker's teachings.

The creep factor of her illegal visit ramped her pulse high enough to force a brief moment to collect herself. Closing her eyes, she willed her mind to calm and her heart rate to slow.

She couldn't find anything else to search and decided to call it a wrap. If she approached him right, Tucker might teach her how to pick locks other than handcuffs. That would mean a return visit.

Meanwhile, she'd swing by the peculiar address on the way home. It wasn't like she'd be able to sleep soon anyway.

Flashbacks of a conversation where Harock detailed his plan for expansion came to mind. She might find a vacant lot. Her phone's app would mark the spot well enough.

Her relief at finding no glaring proof of underhanded transactions huffed out in a sigh when she closed the CEO's door. The hall was dark with the promise of retribution for trespassing. Shame at suspecting her employer's trusted staff dulled her earlier heightened senses. In her heart, she didn't want to find anything but didn't know where else to look.

Two steps toward the exit, her foot halted midair when a faint noise caught her attention. Every muscle in her body clenched tight.

Someone was in the southern stairwell.

Not waiting, she took off, her wet sneakers squeaking from her woodsy trek. Peels from the shoes' soles brought vomit to the back of her throat. She couldn't have been noisier before shoving the exit bar.

"Hey, chickie-chickie. Let's have a chat." From the opposite end of the hallway, a now familiar, deep chuckle filled the space.

Shit. Her legs wobbled with each step.

She'd known. Warning had come from her sixth sense. Had he been lying in wait, knowing she'd show?

Half-turn stairwells meant fewer steps to vault. She bounded down each, landing at the bottom with a thud along with pain in her right ankle. The combination spurred her faster toward the exit.

Karma dictated one of the bastard's cohorts waited to snatch her up. When she shoved through the door to the first floor, she expected a fist in the face. But what she could see of the hallway was clear.

By the time cool night air swept her bangs aside, sweat drenched her skin. Muffled curses drifted from inside. Praying the killer didn't know which exit she took or where she was parked boosted her morale.

Regular exercise prepared her for the race of her life. Fear drove her faster over the neatly trimmed lawn. The wood's silent offering of protection had never felt so welcoming.

Her movements, surroundings, even the wind sloughing through gnarled branches all decelerated in her mind. She'd read and understood the theory but never experienced her body's response to hormonal dumping firsthand.

Every sound from the breeze whipping though nearby trees and shuffling dead leaves to and fro, every sight occurred in high definition. Cortisol and adrenaline hormones would boost her reserves and then manifest in shaking, sweating, palpitations, and nausea. Her vision wavered with the flat pine needles of a low branch slapping her face.

Lack of signs indicating pursuit could be good or bad.

If he'd known where she parked, he might have someone waiting. Of course, taking time to observe once she got close might give the killer time to catch up.

When she reached her vehicle, she plunged forward without hesitation. No hands reached for her and no one waited on the back seat to slit her throat.

Leaving her drone behind could be explained if not for the cloth hanging down to cover the lens, but that was a problem to solve once safe. One hand on the wheel to guide her car, the other shoving the gearshift in reverse, she peeled out.

On the road, she snatched up the controller and flew the drone toward the woods. Her car's speed soon outstripped the controller's range, but losing it in the treetops was better than leaving evidence at the scene.

Absence of headlights in her rearview didn't mean she wasn't followed. She needed time to think things through.

Leading a killer to Carolyn's house wasn't going to happen. Nolan's house wasn't an option either. Working rapport with Tucker didn't include concealing a crime, and Gabby was MIA.

The killer anticipated her moves at every turn. How long could she stay one step ahead?

Chapter Nineteen

Nolan's suspicious nature dictated she might go to Harock Industries. Futile attempts to warn her away from the investigation spurred her determination to move forward.

He'd parked a short distance away and decided to give her a couple hours, then disable her vehicle to prevent her escape. It was a neutral place to talk.

Waiting was the most difficult part of the job. Tonight was no different. Field glasses kept in the back seat offered little to view through thickened woods.

This wait proved shorter than anticipated.

When twin headlights pierced the night and headed back toward his direction, he followed. Erratic driving wasn't his imagination when she took a turn too fast and didn't slow to navigate a roughened patch of road. All four wheels of her abused car left the pavement on a sharp ridge.

His little snoop had found something which scared the shit out of her.

After pulling onto the asphalt, he didn't turn on his lights and thanked heaven for the light misting and cloud cover. Wind tugging at his heavier vehicle forced him to wonder what demons were making her so reckless.

Over time, she slowed to a more reasonable speed.

Trailing someone in a desolate area required two vehicles minimum, but he wanted to follow his hunch without Coyote interjecting random strategies. *How much trouble can she find?*

Instead of heading home, she wound her way through rolling countryside, slowing after passing the nature preserve. It was nights like the present he was thankful for keeping a full gas tank.

He went on alert the instant her lights went dark and she slowed to a crawl. The road's shoulder was almost nonexistent, but he saw a few trampled paths in the woods, one of which offered her an advantage, a place to hide her vehicle.

If she suspected someone had followed her, the current action made no sense.

No, she thinks she's onto something.

It didn't matter that she'd selected dark jeans and jacket while carrying a light with shielded lens. The ridiculous cap would mark her location and identity in a heartbeat.

With a sigh, he hid his SUV and shadowed her movements. If she made half as much noise as she did the day he led her to his house, he'd have no problem despite the increasing wind and light drizzle.

At least in the woods, they'd stay drier. To his knowledge, there were no homes and no businesses nearby. Timing and circumstances boded ill.

It proved more difficult to withhold laughter over her muffled curses than to keep track of her whereabouts. It seemed an overabundance of determined thorns slowed her effort.

When he crossed a well-traveled dirt path, he wondered if she knew where she was going and what to expect. As a local, she should have some idea.

Careful to close the distance with as little noise as possible, he paused several times when hearing a quiet snap. He couldn't discern its direction but figured the likelihood of *him* being followed was small.

If he were wrong, then the other person was good. To be fair, it didn't help that he was a walking advertisement for sticky confetti. The sooner he could collect his little snoop and get her the hell home, the better.

She stopped and assessed her surroundings after muffling a cry. More curses declared her a non-fan of adrenaline inducing activities. Her colorful cap snagged on a branch and she yanked it back with another epithet.

He froze when she stopped at the edge of a clearing, waiting to decide on her next course of action. Any faults she had didn't include cowardice.

A few minutes passed while Nolan waited.

Like a villain in a cartoon, she crept forward in a hunched position. No doubt her defense of the ill-suited cap would be its coverage of her thick blonde hair. Deciding the lesser of the two evils correlated to a toss-up unworthy of consideration.

In the clearing, a large warehouse stood sentinel on a small rise. Two stories of fabricated metal siding, no windows, no proper driveway, and no landscaping. Overgrown weeds stood thigh high right up to the metal siding.

The place even warned him to approach with care.

Out here with no designated parking area, no marking at the entrance, and no sign on the door. Not good, kid.

It was too much to hope she'd turn around.

Either the wind kicked up his paranoia, or another person circled the perimeter. Regardless, he was committed.

Calling his partner was no longer an option once he'd trespassed on private property. He could argue the point of following a suspect, but that debate would only go so far.

Keiki had sense enough to draw near from the back. He waited for her to try the door, find it locked, and return to her car.

The door opened.

Shit. Don't go in there. Come on, Keiki. Show me you've got some sense.

The darkened interior swallowed her without a sound, and he shook his head.

Technically, he could follow under the guise of witnessing a break-in. He'd never bent so many laws in his life.

He had no doubt that whatever she now stumbled onto wasn't good, or safe.

Fate would dictate her either the gutsiest or dumbest coed he'd ever met. Thinking of her as a kid kept their non-relationship in proportion, until he remembered the picture by her bedside.

The tree line offered the last cover to listen for anyone else dumb enough to sneak around the woods of an unknown area while wearing a bullseye on their head.

Nope. It seemed he was alone.

If someone shot him and left him in the woods, it would serve him right.

A second's hesitation at the door and internal sigh couldn't prepare him for the intended lunacy. He entered with his gun drawn. Inside, what little light there was came from the metal walls reflecting her small flashlight.

Behind him, the door shut without a creak or rasp.

To his left, a pile of stacked pallets offered a place to observe without being seen if she looked around. At this point, there was no telling what absolute nonsense traveled at warp speed through her head.

On second thought, yes, he did know.

Her gasp of surprise came after light illuminated a stash of drones on a long low table. Multiple tables held a variety of devices.

Several clicks indicated her taking close-up photos of those which held particular interest. She leaned in to get a look at what he suspected were her initials on the legs. Whatever she discovered inspired a new round of epithets.

She's not wearing gloves. Damn it.

At least she didn't have her gun for part two of her idiotic trifecta. The girl didn't think like a criminal or a private investigator, which put her in more danger. Her heart was in the right place, but she lacked training and experience.

At least the PI hadn't taught her his tricks. *Yet.* Her entanglement with an experienced sleuth generated an uneasiness for reason's he wouldn't decipher.

"Nice that phone cameras have flash nowadays, isn't it?" His voice carried clear in the open space as he stepped forward.

She dropped her cell on the table without turning around. "Detective Garnett? What are you doing here?"

"Oh, just seeing what my favorite pain in the ass is up to. Whatcha got there?" He approached with caution, striding to her side before returning his gun to its rig.

She hadn't moved.

"Where are your gloves?"

"Took 'em off 'cause they got wet."

"Who owns this place?"

"Don't know. I found the address in Franklin Harock's card index."

Suppressed giggles erupted after her light reflected the myriad sparkles covering his form. She didn't remark about him glowing like a neon sign with all the glitter stuck in his hair and clothes. It would take many showers to clear.

"You've never been here before?"

"Nope." Another giggle.

"What have you touched?" Bending laws, aka giving advice rather than retrieving cuffs, entailed a slippery slope he'd never thought to travel, until now.

"Um, nothing but the table here."

"Note to future burglars, go waterproof."

She looked at his bare hands and arched a brow but was smart enough to not speak.

Nolan took his handkerchief and wiped the table, then asked, "Did you use telekinesis to turn the door knob?"

"Oh, yeah. That too."

When she picked up her phone, he took it and stuffed it in his jacket. "I'll keep this for now. You can get it back tomorrow. Okay?" Rhetorical questions were becoming the norm when around her. "It's time we got the hell out of here."

"Wait! You have to see this. It proves my point."

"I'll look at your pictures later and then we'll talk. Right now, we leave." A slight tug at his pocket forewarned she'd retrieved her phone. It wasn't like she would erase the pictures.

"But it proves someone's cloning my devices."

With a tighter grip on her upper arm, he towed her toward the exit. "Later. Damn it, Keiki. I'm not sure we're alone here."

Her acquiescence came with a nod and shuffling toward their escape. When she opened the door, he yanked her back.

"Wait."

His first step outside coincided with her gripping his jacket. Turning to see what snared her attention proved one distraction too many.

Pain exploded in his temple before everything went black.

* * * *

Keiki had opened her mouth to protest, frustrated when he hadn't listened.

From behind the door, a flash of movement caught her eye, a

shadow moving at lightning speed toward the detective's head. The shadow arm swung the butt of a gun in its second most popular method of use.

The detective crumpled face down in the dirt before she could maneuver to catch him.

"Nolan!"

"You should be more worried about your skinny little ass." The accent tingeing the voice thickened on a low chuckle as the prick toed Nolan in the ribs.

Keiki looked up to recognize the glint in eyes staring daggers at her through a black knit mask. *Beady eyes.* From her kneeling position, she felt the steady pulse at Nolan's neck.

"Jesus, what the hell do we have here?"

"He didn't see you." She didn't rat out Nolan's cop status as she slipped her phone from her back pocket and slid it under the leaves.

"Oh, I'm not going to kill him. No self-respecting man would cover himself in glitter then follow a girl through the woods. Looks like he's preparing for his part as a fairy princess in the school play. Who would take him seriously? Though he does look kinda familiar under all that shit. Who is he?"

She swallowed hard but didn't speak.

Two other men approached from the woods, each wearing dark clothing and a mask. Both snickered when shoving the detective onto his back.

"Kinda old for you, isn't he, girlie? Does he help you build your little toys?"

"No. He's a classmate's brother. We just started dating. Who are you?"

Beady eyes spoke up. "You can call me Porter."

Porter shook his head in disgust. "You like the older guys, huh? Looks like we're gonna get along just fine. But first, let's make sure the boys in blue go on a wild goose chase when they find this place."

"You want the police here?"

"Absolutely. S'all part of the plan. Wonder how long it'll take 'em."

Before she could react, he'd snatched her colorful knit cap and tossed it back though the door and to the side. "That oughta give their forensic meddlers something to think about."

"What about the fairy here?" One of the thugs shoved Nolan's shoulder.

"Dump him in the woods down the road. By the time he finds his way back to civilization, this place will be wiped clean and we'll have all the drones needed to continue our own little venture."

"We didn't find another vehicle." The third speaker was shorter and bore a stronger accent. "They must've come together. Why didn't they go inside together?"

"He came with me," she blurted. "Kept some distance to see that we weren't followed."

"Definitely not a cop." Porter sniggered.

When the underlings suspended Nolan's limp body by his shoulders, he made no noise and gave no indication of reviving.

A low hum rumbled up Porter's chest. "Dump him in the woods, but leave him alive. Boss gets upset when the body count rises."

"What is it you want?" Even if she could outrun his leaded projectiles, Keiki wouldn't leave Nolan in her stead.

If the killer kept his word, the detective would find her phone and live to finish what he started, albeit sporting a nasty concussion.

He'll search for me.

"I deal in precious commodities. Today's flavor is information. If you and your whorish friend are nice enough, I may let you live."

"My friend... Gabby? You have Gabby?"

"Helluva nickname. I have to admit, though, it suits her."

Keiki struggled when he snatched her up by the collar. The gun he returned to his holster proved unnecessary considering his sheer size and strength.

From his pocket, Porter retrieved a flashlight and flicked on a beam of light to mark their path.

With a last glance in Nolan's direction, she stumbled beside her kidnapper as he dragged her back through the woods. The new direction threw off her internal compass. She cried out when thorns tore at her hands and clothes. Heavier rain cooling her body temperature added to nature's conspiracy to see her humiliated for foolish behavior.

New foreboding set up shop in her chest with the dawning that her kidnapper didn't care about her condition, only that she arrived at their destination. Unsuccessful attempts at suppressing sobs ended with a firm slap and muttered threats.

If life had taught her anything, it was that there were many variables to any situation, including the opportunity to escape. Any information she could gather would help. "Looks like you know your way around."

"Stop fishing. Won't do you any good. You should be concentrating on how to please me."

When Nolan regained consciousness, he wouldn't be able to track her, but he'd have evidence if he found her phone.

Keiki read people's body language as a matter of experience. It was another thing her PI friend tried to teach her. From what she understood, her future encompassed darkness, fear, and pain.

Fate would finally convince the detective of her innocence.

Karma made sure she wouldn't get to gloat.

Chapter Twenty

Keiki woke to the sound of soft whimpers and the distinct aura of fear pressing in from all sides. Panic invaded every aspect of her emerging consciousness.

Both eyes snapped all the way open to focus on Gabby, whose unmistakable whisper added a smidgeon of light to their darkened confines. Her friend's jeans were ripped and covered with dirt while shreds of her shirt hung askance under her jacket. The brave smile she wore fooled no one.

From her viewpoint, she could see treetops through a high and narrow grimy window. "Any clue as to our location? Hell, we could be on the cul-de-sac of a development for all I know."

"I have no idea, Keeks. Sorry."

Attempts to shake off the firm band of metal clamped on her wrist directed her full attention to the handcuffs as opposed to the hard dirt floor comprising her resting place.

Scooching her body back and inching her numb fingers along the attached chain links, she found the metal ring attached to the wall mere feet away.

Glancing around, she estimated the entirety of the space comprised a twelve-foot square with a wooden door set on one side. A small bulb inside its wire cage offered weak light from high in a corner.

In lieu of speaking, Keiki scanned the perimeter to get a better idea of their predicament. Block walls with tiny windows set high signified their location in a basement with one possible exit. The door.

Vestiges of fear saturated her underarms and between her shoulder blades. The scary movies she'd loved to watch came alive around her in the gravelly jabs of dirt in her hip, the musty smell of damp block, and the dark foreboding in her chest. "Gabby?"

"I'm alive. That's something." On a small square blanket, Gabby lay curled in fetal position. In sitting up, she offered the first sign of inner strength.

"The last thing *I* remember is being shoved in the backseat of a car and Porter sticking me in the shoulder with a needle."

"I'm scared. He told you his name?" Gabby hissed in a subdued voice.

Without words, they both understood that significance.

Keiki nodded. "Yeah. Since he wore a mask, he might not have given his real name."

Or they could've been leery of Nolan waking up and seeing their faces.

"Are you... injured?"

A trembling smile crossed her roommate's face, as if knowing the final outcome yet to play out. "Nothing that won't heal. Will anyone know you're missing?"

Keiki's odd hours and loose schedule allowed her freedom from strict routine. Depending on Nolan's survival, no one would miss her until Tucker or Harock came looking, which could mean weeks or even months.

"Actually, I was with a cop when we got ambushed."

"Is he... dead?"

"I don't think so. I think they're planning on framing me for everything." Keiki had no guarantee the thugs hadn't killed her detective. Odd how she'd come to think of him as belonging to her.

"Jesus, Keeks. I'm so sorry to drag you into all this. It's all my fault." Sniffling interrupted by hiccups testified to flagging courage.

Keiki could just make out her friend's tear-stained face in the few rays of early morning light. She'd obviously been held prisoner for days, her mahogany hair hanging in limp tangles about her face and shoulders.

According to one of Tucker's lectures, the yellow tones in her cheek's bruises indicated the injuries occurred at least eighteen to twenty-four hours prior. The red and purple shiners denoted fresher injuries.

Gabby's attempted bravery covered a world of pain, but they needed to collaborate and work together to form an escape plan. Guilt and explanations could wait.

"Can you describe the prick who took you?" Keeping her friend talking would prevent Gabby's mind from turning inward.

Odd but descriptive details identified Porter and formed a more complete picture in Keiki's mind. She still hadn't seen his face.

Gabby scooted on her butt a little closer.

The fact her friend wasn't tied down remained a mystery until she cradled her right arm against her chest.

"How bad are you hurt? I need to know to plan our escape." Keiki nodded to the cradled injury before scrutinizing their prison again. "There doesn't appear to be any type of surveillance in place."

"Not in here." The odd tone required further questioning, later. "My wrist is broken." A spark of defiance, indicative of expanding intent, lit her determination.

"What aren't you telling me?"

"Nothing, Keeks. Now, how do we get out of here?"

"How many of them have you seen?" She knew of three dirtballs, the two who carried Nolan off and Porter, who'd shoved her into a car.

"I've seen two, but I think one left." Shame lengthened Gabby's face, her jaw opening while her good hand covered her mouth. "Porter's the one who... *questioned* me."

The one-word emphasis combined with Gabby's physical state testified to unimaginable horror.

"Gabby, did he," she swallowed, "rape you?"

Her roommate turned away before murmuring, "There's another room down here. It's where he takes me."

"He's got balls." Anger flooded Keiki's veins, blistering her thoughts and filling her mind with hatred.

The man would die. It would be brutal, and with as much pain as she could inflict. "God, I'm so sorry. Let's get the fuck out of here."

"You happen to have a key?" Sarcasm flickered to life as Gabby closed the distance and offered a one-armed hug. Her one-footed scoot indicated injury to the other ankle.

"Of sorts. Yes."

"Thank God. I've been thinking for days that I'd die down here."

"Gabby?" Keiki nodded toward her friend's ankle.

"It's fine. Let's make a plan."

It was all the incentive Keiki needed. Her thoughts flashed to the picture on her bedside, the grit and determination written in Nolan's face. If she survived this ordeal, she'd damn well act on the tentative feelings growing between them.

"How often does Porter visit?"

Glassy eyes stared in the distance as if willing the answers to come. "At least twice a day. Once to feed me. The other to, um, ask questions in the other room." Using her good hand, she made an impatient gesture, a *show-me* sign indicative of prior strength. "You mentioned a key?"

"These cuffs don't feel similar to Tucker's, but I'll get us out." Escape no longer equated to a parlor trick. It was survival. If she could unlock the cuffs, it would help even the odds when their kidnapper returned. They'd have to move fast and quiet.

Preparation for the break-in at Harock Industries had included arming herself with her mini arsenal of supplies. At the moment, her belt was worth a million bucks. Due to its special design, removal wasn't necessary to access the specific tools hidden within the small compartment.

If she survived this, the paltry stock would grow exponentially. Tucker was in for some lengthy Q&A time, while Nolan's self-restraint would suffer serious abuse.

What Nolan would say when she gloated about how she and her friend escaped crossed her mind.

"The idiot kidnappers thought you college kids were nerds and partying airheads. You were lucky—this time. Go back to school and act like a student."

It was time for his wake-up call.

"What does Porter want from us? He searched my apartment but I've no idea what he was looking for. He didn't get too far before a cop showed up."

Her friend's gasp filled the moment's silence. "He wants to use you to make me talk. Did the officer...?"

"No. He'd worn his vest, but did have to undergo surgery. He'll be okay after therapy. So, what does Porter want?"

"They want my formula."

"What? What formula?"

"Keiki, I never meant for you to find out. Things aren't what they seem. Professor Bayler and I have been working on a project. Please don't ask for details. You're not involved in it. Not really."

"What the hell? What do you mean, not really? My life has turned upside down. Trust me. I'm involved. What have you gotten us into?"

"You know I hover at the edge of the party scene. There's a reason for it. I've been working on a formula to improve a drug the kids are using."

Keiki shot back until her shoulders hit the wall. "What the fuck? Why didn't you tell me? Most of all, Gabby, why?"

"At first, it was a challenge. Something I could do that others couldn't. I wanted to prove myself, to know that I *could* do it." Shoving limp hair from her face, she continued, "Do you remember Janquin?"

"Yeah, she died of an overdose. Everybody in school remembers that."

"She was a friend. Listen, Keeks, kids are going to take drugs, no matter what. It's a fact of life. I thought I could make it safer."

"Jesus. Drugs? I knew you smoked a joint now and then, but I never figured you'd be involved in this shit."

"I didn't want to see this look on your face, the disappointment. I swear I only wanted to help."

"Porter wants this formula?"

"Yes. He's also looking for a distribution list, which I don't have. I'm not involved in that, but I've heard a bit from my friends."

"For Christ's sake. Who's distributing?"

"I'm sorry, Keiki. I'm so sorry. "

"Who, Gabby?"

"It—it's Franklin Harock."

"What? Since when?"

"I don't know. As I said, I'm not involved in that side of the operation."

"So, they think you have this list and want to use me to make you talk?"

"That and, well, Franklin wants your drones to deliver the drugs."

"No."

One sentence, so simple and short, splintered the rest of her world. She had nothing left, nothing real and honest.

It was a wound from which she'd never recover. "No wonder the cops are all over this." Memory of specific questions from Coyote and Nolan and their skeptical acceptance of her statement came to mind. "Oh my God. Harock has ruined everything I've worked for in one fell swoop. But why'd they kill Shelly? That makes no sense."

"They wanted to send a message to Harock. He's the man behind the scenes, playing us all like puppets."

"I thought it was a case of mistaken identity." Devastation crumbled her world with the realization even her surrogate family had turned on her, used her for their own ends. She was the ultimate throwaway orphan.

"Was Shelly involved?"

"She knew nothing about it." Gabby reached out then retracted her hand when Keiki flinched away.

"This formula, where is it?"

"I wasn't going to give it to him, but I will now that he has you. You shouldn't have to pay for everybody else's mistakes." After retreating to her blanket, she pulled a filthy notepad and pen from between its layers.

"What are you doing, Gabby?"

"Giving him what he wants."

"No. He'll kill us when he gets it."

Gabby paused. "Not if we stay one step ahead of him. I'm counting on your resourcefulness to unlock those cuffs."

"We'll need proof to take to the cops." Determined, Keiki cleared her mind to envision the inner mechanisms of the cuffs. She worked a slim pick from her belt into the hole to first disengage the double lock bar, then placed enough pressure on the single lock bar to nudge it off the arm's ratchet teeth, allowing her to push the cuff open.

Rubbing her wrists restored circulation. She'd expected the pins and needles sensation, but not the accompanying pain.

Gabby went on, "I have a flash drive with my notes on it. It's in the place where we first met. Remember the loose brick?"

Memory of their trio's grade school encounter remained embedded in the deepest recesses of Keiki's heart. A treasure for all time, not to be tainted from time or events.

"I remember wanting to brain Calvin with that brick. Is it still there?"

The small, deserted school had undergone transformation and expansion as time and necessity dictated a modern building take its place. The county's resource center held departments for various regional offices along with classes for special needs children.

"Yes. It contains all the information you need, an insurance policy against Harock drawing you into his freaking web of lies and deceit."

Jingling outside their door warned of the kidnapper's return. Keiki snatched the cuff and draped it over her wrists before realizing she and Gabby were on opposite sides of the small confines. She'd make it work.

The prick would have to turn his back on one of them. Under current circumstances, Keiki was the strongest.

The door opened with a low groan and a *whoosh* of less-stale air. Milliseconds drew out, once again narrowing her focus to the smallest details.

Chapter Twenty-One

Backlighting shadowed the visitor's face, but the shape was unmistakable. Broad, muscled shoulders took up a large portion of the small opening.

"*Hola, mi cariño.*" A confident swagger pointed to his need to flaunt both power and strength.

"Hey, asshole," Gabby sneered with false bravado.

Porter swung his attention to his first captive.

In a show of defiance, Gabby shoved the small notebook behind her. The increased distance would force Porter into a more vulnerable position in leaning forward to retrieve it.

Low, soft chuckling indicated his amusement. Murmured threats went unheeded until she grabbed his shirt with both hands and pulled him forward and off balance. Her scream demonstrated one part pain and two parts rage.

Keiki bolted up as her friend used her good hand to hit and scratch. Nothing motivated a victim more than the will to survive. Fisting both hands together, she slammed the meaty side of her clenched fists against Porter's skull.

A short grunt coincided with his sprawling to all fours.

"Time to test our theory, Gabby." With as much speed and strength as she could muster, Keiki drew her foot back and aimed for the soft bits between his legs. Pent-up rage and fear intensified her force, the result sending her kidnapper toppling forward with a high-pitched yowl.

Gabby grunted, then wiggled out from under his weight.

"Hypothesis proven. He's got balls. C'mon, let's get the fuck out of here." He was too big to take on, even if her roommate wasn't injured. The best she could manage was straightening his legs and slamming the metal cuffs around his ankles.

In shock, he turned to see her jump out of his swiping grasp. "You're gonna pay for that, smartass bitch."

They had no weapons, no fighting skills.

"C'mon Gabby. Time to go."

Porter reached into his pocket.

For a key?

"Go, Keiki. I'll follow. Get moving!" Desperation and a certain sadness sent the message loud and clear. She couldn't.

"My ankle is broken, too." She confessed. "Don't wait. I can keep him busy for a bit. Go, damn it! I'm the one with the information he wants. He won't kill me."

Tears blurred Keiki's vision in the sallow light leading to freedom. From the hallway, she looked back to see Gabby's frantic scrambling to knock the key from Porter's grasp.

He slammed her down, but she rolled her body back and used her remaining strength to attack as she screamed out, "Go, Keiki. Now!"

Dirt and cobwebs covered the block walls leading up decrepit wooden steps. Her prayers were answered when the door at the top opened under her urgent wrenching.

Behind her, remnants of scuffling, curses, and a distinctive thump of flesh hitting flesh filled her ears. As long as she heard Gabby voicing her rage, she knew her friend fought tooth and nail.

The basement opened to a seventies-style kitchen, complete with avocado-green cabinets, cracked and chipped tile flooring, and a door leading to the outside.

Other than filler space, the room had no apparent use. Thick layers of dust covered every surface to further the creepy ambiance.

Drawers stood open and empty, the countertops bare except for several dead cockroaches. No proof of anyone having cooked in the space confirmed its function. Several cabinet doors hung by a hinge. *No knives, no weapons.*

Mullioned glass panes in the back door's inset allowed a limited view of thick forest beyond. Without a deadbolt to slow her down, freedom was mere feet away. It took a second to thumb the old-fashioned lock open once her friend's scream cut short. Keiki's fingers shook.

Porter wouldn't kill Gabby without having the formula and the distribution list. If either was incomplete, Gabby should survive. Keiki, on the other hand, was expendable, but could send help if she escaped.

Heavy boots thundered up the steps even as she jumped off the back porch into knee-high weeds. Snakes and other critters presented less threat than the roar echoing from inside the house.

She was a runner, in decent shape, and motivated. The hounds of hell couldn't instigate more incentive to flee. Her wild dash for cover led to a deer trail winding through the thickening forest.

Behind her, the sudden bark of a gun punctuated Porter's low laugh filled with the promise of torment and suffering.

The dull thud of the bullet hitting a nearby tree compelled her to duck while running. Her heart hammered in her chest and her breath came in quick pants.

Blind panic pushed her through barbed vines seizing her shirt and flesh. At this rate, she'd leave a bloody trail any search and rescue dog could follow.

The thought of snaking her way in and up an evergreen tree held merit until she thought of Porter getting ahead of her and meeting her when doubling back. He had the advantage of knowing the terrain.

A stitch in her side forced her to stop and catch her breath while leaning against a tall oak. Once she put greater distance between herself and death, her mind would clear enough to form a plan.

The screech of a large hawk conveyed a sense of urgency and kicked her metabolic system to a higher gear. Fear overriding pain compelled her shaking legs to carry her forward, her senses hyper alert to every sight, every sound.

Thick branches intertwined overhead to foster a sense of surreal tranquility when, with every step, she expected a heavy hand to drag her to the ground. Each whisper of nature's breath swirled in from the collecting shadows to add a new layer of fear twisting in her gut.

Vaulting over a log and dodging a snarled thicket of thorns brought her to an opening in the path. Sunlight stung her eyes.

She found herself positioned at the edge of a deep ravine which would take precious time to navigate. Her first step down the descending slope sent her skidding on her ass.

Her blonde hair would stand out against the darker shades of fall as she skidded downslope to the ravine's bottom but couldn't be helped. Gravity had done most of the work.

If Porter made it to the ridge before she topped the other side, she'd prove easy pickings with his height advantage. If she'd taken a zig-zag route or at least avoided a straight path, she might've thrown him off course.

A fact to remember if I make it to the other side.

The steep grade presented less opportunity for trees to take root, and therefore less cover. Climbing the opposite side proved more treacherous after the previous night's rain. Twice, she slipped and landed face first in the briars. The warmth of blood stinging her eye goaded her to scramble up and regain lost ground. Once at the top, she couldn't help but look back.

Porter was taking aim at the same time she dropped to the ground. Small spurs from a broken branch gouged her calf.

Another bark from his pistol kicked dirt up and into her face. She imagined her scream strengthened his sense of power and sadistic intent.

Shit.

Porter carried at least an extra hundred pounds with a disproportionate few extra around his middle. As long as she maintained her pace and avoided his cohorts, she could outrun him.

One up for not drinking booze.

Already, she'd gained distance and time. Unfortunately, he held the advantage of knowing the terrain. She ducked into the cover of woods and kept running as another bark of his gun ruptured the quiet.

Tall trees thickened with late fall vines had surrounded the kidnapper's house on three sides. Karma and fate probably conspired to set her in the middle of nowhere, headed for miles and miles of treacherous wilderness ahead.

Better than the killer behind me.

Low dishrag clouds covered the sky, or what she'd seen of it before her mad dash for survival. If it rained again, it would wash away her trail and make it more difficult for a SAR dog to retrace her steps and find her friend.

When animals fled, instinct urged them downhill. She'd be no exception, able to make better time and cover more distance.

Increased odds of reaching civilization guided her current if erratic path. She hadn't heard another shot. It would take Porter longer to cross the deep ravine.

Her heart raced, and her breath puffed in the cool morning air, punctuated by quiet curses with each cut from barbed vines. Stealth wasn't as important as distance for the time being. Keiki was young, and had the physical advantage. She held no misconception of what motivated her enemy.

Minutes passed while each step added physical evidence to her panic. Her clothes ripped, her hair snagged in passing, and her flesh leaked a crimson trail. She had no idea where she was, where she was headed, or what awaited her.

What felt like ten miles probably equated to a five K run for someone not fleeing for their life. When she had to catch her breath again, she hunkered down behind a broad oak and listened for the telltale signs of pursuit.

Normal woodland sounds provided a small measure of hope. At the time of her capture, she hadn't heard Porter's approach. In her defense, she'd just exited a building. The depth of her enemy's skills remained a mystery. One thing was clear—he'd cross any line to accomplish his goal.

If anything could be considered lucky, she knew where to find Gabby's evidence. She just had to live long enough to get it.

He could've transported her across state lines while she lay unconscious on the back seat of his car.

Exposure to the elements wouldn't become a factor as long as temperatures didn't drop too low at night. If she didn't run afoul of critters looking for a meal, she'd survive. Several forays into hiking had given her basic skills, which she used to head south.

Her mind forged links between Gabby's confession and past conversations with Harock Industry personnel. It still wasn't clear if the engineers she'd worked with were part of Franklin Harock's scheme or whether he used *outside* help.

Porter's demand for precious information declared him a competitor in the drug trade, but not the identity of his boss. It could be a local gang, or heaven forbid, something a lot bigger and more sinister.

The sound of water rushing ahead drew her to the source. Rivers meant bridges and roads, which meant people. Her intent to avoid anyone in the immediate vicinity made her shy away to a parallel path in hopes of reaching a small town. Any place with a phone would suffice.

Navigating down a steep hill took longer than expected after a misstep sent her tumbling a solid thirty yards. Scrambling up the next hill proved worth the effort when she looked back. The forest was far too dense for Porter to track her without a dog or keen skills.

He didn't strike her as the outdoorsy type.

From the top of the next ridge, she stood at the edge of a small clearing, careful to stay behind cover. Nonetheless, skin on the back of her neck itched with the feeling of a cross hair centered on her spine.

Deep breaths while resting against a trunk provided a view of the small valley below. Down and to her right, an old narrow bridge didn't appear to be in good shape. Four groups of concrete piles spanned the river and supported questionable decking. It didn't look well used—or safe.

It could be the first place Porter stations someone to grab me.

Her sense of self-preservation dictated she turned in the opposite direction. The water may or may not be deep and would be cold, but she was a strong enough swimmer to make it. She hadn't put enough distance between herself and her captor would to take chances crossing the bridge.

Several hundred yards north, the river curved into an S shape, the middle of which she chose to forge. Daytime air temperatures were comfortable enough, but sundown would bring cooler air to drop water temps by a significant amount. She'd cross as fast as possible then pray to find a safe place to dry off and get warm.

Initial steps into the cold water bit deep, the combination of fear, temperature, and exhaustion slowing her strokes. Despair edged the periphery of her thoughts before she reached midpoint. Desperation focused her mind on the picture on her nightstand. Nolan's intense concentration animated and reinforced her flagging will.

At each turn, she hadn't been honest, either concerning the investigation or her feelings. He'd turn her away, but life had taught her a valuable lesson. If she never let him know how she felt, she wouldn't give him a chance to prove her wrong.

The current's fury overwhelmed her diminishing energy. Assuming an *armchair position* and floating for a short break restored a small portion.

The approaching bend where she'd become visible to anyone lurking near the bridge encouraged her to resume her desperate bid for survival. She hadn't seen any traffic, which meant a sniper could pick her off and leave her for dead with no one the wiser.

Once she sprawled on the far bank under a tangle of vines, chattering teeth promoted the warning of advancing hypothermia. Her fingers were numb and her mind sluggish. As much as Keiki wanted to rest, a sense of foreboding urged her to stand and resume her woodland hike.

When the trees began thinning, a moment of truth approached, a decision to be made. Once she reached the outskirts of a town, she'd be vulnerable and out in the open. It was a necessary risk.

Shaking, numb, and depleted of energy, she couldn't hold out much longer before succumbing to the inevitable.

Small houses dotted the landscape ahead, the closest of which appeared to be a double wide planted in the middle of a field. An aroma, the slight dusty sweet odor of fresh cut corn, registered another sign of fall.

A child's swing set, a seesaw with a twisted two-by-twelve weathered plank, and a rusted sliding board deemed the home unapproachable. Bringing trouble to a stranger's door didn't sit well. A home with children even less so.

Similar dwellings dotted the surrounding area, which gave hope of finding access to law enforcement of some type.

Skirting the small development lengthened her journey but in the end might save lives. With great effort, she forced one foot in front of the other until more signs of civilization pricked her attention.

The first thing she noticed was the sun's reflection off something shiny through the thinning trees. A parking lot and moderate sized block building.

Dozens of cars meant people, and phones, and the chance to find out if Nolan survived. If he was in the hospital, Coyote would blame her.

Every town had some type of law enforcement coverage. One with a few small businesses might warrant a small police station.

In a desperate bid for survival, she broke cover and shuffled out into the open. The sun's warmth on her face contrasted her cold squishy footsteps leading to warmth if not safety.

Instead of relying on her bedraggled appearance to thwart anyone's attempt to stop and ask questions, she skirted the business. It was the first sign of public safety and a place Porter might stake out.

The town was small but quiet. Maple trees lined the quiet streets where modest homes and small yards offered no hint of her desired direction.

A young woman opening her mailbox to retrieve letters paused to take in her limp, damp hair, and clothes. A brief if false explanation ensued, along with directions to the local sheriff.

Her thoughts drifted to what might be Porter's next move. If his men hadn't killed her detective, he'd be the greatest source of help with the least amount of time wasted in explanation.

Circumstances forced her to accept the reality of what her heart knew and her mind repeatedly crushed. She cared for the man behind the badge. His fierce determination and unwavering intent to protect her at every turn had eaten away her veneer of virtual armor. The next time she saw him, *if* she saw him, she'd confess.

And he'll laugh in my face.

At least that would end her private fascination bordering on obsessive infatuation.

It stood to reason that some law enforcement officials would work within the drug operation's circuit, which meant she needed a well-concocted, vague story of recent events.

The local sheriff could contact Nolan's department and ascertain his status. If last night's thugs had killed him, Detective Waylin would never believe her story.

Chapter Twenty-Two

Nolan woke to the annoying sound of chittering and rustling. His teeth chattered, and his fingers were numb.

Blurry vision and a pounding headache counteracted the softness of damp forest floor cushioning his head. Every bone in his body ached.

Something flitted about in the leaves several feet away. A curious squirrel flitted around the fallen leaves and watched the intruder invading its domain.

Closing his eyes helped stem the rolling wave of nausea. Each thundering heartbeat in his ears emphasized another fragment of memory to piece together his predicament.

He prayed to find Keiki nearby in like circumstances but fate hadn't favored him so far.

His arm had gone to sleep while lying unconscious on his side. A tentative touch of his skull revealed a lump on the side with a crusty line leading down his neck. His moment of distraction had cost Keiki her freedom, possibly her life.

Again, his feelings for the young woman got in the way of following procedure. No wonder his partner stayed on his case.

The moon had sunk below overarching branches with the faint light of dawn breaching his tightly clenched lids. Even dim light blinded him with pain. Finding his way back to the warehouse and his vehicle would be problematic since he didn't know his current location. *Always pick up where you left off.*

A wave of dizziness sent him crashing to the ground when he tried to stand. Blackness closed in and took him under. His last thought included a prayer for Keiki.

Bright sunlight stabbing his closed eyelids produced a veil of red. If not for sudden panic, he would've ignored his surroundings and let unconsciousness snatch him again.

Nice of the bastards who'd taken him by surprise to leave him with his watch to time the pounding throbs in his brain. Shoving his hand around his back, he realized the thugs had taken his gun and cell. Forthcoming paperwork involved the least of his problems.

Keiki must've been savvy enough to avoid announcing his cop status, or he'd be dead. It helped his cause that no sensible officer would cover himself in glitter.

Light drizzle during the night dampened his clothes, but not enough to remove his psychedelic camouflage.

Precious time ticked by in his attempt to get his bearings. Until familiar markings or an epiphany could guide him, he couldn't get a fix on direction, so he sat and collected himself, taking a few precious moments to recall any significant detail that might help identify Keiki's soon-to-be-dead kidnapper.

Multi-tasking permitted the addition of remorse to his shame. He didn't need to see the evidence on her phone. His instincts confirmed as much from the sincerity in her eyes and the truth in her voice.

A small part of him had doubted her then listened to that insignificant whine instead of his instinct.

Or his heart.

As much as he couldn't admit it out loud, he wanted her, with all her quirks, stubbornness, and bent for devious pranks.

Two furrows leading to his position presented him with a path to follow. Fear for her quickened his step. He could follow the trail of broken limbs and trampled grass back to the warehouse. He never thought he'd be glad someone had dragged him through a forest.

The killer would be gone, thinking to vanish, but there always remained a thread of evidence.

In this case, it was like silk in a spider's web that drove him to consider the bigger picture, fitting all the pieces together. Whatever detail his little snoop uncovered in that building had lit a fire in her soul. *There will be some type of evidence even if they took all the drones.*

When he reached the edge of the clearing, the building's door stood ajar. No sounds or slight movement reflected another presence. Whoever they were, they'd left without a trace.

If the bastards hadn't yet destroyed her phone, and at least three towers received its signal, he could track her.

Once he found her—and he couldn't stomach the image of her with anything more than a few bruises, he'd contact Tucker for help.

Should've already done so.

The PI would employ a bit more vigorous approach with less respect for restrictions when it came to her safety. All Nolan had to do was insinuate she was in danger.

He'd make it perfectly clear how Keiki liked her black jacket, and the benefits of them knowing where she was in case they had questions. Then he'd *inquire* about Tucker's newest devices. He'd deliver the message without breaking any laws. Any *more* laws.

Memory of Shelly's body left in the forest debris for scavengers caused a violent shudder. Nolan picked up his pace.

Concern over leaving his prints in the storage building wasn't an issue since he'd be present when the team of forensics arrived. Before opening the door, he took a deep breath, acid boiling in his gut at the thought of finding Keiki's lifeless body inside.

Instead, the first thing he saw was a kaleidoscopic cap lying in the dirt next to a wooden post. Snatching it up was part instinct, part intuition.

I'm not tampering with evidence. It's cold out and she'll need it. He followed the letter of the law splendidly.

A quick visual verified the building was empty, cleared of the drones. He'd suspected as much. It would take time for forensics to decipher trace evidence, time his little snoop wouldn't have.

In backing out, something hard underfoot made him step lightly and stoop to explore. Leafy debris covered Keiki's phone. The significance of her gesture knocked the breath from his lungs. By hiding it, she'd given him the evidence to prove her innocence. She may also have signed her own death warrant.

His first call went to Coyote. The call to Tucker could wait a bit.

Rumor mill stated the PI had quit after an innocent bystander got pulled into an ongoing investigation and charged with conspiracy. Keiki traveled a similar path.

The private sector experienced more leeway in certain situations and were held to different standards, for which Nolan found a new respect. Friendship with the PI would hold merit.

Regardless, determination and instincts would keep Nolan wearing a badge.

It took ten minutes to make his way back to his vehicle, time to gather his thoughts. Relief washed through his chest to find the doors locked, windows intact, and no evidence of tampering. After checking the undercarriage for quickly planted devices, he retrieved his spare key and grabbed his backup weapon from the glove compartment.

By the time the neighboring sheriff's call came in, Nolan had endured enough teasing from fellow officers and the CSI techs searching the building. Repeatedly combing his hair, swiping at his face, and brushing the remnants of glitter from his clothes hadn't helped.

Saving grace came in the form of his partner acquiring his own share of sparkle after sitting in the passenger seat.

"You sure you're up to driving?" Coyote nipped his lips between his teeth to stifle a smile.

"Yes, I see only one asshole sitting beside me. And before you ask, I'm not going to the hospital. My vision is clear enough to do my job."

Coyote held his hands up in surrender. "Okay, okay."

"Damn kids these days. Who the hell knows what goes through their minds." Nolan stomped on the gas, aware of his partner's mocking grin. "Fuck you, too. You're here to help. Remember that."

"I didn't say a word about the glitter, Tink. Although I am concerned about you being behind the wheel while sporting a possible concussion. The reason I'm letting you drive is because I figured it would keep you calm."

"Think of it as a fast fan boat if it helps. And the reason I'm driving is because you don't feel like wrestling me for the keys." He prayed the new moniker, *Tink,* didn't follow him through the rest of his career. "At least give me some dignity and make it something like, I dunno, glimmer man?"

Coyote grinned wider. "Nope."

"Do you think they're listening in on our airways? Damn sheriff should've known better than to announce her presence over the radio even if he didn't give her name."

"We don't know exactly what she told him, Nolan. You're more wrapped up in this case than I suspected. Anything you'd like to share with the rest of the class?"

"Someone cleared out that building in short order. I showed you the pics on her phone. What you didn't see was at least four other tables, all holding dozens of drones. Devices we can't prove how Harock intended to use."

"Harock must own the building through shell corporations and dummy companies. That combined with what we do have is a good clue. The drones he uses in legit day-to-day business come from the main headquarters," Coyote countered.

"But it's not the proof we need. It still leaves Keiki lumped in with the bastard."

"You said it wasn't her who knocked you unconscious. Are you certain?"

Nolan glared at his partner. "Yes. I don't know who did, though, which won't prevent the captain from thinking she's in league with whoever dumped me in the woods." The knit cap he'd stuffed under his seat remained a piece of evidence they *wouldn't* find.

"Harock has lines of drones, either to deliver *something* or spy on others. Maybe both." Coyote drummed his fingers on his thigh, an aggressive we-gotta-figure-this-out-now signature.

"I'm betting on drugs as the primary goal. The fact he tried to tell us his competition could be running interference with his operation was a red herring." Nolan berated himself for not figuring it out sooner.

"According to Baltimore vice, this has cartel stamped in the background." Coyote wouldn't back down from a challenge, regardless of its size.

"Which I don't think Keiki knows. She's not foolish enough to take *them* on." Even as Nolan spoke the words, he prayed it was true.

"You think Harock wasn't referring to Cannon Industries as his competition? The cartel might want your girl to build drones for them."

"First, she's not now, and never will be, my anything."

Liar.

"Hmm, could've fooled me."

"Well, okay, we're friends. Both Carolyn and Faye have taken a shine to her. If not for my neighbor's probing, we wouldn't know how thick Keiki is with the damn PI. I wish we knew more, to be fair. I just don't understand that connection."

"Death of a parent affects everyone a little differently from what I've learned. Sounds like she's determined to right other people's wrongs in her own way. Despite the different paths, you two share a lot in common."

Embedded in Coyote's words existed a warning Nolan couldn't deny. "We are nothing alike. She's impetuous and goes off half-cocked. She's unprepared for the things she's facing. Most of all, she's too damn smart for her own good."

"Kind of like following a girl to Harock Industries, onto secluded private property, and into a building without backup?"

"Fuck off."

"I agree she shouldn't have gone out there on her own. Plus, you should've called me before you got out of your vehicle." Coyote delivered his parting salvo. "We are still partners, yes?"

"Shit. Okay. Next time I'll call you in the middle of the night to interrupt whatever wild orgy you're hosting to sneak around, trespass, and get conked over the head with me. We share that stuff, right?"

"Damn straight. And for the record, any *activities* I may be involved in, end by eleven. I do need my beauty sleep, after all."

"I'll try and remember that."

"Nolan, you've finally met your match, and that's what has your drawers in a twist." Coyote took a swig of the flavored water and returned the bottle to the cup holder.

"Damn it. She. Is. In college! Don't you get that? We're worlds apart. There is no physical involvement here. And there won't be. Granted, she's endured a lot of shit in her life, but she'll have a fresh start and needs to take advantage of that. Graduate, start her business, get married, have kids."

"I agree, and she graduates soon." Coyote smiled his shit-eating grin. "There may not be physical involvement, but there sure as hell is emotional attachment and the makings of a solid friendship. Who knows what could grow from it in time?"

"She doesn't need a cop as her other half. You know that as well as I do." Nolan's taking the curve too fast earned a curse and exaggerated throat clearing from his partner.

"I agree, for now, but after we officially clear her name and solve this problem, then no. She's a mature young adult."

"For all I know, she's never had a serious relationship."

"That's possible. Still don't see your issue. And speaking of issues, if you don't let up on the gas, you're gonna miss our turn."

"Shit." Vehicular training in the academy was the last time Nolan had left skid marks on a road. Until now.

The township was small, the streets lined with oaks and maple trees sporting more vibrant colors he couldn't tolerate.

A sleepy little town unprepared for the likes of a drug cartel's raid.

"Sherriff's office is ahead on the side-street to the left, according to my map." Coyote pocketed his cell.

Nolan unclenched his fists after pulling to the curb. His partner again commented about keeping his woman in line. He didn't bother arguing. It wasn't worth the energy.

"Remember. Vice says these thugs have a long reach and deep pockets. Keiki's smart enough to not say much, depending on her emotional state."

The small brick building with two marked vehicles in front stood on a low rise, as if keeping watch over the vicinity. If not for the sign posted in the front yard, it could've been a quaint house nestled against the woods.

Nolan heaved a sigh after pocketing his keys. "Let's see what kind of shape she's in."

They each stepped over the section of walkway heaved from the many freeze-thaw cycles of winters past.

Coyote reached to get the door, then paused and gave Nolan a measured look. "If this is cartel related, we need to figure out how to keep her safe. She seems to be some type of lynch pin. We just don't know whose yanking the strings."

The nonverbal, *they may be wearing a badge*, came through loud and clear. Nolan nodded.

"Right now, I just want to see she's all right—then ring her neck for pulling such a stupid stunt."

At that, Coyote yanked the door open. A sudden gust of wind necessitated a quick grab to keep it from swinging wide. Modern facilities generally had glass doors, but this wooden throwback in time fit the surroundings.

"From what I can tell, she's on the road to becoming a licensed snoop unless *someone* can manage to guide her to a different path," his partner teased.

"Damn it. I knew she was going to spy. I should've handcuffed her to a bed." Realizing his partner misinterpreted the statement prepared him for the retort.

"Maybe you could try talking to discourage her from the super spy business. If not, at least discuss safe words first?"

"Damn it, Coyote!"

"Hey. The sheriff told you when she ran into his office, she appeared relatively unscathed after reporting an *attempted* kidnapping. You'll help her recover."

"Because we can see and bandage all the scars?" Nolan's retort was lost in the slamming of the door.

Nothing about the facility resembled a typical county office building. The receptionist's desk sat to one side and merged with a long low counter. Behind her, six more desks filled the open space. Three doors to each side signaled private offices.

"Hello, gentlemen. What can I do for you?" Tortoise shell glasses and auburn hair pulled back in a severe ponytail stereotyped the petite woman as a bespectacled book pusher, at home among thousands of leather-bound tomes.

Once the secretary removed her specs, intelligent green eyes betrayed an active mind imbued with excitement and a tinge of anxiety. As was common in small departments, unusual occurrences threw everyone off balance, especially if they didn't have specific details.

"Detectives Garnett and Waylin to see Sheriff Finley." Coyote stepped forward to offer his hand and a warmer-than-necessary smile.

Southern charm evolved in slow degrees of confidence, swagger, and intuition. He could settle witness and victim alike with amazing insight.

"Oh, certainly. You're here for—the girl who wandered in. What happened?" Her hands tapped her desk in search for who knew what then gestured to a closed door bearing the nameplate *Sheriff.*

Second one on the left." Her motion indicated they help themselves, but her focus slid to Coyote's left hand before a small smile graced her lips.

A nudge moved his partner ahead to the door, behind which, Keiki waited. He hadn't spoken to her on the phone, instead being disgruntled with Coyote relaying information. Until standing nose to nose with his errant hell raiser, he couldn't draw an easy breath.

As he lifted his hand to knock, the door flew open and out barreled one frantic and bedraggled ball of energy in baggy sweats. Her arms circled his waist and held on for dear life.

"I don't know whether to hug you, scold you, or put you in protective custody." His last option included forbidden contact.

Keiki's breath warmed his chest through his shirt. Instinct urged him to hold her snug to feel the beat of her heart and expansion of her chest against his own. He closed his eyes and breathed in the heady scent that was all Keiki.

"You're all right. I didn't know it was you coming to pick me up. When they hit you, I checked your pulse, but then they dragged you away..." A higher-pitched voice and words that rushed over each other corresponded with her quick, uncoordinated movements.

Despite not seeing her hands, he understood she used them to speak when riled.

Coyote's knowing grimace was something he could deal with later.

"I'm fine. Are you okay?" A light clasp of her shoulders allowed him to separate them a few inches so he could see her face, scratched and dirt-smudged. The oversized sweat pants and sweater she wore contributed to her waif status.

Farther inside the office, her bagged clothes were filthy and ripped, waiting in the corner. Small smears of blood would match the rips acquired during her mad dash through the woods.

"Yeah." She hiccupped before tears trickled down her cheeks. "I don't know about Gabby, though. She—"

"I've called in my off-duty officers and the state has two tracking dogs on the way, along with a local S&R team willing to donate their time. We're about ready to go." Finley nodded for them to take a seat. "We found some dry clothes for her, but she refuses to go to the hospital or tell me anything other than her friend is missing. Wanna fill me in?"

Nolan winced but knew her caution stemmed from experience. "Tell us everything you remember."

A soft touch guided her to one of the wooden chairs in front of the desk. Unable to tolerate any distance, he stood beside her with his hand gentle on her shoulder. Bruises and small cuts marked her face. The way she favored her left ankle tallied another source of pain.

"I thought they were gonna kill you." Keiki drew her lips between her teeth and stifled a sob.

If not for Finley's presence, Nolan would've sat and pulled her onto his lap. Growing up with four younger sisters magnified his protective instincts and solidified his empathetic traits.

Instead, he offered his handkerchief. "I'm fine. A bit of a headache is all."

She raised her hand as if wanting to touch his head, then stopped when he cleared his throat.

Details of her harrowing experience spilled out among broken sobs and hiccups. The coed kept things almost together until reaching the part where she'd left her friend behind.

Agitation forced her to pace the small area. Her story ended with entering the station and changing clothes.

Nolan moved to stand before her. Wrapping her in his arms calmed his erratic pulse and the flashed scowl warned Coyote to keep quiet.

Baggy clothes didn't detract from her unyielding resolve. He knew better. Underneath the shaking limbs and sniffles beat the heart of a fighter who wouldn't concede.

"I didn't know how much to tell him." She nodded toward Finley. "I'm sorry."

To his credit, the sheriff bobbed his head in acknowledgment. "Understood, Katherine, I would've done the same thing. I think it's time for me and my team to search for this cabin. From your description, I have a fairly good idea where to start looking. Detective Garnett can take you to the ER."

"No! I mean, yes. Look for her." Pleading eyes turned to the man on whom she held a death grip. "We have to go. Now."

The unrehearsed message delivered another punch. Once again, she squirreled information. The question remained, how much would she share this time?

Chapter Twenty-Three

Nolan kept his arm around Keiki through the station and out the door, observing the way she moved. When she stumbled over the uneven sidewalk, he plucked her up and cradled her against his chest.

Ignoring his partner's murmur avoided bloodshed.

Exhaustion, pain, and fear warred for dominance in her tightened frame. She didn't speak until he'd buckled her into the back seat and tossed the keys to his partner.

"Now you let me drive," Coyote growled.

In lieu of Keiki's possible unvoiced trauma, Nolan sat in the front passenger seat and twisted cattycorner to face her, needing a visual of nonverbal gestures to measure degrees of stress. His partner jumped the gun.

"Were to, Keiki?" Astute as ever, Coyote backed out of the space and slipped the vehicle into drive.

"Spinyneck grade school." Though her fingers trembled in her lap, her voice signaled her spirits bolstered.

"What?" The vehicle's tires dipped onto the road's dirt shoulder as Coyote pulled to a stop. He'd reached the limits of his endurance. Nolan knew he drew the line on anything involving children.

"It's Sunday. Shouldn't be anybody there," Keiki mumbled just above the motor's soft hum.

"What's there, Keiki?" Though others weren't entirely convinced of her innocence yet, Nolan knew she'd proven herself clear of murder and involvement with drugs.

"The proof Gabby hid. We have to get to it before anyone else does."

"Do the kidnappers know about it?" Nolan waited while she considered her answer.

Beside him, Coyote kept an eye on the rearview mirror with frequent glances at the sky. If Porter was tracking them via a drone, he could be following outside their sight line.

"I don't know. When I ran, Gabby was struggling to keep him from unlocking his cuffs. She knew all along she wouldn't be able to run, but she saved my life." Keiki didn't bother to wipe away the tears, this time. "I don't know what she told him after I escaped, but she'd told be about the stashed evidence. I think she got suspicious."

Neither detective pointed out the fact her friend had put her in danger in the first place. There was too much grief weighing her shoulders to digest anything more.

"Gabby was working to perfect a formula. I don't remember its name. A friend of hers died from an overdose, so she wanted to make the drug safer. It's not like you can get them off the market, but she *could* save lives by making it more stable."

"Serenity," Coyote supplied the information with a sigh.

"Yeah, that's it. How'd you know?" Keiki looked from Coyote to Nolan.

"We've talked at length to vice. The drug being shipped to the states is killing people. I'm guessing Gabby, with her background in chemistry, found a way to alter it."

"She just wanted to protect her friends. She didn't want any part of the business."

"Was Shelly involved?" Coyote's loosening grip on the wheel and softened tone suggested he understood her pain.

"No. They killed Shelly because they mistook her for me. People used to call her my doppelganger. When Porter realized he had the wrong girl, he killed her to send a message to Mr. Harock."

"And you didn't trust us enough to tell us?" Nolan tried to keep the hurt from his voice.

"I was afraid that until I found proof, you'd think I was involved in all that shit. I don't take drugs, deal drugs, or have any involvement with those who do. At least I hadn't known about it." Her words vibrated with the intensity of determination and truth.

"Believe it or not Keiki, I do know. And I do believe you're innocent of all the crap that's gone down," Nolan wasn't sure how to convince her.

"We need to get her to a hospital, Nolan." Coyote continued down the road and merged onto the highway.

"No. I won't go. It's just a sprain. I've had worse."

The trip back, longer without the urgent need to shave time, allowed them to digest new details.

"Let's go over Franklin Harock's specific involvement." Nolan retrieved a file tucked between his seat and the console.

"From what I gather, he's using my drones to deliver drugs. I think that pissed off the supplier already in place."

"Porter?" Coyote suggested.

"No. He's just a crony. I don't know who *they* are, but hopefully we can find out. Maybe Gabby left a clue on the flash."

Conjectures and suppositions filled the remainder of their drive with no definitive answers but multiplying the determination to get them.

Spinyneck School sat at the end of an outlying, sparsely populated street. A chain-link fence surrounded the side yard inhabited by monkey bars, swing sets, shortened basketball hoops, and teeter-totters. Parking spaces in the front were minimal due to recent expansion.

Coyote pulled into the circular bus loop and cut the engine. "Do we need to go inside, Keiki?"

"No. Around the side, there's a place we used to hide stuff when we were kids."

"What makes you think it's still there, not degraded by time or changed with the renovations?" Coyote paused in opening his door.

"Because Gabby said it was there. She hid the flash within the last two weeks. Our wall is on the south end and protected by an overhang which extends from the side entrance."

A soft expletive accompanied her sliding off the seat to stand beside the vehicle. Obvious pain from an ankle injury forced a slight hobbled step. Her outstretched hand prevented Nolan from scooping her up.

"I got this."

If she thought she deserved the discomfort for leaving her friend behind, she was wrong. Still, Nolan wondered about what she *hadn't* said. Her best friend endured rape and beatings. Keiki was with them long enough to have suffered the same.

Either way, the world as she knew it, had further disintegrated before her eyes, again altered by death and deceit.

"Don't touch the flash once we find it, Keiki. Its evidence we don't want altered." Nolan's reminder stiffened her shoulders.

We especially don't want your *fingerprints on it.*

"Yeah. I know. We need it to incriminate Harock. He's ultimately responsible for Shelly's death and for Porter kidnapping Gabby."

Nolan shook his head, following Keiki's limping form around the building's corner. "This is no longer a *we* situation, kid."

"I'm in this, too, and I won't back off." Her warning held the steel of a determined mama bear.

Low-growing shrubs fronted the building but ended at the corner. The west side included a tidy lawn without flowers or shrubs, its smooth expanse interrupted by a large compressor for the system's heat pump.

"Let me guess. You'll enlist your PI buddy's help and use your drones to do your own investigation?" Frustration nudged Nolan's voice a little further south. He intended to protect her, despite her penchant for meddling.

"I'm guessing its been cleared out after they took me?"

"Yeah, they did a pretty thorough job." Coyote halted when she indicated a brick in the wall. With a frown, he crouched beside the boxy compressor to examine the mortar around each piece of masonry. "How'd you know which one?"

Keiki pointed toward the roof. "See the light? When they expanded on the other side, they didn't move the wiring. The old compressor used to be a lot smaller, but the light marks the spot."

Nolan snapped on a pair of gloves and knelt beside his partner. Gentle probing near the base revealed a loosened piece. "Here." Dirt packed around the joint didn't crumble as he expected when he jiggled the brick free. "What did she use to pack around this brick?"

"Who knows? She's a chemistry whiz, remember?" She leaned over Nolan's shoulder, and her warm breath tickled his ear, sending a shudder washing down his spine.

His partner shook his head and scrubbed a hand over his nape.

Once out, the half brick exposed a tiny compartment. In it, a baggie containing a small flash drive rested against the back.

"Got it." Nolan stood, holding the evidence.

Coyote held a paper bag open expectantly. A twist of his lips granted a single outward sign of indecision as he tucked the bag in his jacket. "If we take this in and something happens to it..."

"I'd like to see what's on this before anyone else does. Make a copy?" Breaking procedure didn't happen often for either detective, but Nolan's glance flicking in Keiki's direction conveyed all he couldn't say.

His partner nodded.

"We'll take this to my house and not—" Hair raising on his nape forced Nolan to glance back the way they'd come. The ensuing click and slide of a gun impelled him to draw his own after yanking Keiki down behind cover.

The first shot pinged off the compressor inches away. Considering its construction, it offered little protection.

"Shit." Coyote's weapon was drawn, and he faced the back of the building. "Clear this way. I'll go."

Thirty yards of open space meant an unhindered shot for anyone circling behind the building.

"She'll follow." Nolan leaned to the side and returned fire as Coyote ran in a crouched position to the back corner. No shots came from that direction, and a quick thumbs up indicated the coast clear.

Keiki nodded.

"Give me the flash and I'll walk away. I've no desire to kill a few more but won't hesitate."

The accented voice struck a familiar chord in Nolan's mind. "Is that Porter?"

Keiki's fear became a living, breathing beast in Nolan's mind. No one should cower like a beaten dog. "Stay down. As soon as Coyote makes it around the front edge, he'll double back and give me a signal. Once he does, you high-tail it to him. Any problems, you head for the woods, then follow the copse of trees to Langdon Street. It'll screen your route out of town. Got it?"

"What about you?"

In that second, he wanted more than anything to hold and comfort her, kiss her senseless, and tell her it would all work out. Life seldom happened that way. She'd already experienced the dregs of fate's offerings. "Pincer's move. We'll sandwich him between us. Go. I'll provide cover. Stay low and don't slow down."

Porter fired three more shots but failed to hit a target.

Nolan returned fire, each shot a reminder of what could happen. Each bullet struck the brick where Porter's head had been a split-second prior thrust home the division between himself and Keiki. The life she led shouldn't include firefights, kidnapping, and rape.

Fate and unpredictable circumstances dictated the shifting world they faced.

In loosening his guard, he'd placed his witness in the thug's crosshairs. Seconds passed. Sweat trickled between his shoulder blades. Bullets ricocheted off the brick to his side and the unit granting spotty cover.

Knowing they couldn't guarantee her safety rekindled his memory of waking up in the woods and not knowing what had happened to his charge.

A short whistle marked his time for procrastination at an end. Coyote and Keiki had made it to the opposite corner. He'd continue with minimal cover, leaving her at the front edge.

Seventy-five yards separated the building and the trees lining the perimeter's back and other side.

Silence stretched out. Either Porter fled, waited for his target to break cover, or anticipated reinforcements. None of the options suggested Nolan's dawdling a good choice. If they waited for backup, first arrivals might be hostile forces.

Nolan shoved to his feet and bolted away from the building in a brazen move to draw fire. His partner was in position to end the threat.

His gaze swept the area for signs of movement. Thirty yards out, and no bullet pierced his flesh.

Angling back toward the front corner, he noted shadowy movements darting through the copse of trees ahead. Catching Porter took a back seat to protecting Keiki.

Instead of giving chase, he returned to the vehicle where Coyote waited. Keiki's slight frame hobbled forward with a quick gesture.

"I'll check for trackers." Dropping to the pavement, his partner searched the undercarriage.

Magnetic pucks could be slid into place in less than ten seconds. Porter wouldn't have had time to plant a more sophisticated device.

The all-clear gesture signaled it time to leave.

Keiki's legs wobbled when scrambling to the back seat. Her exhale filled the small confines.

"Keys." Nolan held his hand out. "Change of plans."

"Yeah. Straight to the office." Coyote slid his weapon back into his shoulder rig. "They want this thing real bad."

"Which means Gabby told them what's on it." Keiki didn't have to finish her thought.

Nolan exchanged a measured glance with his partner.

In the rearview mirror, slumped posture and head down signaled her understanding.

Once Porter confirmed the information, he had no reason to keep the chem student alive.

The neighboring sheriff's mission had become one of recovery, not rescue.

Chapter Twenty-Four

"Coyote arranged for your car to be moved to the impound lot. Since they've seen it, you shouldn't be driving."

His partner suggested a divide-and-conquer strategy.

Nolan dropped Coyote at the office then took Keiki to the ER, where they collected fingernail scrapings and documented the myriad cuts and bruises.

Her statement he'd collect at home instead of an interrogation room. Silence in the back seat disrupted his ability to sort priorities. He could feel her defeat.

"I'll need you to write down everything that happened." Making her relive the horror was reminiscent of dealing with a rape victim. Resurrecting her terror would bring the horrific experience closer to the surface and prolong the nightmares to come.

She'd need to talk to someone, someone she trusted, someone who could reach her on her own level. That number now amounted to two. Coyote would defer to him.

Once at his home, she shuffled in, each step an indicator of her mood. He didn't interrupt her silent introspection, his silent prayer her path would lead back to him.

On the sofa, she leaned forward to scratch behind the dog's ears when he plopped his butt down in front of her. He set pen, paper, and a glass of water on the table beside her.

It didn't take her long to write her statement.

She drank a little and continued to pet Horace. Her mind would rewind and replay until every detail was searched for fault and negligence.

He gave her the space, reviewing his notes and the file until she was ready. She no longer had the stamina to resist or hold anything back.

The silence broke when she started cooing over the dog.

"I think you should've let them X-ray your ankle." He wanted to soothe her pain, to provide a balm for her shattered soul. Instead, he was helpless.

A vehement shake of her head closed the subject for the time being.

Everything she'd known, every one she'd believed in, either died or betrayed her. Trust was a precious commodity, more so for those alone in the world and who endured deceit and treachery at every turn.

"She saved my life. Her ankle was broken, and she knew from the start she wouldn't escape."

Unable to sit, Keiki paced, ending in the middle of the kitchen. Her eyes glazed over as if little mattered. "I know she's dead. I feel it."

He couldn't deny her gut instinct nor defend her long-term friends, not without knowing more. "You said you had little physical contact with Porter. Still, we had to send your clothes to forensics for trace evidence. Just being—where you were—should pick up something that might help us nail him."

"God, I hope so."

"When you're ready, you can get a shower. I can find you something else to wear." Helpless agitation carried him to stand in front of her.

She was so lost, so alone.

To hell with appearances. He wrapped his arms around her shoulders and pulled her close.

She inched forward with a sniffle and a sob, followed by more of the same. "How did I not see any of this coming? I've thought of Franklin Harock as a second father for years. He's family."

"It's the people closest to us that hurt us the most."

Filtered light dappled the borrowed clothes big enough to house a second body. The end result reaffirmed her status as lost waif.

Nolan held her through the tears and self-recriminations, knowing time would wear away the rough edges enough for her to see the truth. Until then, he'd offer whatever support she'd accept.

"I'm all alone now. I've got nobody."

Gripping her shoulders, he tightened his hold, needing to make sure she understood. "No, Keiki. You're not." Ticking of the grandfather clock timed her calming breaths. He waited until she met his gaze, needing her to understand the depth of his commitment.

"I may not be the friend you want, but I'll be around for as long as you need."

Keiki leaned forward and rested her forehead against his chest. "You're a detective, one who saved my life. I have no idea what to do with that information."

"I'm also a man, a friend, and a good listener."

Moments passed, her steady breath warm through his cotton shirt, stirred sensations he had no business feeling.

"I never thought a cop would be my friend."

"That's because you're still in college. Life will change and offer a new perspective once you graduate."

"You're wrong. I've been on my own for the last four years, making my own decisions and mistakes."

Maybe Carolyn was right, and the distance he'd forced between them stemmed from his need for self-protection. "You want to get cleaned up now? I can find some clothes that fit you better." Against his chest, she nodded.

"I want a dog. They're always honest about what they feel, never hold a grudge, and don't know deceit."

"Sounds like a good idea. I think Carolyn would love it. She often *borrows* Horace for the day." Deep down, he hoped she'd opt to stay at Carolyn's after this was all over, where he could keep an eye on her.

"I have time to train a puppy and enough funds to take a break after I graduate. 'Sides, I plan on working at home for a while."

The way she hesitated sent up a red flag. "You're planning on continuing to work with Tucker, aren't you?"

She shrugged a shoulder as if nothing mattered. It was a discussion for another time, an argument suffered through once clearer heads prevailed.

When she snuggled closer against his harder frame, he noticed the subtle change, the softening of her body as it molded against him. *Shit.*

Certain parts more interested in a physical relationship responded immediately. When he pulled back to step away, she tightened her hold.

"Please? I need the contact."

He wasn't sure which she desired most. The comfort of a caring human or the continued response of a man who wanted a woman.

Not just any woman. This one.

He hadn't remained celibate after Clare's passing, but he hadn't become emotionally involved with another woman or brought one to his home.

Keiki was a young lady in crisis. Now was not the time to take the plunge into a sexual relationship.

When she lifted her head, the look in her eyes gutted him, destroying all thoughts of resistance.

"Keiki? I... you're vulnerable right now. I don't think—"

"That's the problem. Too much thought. I swore if I escaped I'd let you know..."

She closed the distance before he could react, not that his body was capable of retreat.

The soft brush of her lips started a tingling sensation in his own which soon spread through his chest. Butterfly wings couldn't have been softer.

He fisted his hands in her hair and held her in place with gentle assurance, offering himself to any degree she would take. Gone was the guilt of yesteryear, replaced with a need so strong, a hunger so wild, it would consume his soul.

Her hands drifted up his back to clutch him tighter, her body melting into him so every curve, every soft, rounded, supple inch of her molded to him like a gift fashioned by cosmic design.

He'd done nothing to deserve this, nothing to merit the potential paradise her arms offered. Yet his body overrode conscious thought, delving into her tender submission with a zeal matching her passion. Tilting her head to the side granted better access, a groan escaping when she opened her mouth at the touch of his tongue along the seam of her lips.

Inside, he found ecstasy. The kind of bliss which could sustain a spirit for a lifetime, a hundred lifetimes, an eternity of never-ending euphoria. Outside stimuli became white noise where nothing could intrude on the enchantment of their moment, frozen for all time.

A soft whimper resounding in her chest compelled him to deepen the kiss, tasting, exploring, exalting in a union of minds and souls.

The sound of his front door opening equaled a bucket of cold water. *Damn!* If he didn't kill whomever had entered, they'd be lucky.

Both his family and Coyote had keys. The current situation forced a re-examination of priorities.

His partner's throat clearing then feigned retrieval of an envelope from an inner jacket pocket claimed his attention, negating the sight of Nolan's transgression.

Keiki backed up, her eyes glazed and her hands trembling. "Hi, Coyote. I was just, um, talking with Nolan."

"I see. Awful quiet."

"Sign language."

"With your tongues?"

"Yeah, it's a new fad."

"Hmm. Maybe I'll have to take lessons."

Coyote smiled in the face of Nolan's groan.

"I'm gonna go get a shower." She didn't look higher than Nolan's chest. "Can you set some clothes out on the bed?" Crimson cheeks and a somewhat less than steady stride accompanied her sight line never leaving the floor in passing to the hallway.

"Sure." He didn't need to see Coyote's face to know what thoughts rambled through the man's mind. Once the door shut to his bedroom, he focused his full attention on his partner. "Don't say it. It won't happen again."

In the back of his mind, an inner demon replied, *At least not while my partner is present.*

Reminding himself of the vast differences between a college student and detective didn't shore up his emotional reserve. There seemed no way to shove the situation behind self-protecting walls.

"Uh-huh. Wasn't gonna say a word, well, maybe congratulations. And it's about time. But..." Coyote's grin spoke volumes. "I think the timing, well, could be better. You know, distractions, killers on the loose and all that."

"No. Damn it. Mind out of the gutter. Now, what'd you find on the flash?"

"I duped it before turning it in. Captain wants a report by morning." Coyote strode to the table and sat. "Got any sodas?"

"Nothing made with swamp water." Nolan retrieved two drinks

from the fridge and joined him.

"We've got work to do. I spoke with Sheriff Finley. State forensics has her clothes and joint agencies are combing the woods for Gabriella Kiernan."

"Or what's left of her." Coyote kept his voice low, his watchful expression lingering on the hallway to the bedroom.

"I'll be back in a sec. I need to find her something to wear."

"She'd look cute in one of your flannel shirts."

Nolan flipped him off. Once his partner got something on his mind, it took a nuclear blast to change it.

Coyote booted up the laptop on the table as Nolan headed toward his bedroom. Despite a penchant for tidiness, living alone offered certain liberties, ones he wasn't sure he still wanted.

Like keeping the seat down, having toilet paper roll under not over, and tampons in the cabinet.

Both men paused at the sound of an engine's throaty purr out front.

"Tucker's here. Make him comfortable."

"You're sure we should pull him in from the side?"

"Yeah. We can't be everywhere. She doesn't have the sense to let us solve this mess without her help, and I don't want her hurt." Nolan would rather endure another concussion than the PI, but realized the ex-cop had experience and good instincts—both things Keiki lacked.

Chapter Twenty-Five

Keiki closed her eyes against the warm water stinging her flesh amid the many cuts and scrapes. Shades of brown and crimson circled the drain to take away the physical remnants of her ordeal.

In her mind, seeds of doubt grew and remorse blossomed into full-blown shame over leaving a friend behind. Perhaps destiny configured her life to be a series of disasters. One after another, ever circling, never finding peace, except for the stolen slice of heaven she held in her heart.

She'd kissed Nolan just as she'd promised herself. And it was more than she could've imagined. He was a cop who earlier suspected her of murder, drug dealing, and heaven knew what else. In his defense, she would've drawn the same conclusions under the circumstances.

Her previous romantic entanglement ended in disappointment and regret, with no plans to duplicate the disaster. Now, she couldn't dredge the least bit of criticism for making the current bold move. Shelly and Gabby would've applauded her initiative.

Both detectives conferring over whatever new information found on the flash indicated a difficult discussion ahead. They'd speak about her friends in cold and analytical terms, not understanding the girls' support after her parents' death.

With destiny embroiling her in new and vicious situations, the difficulties and risks police took to protect others became clear. *My drones can help them.*

A black flannel shirt with snowmen embroidered on the front and a pair of jeans lay on the corner of the bed when she'd emerged from the shower with a new perspective. The shirt must've been a holiday joke, was way too big, and carried his scent. In other words, it was perfect. The jeans were large but a belt held things in place.

Nervous anticipation of the conversation to come slowed her pace down the short hall where Tucker's distinctive bass voice interrupted Coyote in piecing together their puzzle.

From the open living room, she saw the detectives sitting at the kitchen table, poring over documents with murmurs and their usual abbreviated communication.

All three looked up when she heaved a sigh.

"Are you hungry? I can fix us something to eat." Coyote took the lead, shoving his chair back to retrieve lunchmeats and sliced cheese from the fridge.

Nolan studied her as if unsure where to begin. Reasons for the deep sadness radiating from within was something she wasn't ready to contemplate.

"We should have let the ER nurse tend to those scratches. Let's apply some antiseptic so they don't get infected," Nolan directed.

The ease with which he led her back to his bathroom testified to the speed of discounting their earlier interaction. It would be a long time before her body stopped trembling when he stood near or gave that signature look—brow raised, head tilted to the side, and the quiet expectation which made her itch to fill the silence with whatever answer he desired.

His gesture to sit on the counter while he fetched a tube of ointment from the medicine cabinet accompanied a frown when she squealed.

With the graceless and uncouth action of a man who swatted at a bees in his pants, she readjusted the crotch of her jeans. "How do you guys go commando and not get things... stuck?"

Heat creeping up her neck intensified with his smothered chuckle.

"Don't know. Not a practice I follow."

"Boxers or briefs?"

His signature look made her take another gulp.

Attention to detail in every other aspect of his life carried over to his examination and treatment of her cuts and scrapes. Intermittent compression of his lips confirmed his withholding information but not the reason why.

Either way, it couldn't be good news. She didn't want to hear it. "About earlier..."

"Yeah, um. That shouldn't have happened."

"Why?"

"Because we're worlds apart, Keiki, and not just our perspectives on life. We're in the middle of something big, and distractions like that could get us both killed."

"So, later then."

He didn't answer, didn't even acknowledge her spoken words.

That along with his reference to her near-death experience added weight to her already heavy heart. Instead of facing Gabby's probable end, she focused on Nolan.

"I thought they were going to kill you. I'm sorry—"

The ointment landed with a small thud beside the sink. With his hands resting on the counter to either side of her hips, he leaned in so their faces were mere inches apart, but it wasn't in preparation for another kiss.

"What you did was foolish and reckless. If you hadn't escaped, they *would* have killed you, and I couldn't have done a damn thing about it." The fierceness blazing in his eyes spoke of possession, revenge, and least expected, fear.

"I was afraid if I didn't find evidence to figure this mess out, you'd think I was involved with Shelly's death." Unable to hold back any longer, she reiterated her newest truth. "They were my best friends. And they're gone. I—"

"You are not alone and never will be again. You have Carolyn... and me."

His frustration melted before her eyes, morphing into compassion as he wrapped his arms around her shoulders and edged her against his chest. "I'm sorry all this has happened, but I'll never be sorry for meeting you."

"It wasn't a competitor for Harock Industries who started all this. It's been about drugs from the beginning." A sob broken by a hiccup and sniffles interrupted the flow of grief and explanation. "Gabby knew all along. She knew Harock was involved but still wanted to help other kids, even if her methods were a little dodgy. How could I not see what was right under my nose?"

"We often don't see what's right in front of us, for all kinds of reasons. Busy schedules, trust, and security in our relationships. You three girls were so close yet had such separate identities and interests. I do believe she wanted to protect other students. She employed—different methods for going about it."

"But Harock is using *my* drones for the illegal side of his dealings. No wonder he gave me such leeway. He planned on using me from the start. Gabby spelled it all out. That's why she protected me in the end."

The floodgates opened then, and Keiki couldn't hold back the tide of emotions spilling forth. Each detail her friend had spoken in the dark, damp basement had widened the chasm started in their freshman year.

"If I hadn't been so focused on my damn machines, I would've seen it earlier. Tucker always says to pay attention to those closest to you."

Soothing murmurs whispered against her hair and the light touch grazing down her back equaled a balm to her shattered nerves.

"The information on the flash drive lays it all out. Everything she knew. Gabby didn't trust Harock."

"If Shelly had known, she would have told me. I know it."

"It doesn't look like she was involved in any aspect of it, which made her an innocent bystander."

"We have to nail both Harock and Porter. But I don't know how. He's going to try and turn everything against me."

"It's too late for that. Gabriella detailed enough of the operation up to and including the drones. She didn't specify names in that part of his dealings. I don't think she knew anything more."

"I was starting to insert trackers but hadn't turned in the prototype."

"He's already done it."

"You went back and found the ones in the building?"

"No. By the time I returned, the place was empty."

"Does Porter know they have trackers in them?"

"We have no way of knowing what he found out."

The mention of her friend and her probable fate knocked the breath from Keiki's lungs. "How do we get Harock *and* Porter, along with whoever hired him?"

"That's something we're working out now. We'll talk more once we're out in the kitchen."

After her hiccups stopped and she felt able to face the world again, she nodded her thanks. As if on cue, Coyote appeared in the doorway, minus the smirk he seemed to wear most of the time.

"Food's on the table."

Instead of turning to lead them out, he stepped forward in an unusual show of compassion and gave her a one-armed hug. "Sorry, Katherine."

"Only my parents called me that."

The faintest of smiles ghosted Coyote's mouth. "I know you feel some of this is your fault, but it isn't. We'll get these bastards, every last one of them."

Huh, she hadn't taken him for the *huggy* type. When he pulled back, she looked for an explanation in his sorrowful expression but found none.

"I have a brother who got caught up in a situation, kinda similar. It was tough on us all."

She'd wanted his acceptance, his conviction of her innocence, but not at the cost of stripping his soul bare.

Once her minor cuts were swabbed with ointment, they headed back to the kitchen.

Keiki sat at one end of the table with Nolan and Coyote to either side. Nolan pushed a plate of food closer to her, expecting her to eat.

Tucker looked up from the notes before him and murmured, "Hey, kid."

Rehashing current and previous events dulled her appetite, but she'd need the fortification to face what lay ahead.

"We're planning a sting operation," Coyote began.

"First..." Nolan leveled a look at his partner, the silent exchange sharing a wealth of information. Covering Keiki's hand with his larger one, he took a deep breath. "There's something you need to know."

"The rescue team found Gabby," She blurted before either man could continue. In doing so, it seemed she willed the following sequence of probable outcomes to life.

"As it turns out, it wasn't a... a rescue operation. It was recovery." Coyote's confirmation filled the silence with every best friend's worst nightmare.

"They killed her. I left her there to die." Dry heaves forced her to stand and reach for the trashcan. At once, Nolan was there to hold her hair and gently rub her back. "No," he barked out in a burst of determination. "They confirmed one ankle was broken or badly sprained. Considering the old bruising and significant swelling, it hadn't occurred in the prior few hours. She couldn't have hobbled out let alone run."

"I could have stayed, found something in the kitchen to fight him off. A weapon or something."

"There wasn't anything there to use. They searched for confirmation of Porter's contact, but found nothing. The house was clean except for prints and trace evidence." Nolan looked to Coyote to add his assurance.

"There's no way you could have taken him on and survived. From the description, he outweighed you by over a hundred pounds. Besides, we know there are at least two others who work with him still at large. If they'd entered the fray, hell, even if they hadn't, you'd not have escaped."

Tucker said, "You're good at what you do, kid, but you're not trained for this stuff. That means you have to make a decision. Either go through the training or stay on the fringes of investigations. I was wrong to pull you in as far as I've done." Self-chastisement coincided with a concordant nod from the two other men.

Their words made sense in her mind, but not her heart. "How do we nail them all? I want to help."

"You'll have a part in this, from a distance." Nolan's hard glare brooked no argument.

"But—"

"No. This is how it's going to go. You're going to contact Harock and tell him about your *attempted* kidnapping, leaving out key details like Gabby's presence."

"You're taking a chance he won't contact Harock," Keiki surmised.

"Yes." Coyote picked up the thread of conversation. "You'll tell him you're scared, in hiding, and need help. You'll let him know Porter is in cahoots with one of his engineers. Tell him there's a plan in place to take over his business, and if he goes to the cops or contacts Porter, they'll kill both him and his wife."

"That should cut him off from Porter, if only a temporary stopgap," Tucker confirmed.

"Harock's gonna want to meet you," Coyote began, "since he and his wife consider you family."

"Okay, then what?"

Nolan laid out the rest of the plan. "Deeper background checks uncovered a connection between Porter and two of Harock's employees, both of whom have pointed the finger at their boss. It seems the CEO was trying to negotiate terms and Porter didn't like them." Coyote's grimace suggested the entire plan didn't sit well. "Harock's men will arrange a meeting between their boss and Porter's boss."

"And you'll be waiting to grab them all up?"

"That's the goal. However, it's going to take a few days to delve deeper into their backgrounds and coordinate the various agencies involved." Coyote's apologetic shrug belied the determination in the hardening of his jaw.

"Meanwhile, I'll be keeping tabs on you." Tucker grinned at the flash of annoyance crossing Nolan's face.

"Okay then." Keiki respected the raw grit and focused tenacity with which they devised their approach. It sounded like a blueprint for success. "One more thing. I want to carry my gun."

The unanimous "no," didn't surprise her. Nolan's glance flicked from his partner to the view outside his kitchen window. Tucker didn't appear so resolute.

It was Coyote who spoke first. "You're not going to be present. We'll use an undercover officer in your place." He flicked a lock of her hair before adding, "Maybe we'll have her dye her hair neon green for a distraction."

Denial wouldn't placate her conscience, so she introduced her ace up the sleeve with a direct smirk at Tucker. "I want to go to the shooting range. I haven't been in a long time."

"Shit. You're not going to let it go, are you?" Nolan asked.

"Nope. I'm going. It's legal. You have proof I'm not a suspect, so you can't hold me or take my form of self-defense."

Nolan's hard glare in Tucker's direction declared any method acceptable in achieving his goal.

"If you go, we're going with you. Understand?" Coyote's snicker warned of his style of anticipated fun. "Who knows, maybe you'll take my partner down a peg or two."

Chapter Twenty-Six

"Got your lead dispenser?" Tucker clapped Keiki on the back as soon as she stepped from the SUV into the bright morning sun. The ex-cop had followed them from a distance, providing backup.

Nolan had driven in silence, gritting his teeth every time his partner mentioned one of the PI's attributes. Retribution would be slow and painful—and sparkly.

The shooting range was relatively new, one neither Nolan nor his partner had visited. The owner was a friend of Tucker's.

Since Keiki wouldn't give up her gun, they all needed to see she was safe using it. If she found herself in a tight situation with the likes of Porter, the day's practice would help her focus even if she didn't have a weapon handy.

"Hey, Coyote. Nolan. Shall we make wagers?" The PI was closer in age to their witness, with a penchant for flirtation.

Tucker's prior experience on the force, despite its brevity, qualified him to help. He'd proven himself intelligent and shrewd.

"Fine. Next week, lunch is on the loser." Nolan let his clipped answer speak for itself. "This is just between the men."

"Oh, boy. Let me grab my telescopic measuring stick. Or, perhaps I should grab the compact so I can stick it in my back pocket to keep it handy." Keiki smirked when Coyote shoulder bumped her sideways.

Nolan suppressed a groan. They needed Tucker, as evidenced by his help the prior day.

Two buildings formed an L shape with the longer arm housing an indoor range. Nick led them up the steps and inside the office.

"Made friends with any keyholes or prickly bushes, lately Nick?" Nolan tilted his head back to watch a plane overhead.

"Actually, I'm to the point where I take fewer divorce cases and more of the fun stuff. As soon as our girl here graduates, I suspect they'll be enough work to keep us both occupied." The grin flashed over his shoulder declared his intent.

"I've heard this place is top shelf," Coyote inserted himself into the conversation with a frown in Nolan's direction, a clear message to take it easy.

"It just opened up a couple months ago. The setup might need a little tweaking, but the attention to detail is in-depth." With a hand at Keiki's waist, Tucker guided her into the building and to the left where a thick-shouldered man stood belly-up to the counter.

"Hey, Pete."

Straight dark hair peppered with salt and the tiny crinkle lines edging mouth and eyes attested to a middle-aged man who smiled a lot. Well-defined muscles and lack of excess fat indicated he took care of himself. He greeted the PI with a handshake.

"Hey, Tucker. Who've you brought along today?" Intelligent eyes assessed Keiki and the two detectives beside her. "You told me you were bringing your, uh, friend with you, but not two officers." With a smile, he held out his hand. "Hi. I'm Pete. Firearms instructor and owner of Straight Shot."

Coyote stepped forward and completed introductions, finishing with, "Hope you don't mind us tagging along."

"Not at all, the more the merrier. Tuck said she's got a target on her back." Narrowing his appraisal on Keiki, Pete added, "It's always a good idea to be prepared. We've received requests to train quite a few civilians, many of whom are women. I thoroughly approve."

"Okay if we take the long course today, Pete? I'll run her through it." Again, the PI's proprietary hand sifted through the ends of Keiki's hair at her waist.

"Along with us." Nolan pulled out his wallet to retrieve his ID and cash.

"We've made a friendly wager, if there's time," Tucker added.

Pete's quiet guffaw made it clear the competition was for more than targets. His speculation returned to Keiki. "I cleared the course for the morning after you called, Nick. Help yourselves."

Preparations aside, the four made their way to the still target section for initial assessment of gun safety and accuracy. Nolan watched Keiki load and fire her weapon at stationary targets while he reiterated standards of practice.

Keiki's intense focus carried over with a 94% kill rate. Coyote whistled low, and Nick nodded his approval.

"There's a big difference between paper targets and someone firing live rounds at you," Nolan advised.

Keiki leveled a stare at him. "Yeah, been there, done that. More than once as a matter of fact. At least now, I'll be able to shoot back."

"You're not licensed to carry," Coyote reminded her.

"*Yet*. I'm not licensed to carry yet."

The subsequent course resembled Hogan's Alley, used by the FBI. The outdoor range employed three *safe* directions for practical training. Pop-up or turning targets with sudden loud noises mimicked possible situations for a police officer on duty.

The course spanned seventy-five yards, during which the trainee was scored on time and accuracy while moving forward and assessing threats on the fly. While she got her visual bearings, Tucker explained the strategy and various situations she could encounter in a straightforward manner.

"For today, since this is your first time, let's braid your hair. Next time we come, we'll pick a windy day and leave it down to offer a bit of distraction."

Nolan took a step forward when the PI gathered her long locks in his hands. From his back pocket, he pulled a soft hair band. The man came prepared, if nothing else.

"There's no way they could guess we'd be here, right?" Keiki turned to Nolan for reassurance. She shifted her weight from foot to foot, keeping her gun aimed downward.

The flash of pride he'd felt when she looked to him for reassurance cooled as Tucker took his time braiding her wavy hair.

"We're fine. Coyote and I will be with you all the way. Since this is the type of place cops frequent, it's the last place they'd look." As a precaution, Coyote had left his disassembled cell on his kitchen table. The new one he'd brought for Nolan would serve their needs.

"Okay. Let's take a stroll down Main Street, shall we?" Tucker tugged on the end of her braid and redirected her attention. "This'll be a walk in the park."

Cars parked in front of a false bank front simulated a real-life scenario except for the pockmarks from wild shots scoring the painted plywood exteriors.

Nolan and Coyote kept pace behind Keiki as she moved forward with her Glock.

"Most shots are fired from within seven yards of a suspect, hence the road is narrow." Nolan's running commentary offered necessary learning as well as a distraction for them both. The sight of her holding her weapon like a pro distracted the hell out of him. He didn't need another reason to find her hot as hades.

"We'll also show you how a twenty-five pound, handheld battering ram can shatter a lock," Tucker supplied as he remained slightly back and to her side.

"Because I need to know how to break into someone's house? I thought that's why you were teaching me to pick locks, which, by the way, saved my life."

Nolan fisted his hand against his gut to waylay its churning. The fact she escaped at all was a miracle. Doing so before enduring rape saved his sanity.

There were things Nolan, as a friend, would teach her, regardless of her life's future direction. A mental list formed, complete with complementary meals and various diversions in between.

"The reason is so you'll remember the sound if someone breaks into *your* home," Coyote explained. "It's important to use all your senses in assessing a situation to cut down reaction time."

"There are things we realize in a split-second while assessing a possible threat." Nolan paused when Keiki raised her gun and shot the pop-up gunman in the mock post office window.

"Consider how a normal, innocent person would react to a gun pointed at them. They'd raise their hands, make eye contact, and you'll recognize the confusion in their expression, body language, and voice. Learn to take note of it all to determine the threat level."

"Verbal abuse, low light situations, anything that provides distraction, it's all fair game during training." To prove his point, Tucker splayed his fingers on her low waist and began sliding them downward.

Keiki missed her shot. "Hey!"

Nolan gripped the PI's arm and tugged him back as Coyote snickered.

"See? My case in point. You missed." With a knowing grin at the detectives, he added, "At least she didn't swing to shoot me. This is the way some partners train."

That smirk is coming off, one way or another. His little enigma squared her shoulders and straightened her spine in a show of mental preparation. "Next time, I won't let the bastard get close enough to touch me."

"Ah, but shit happens, doesn't it? Consider Tink's concussion." Tucker's gloating would cease when he was unconscious.

Coyote's side-glance expressed his remorse over divulging Nolan's embarrassing debacle. "In all honesty, partner, it *was* a good prank."

Her next two shots struck with a dull thwack, her aim accurate and hands steady. Stretching her neck and rolling her shoulders, she exuded more confidence with each step.

In approaching the final stretch, she relaxed her posture and strode forward with self-assurance indicative of emerging inner strength.

As she raised the muzzle to fire at a man wearing a black ski mask, Tucker retrieved his pistol and fired downrange.

Startled, Keiki shot wide. "What the hell are you trying to do? I could've shot you!"

Tucker wore an idiot grin. "Naw, hon. I had my left hand inches from your elbow. I wouldn't have let you hurt anyone."

"That's why you wanted to stay on my right. You're right-handed." Keiki's voice elevated an octave.

"Yep. Got to learn to expect the unexpected. It's what's gonna let us work great together."

References to their future working relationship proved something Nolan couldn't swallow. He stepped between Keiki and Tucker, facing the PI.

He'd had his fill of the younger man's cockiness and innuendos. "That has to be one of the most harebrained moves I've seen pulled on a novice. With more experienced officers and maybe even trained civilians, yes. But with a complete rookie, no." On second thought, maybe he should've let Keiki shoot the self-assured prick.

"Best way to learn, Nolan." Tucker raised a shoulder in nonchalance.

The PI, with his self-composed yet cocky attitude, volunteered to go next. Although Nolan and Coyote provided various distractions, it was Keiki's subtle brushing against his back that sent the PI's shots askew.

Witnessing it was more rewarding than words could describe. Even Coyote failed to smother his guffaws.

At least Tucker had the good grace to nod to her success.

Nolan and Coyote finished, their competitive streak bringing the familiarity of jokes and remembered situations. Keiki smacked Coyote's ass with a gusto that sent him stumbling forward, but she limited her touches to Nolan on his back and neck. Visible shudders accompanied boisterous laughter when his shots went astray, fodder for future jibes.

"Close, but, you lose, Tink." Tucker couldn't contain himself. "Looks like you're buying."

"Yeah, all right. How about steaks on the grill?" He preferred to keep Keiki close to home.

"Sure. I like mine rare. I'll bring dessert," Tucker replied.

The exercise appeared to remove some of Keiki's strain, even allowing for a smile and small chuckle.

In the end, the specter of Porter and Harock's threat sobered them all when the PI offered a rematch, declaring she needed more practice.

Once back in the SUV, they'd stepped away from the range's pretense of shelter and back into the stark reality of facing life and death.

"I can't go to Gabby's funeral either, can I?" Keiki murmured from the back seat.

"No, I'm sorry. That'd be the first place someone would look, regardless of how good a disguise you put together." Nolan put the vehicle in gear and thought back to the PI's behavior. Part of the flirty demeanor may have been an effort to divert Keiki's focus on kidnappers, deceitful employers, and her friends' deaths.

The ride home was quiet and reflective. Even Coyote remained mute.

When Nolan cut the engine in his driveway, he caught the flash of Keiki's grim determination in the rearview.

"I'm gonna go back to the office and see how things are shaping up." Coyote hopped out and headed for his truck. "I'll stop in tonight, partner."

The reminder was as much a warning as intent to keep Nolan informed.

They had a job to do and one hell of a mess to sort. The final straw would lie in rounding up all the participants.

Her sudden nervousness in entering his house dissipated somewhat with Horace's affectionate greeting.

"Have a seat, and I'll fix lunch."

"You think because I'm in college I can't cook?"

"Not at all. You're a guest in my house. I'm trying to be gracious." He kept the snicker out of his voice per order of his shins.

Bottled emotions would fester, swell, and change a person from the inside out. At the moment, she was ready to burst. She'd grieved for her friends and lost surrogate family. Helping her to remember the good in her classmates could start to balance the scales of sorrow. Neither Shelly nor Gabby had intentionally used her for their own gain.

Chapter Twenty-Seven

"I still don't understand why I can't watch this go down. I'll stay in the background, behind you all." Keiki didn't look up from her keyboard. Extreme focus meant she paid little attention to her surroundings.

"Because you're not a police officer. Operations rarely go exactly as expected, so plans have to be fluid. They change on the fly, and you have no training." Nolan finished putting the dishes in the dishwasher and rubbed his forehead. The dull headache from early morning had circled around and now throbbed mercilessly behind his eyes. It was an argument she wouldn't win but refused to abandon.

He took a moment to bring up the app on his cell phone marking her presence, satisfied when the little red dot appeared on screen. The reminder of Tucker's ability to keep abreast of advanced technology didn't change his disapproval of her aspiration to work with him.

"But Tucker's gonna be part of it."

"Keiki, there's gonna be a few alphabet teams overseeing this operation. Tucker's earned a certain leeway. He's also trained and has experience. With a little touch up, he looks enough like me, sans glitter, to fool Porter's muscle into believing he's your protection."

"When he shows up with the female impersonator, Porter's gonna know it's a setup."

"By that time, it'll be too late. We'll have him, his underlings, and Harock in one fell swoop."

"I don't like it. Too much can go wrong."

"It's not up to you. You're a civilian, and we have enough manpower to cover the bases."

"Maybe I should apply to the police academy."

Nolan shrugged, knowing he hadn't come close to selling his feigned indifference.

Keiki groaned and repeatedly punched one key with excessive force. "Damn. This is an ID ten T issue."

"A what?"

"Write it down. You'll figure it out."

Nolan retrieved a pen and paper and wrote ID10T. "Huh. Smartass. Try pushing other buttons, sometimes works for me." His attempt to lighten her mood earned a scowl.

"That's what's wrong with your generation in dealing with electronics."

He estimated her nod to their age difference a modern version of backtalk. No doubt it shored up her emotional reserves and restored her equilibrium.

On the other hand, if the green screen of her mind focused on their kiss instead of the horrific and repeated nightmare occurring in his head, he'd consider that a win.

"What about Porter's boss? Won't he just send another lowlife to come after us?" she reasoned.

"Not if we can flip anyone we catch. The chances of that are damn good."

"They'd let him off with *two* murder charges?" Disbelief elevated her pitch and volume.

"Not in this lifetime. But most would take life without parole under an assumed name rather than a lethal injection or caged with inmate general population."

"I can live with that."

He hadn't realized he'd been holding his breath until it erupted in a quiet exhale. "You're going to stay with Carolyn until this is over."

She tightened her fists on the table then jerked her head in a reluctant nod. "Fine. Tucker will give me the details, if you won't."

Nolan checked his watch again before fishing his phone from his pocket. A quick swipe of the screen revealed the red dot indicating Keiki's location.

"She still there? It's been what, five whole minutes?" Coyote raised his field glasses to survey the meadow below. "Get your head in the game, partner, we've got killers to catch."

"Yeah, she's still at the apartment. And you're one to talk. What's been eating at you? I haven't seen you this quiet since we met."

"Nothing. Well, waiting on a call. It seems my brother may have stepped in something again. It'll wait."

It was obvious his partner didn't want to elaborate on the matter. "I have a bad feeling about this set up."

"We've covered all the bases we can. Move on."

Keiki had refused Carolyn's company, insisting she was agitated and wanted to rest. He'd taken her car keys then left her disabled vehicle in Carolyn's garage. There was no way she could get it out without drawing her landlady's attention.

They'd taken cover in the woods surrounding the meadow, along with a team assigned to protect the undercover officer and PI. Tucker kept his left arm around Keiki's doppelganger, who'd placed her hand at his back waist where he kept his backup weapon.

Leaning against the hood of an old pickup truck, both decoys chatted as if enjoying the cloudy afternoon before a storm broke. Tucker wore ripped jeans, a chamois shirt, and boots. The undercover officer sported dark corduroys, a knit pullover, and a baseball cap with the brim pulled low.

"What's the worry, Tink? She has her new phone. One that Porter hasn't accessed."

References to the glitter fiasco had earned him a steady supply of gleaming confetti on his desk every day along with several animated children's movies and fake tickets to a nearby children's park.

"Doesn't mean she hasn't called other friends. If Porter's men have locked onto other classmates, Keiki can be traced."

"Look, you told her no calls unless it's an emergency. I know it's driving you nuts, which by association, extends to me."

"Fuck!" The little nag at the back of his head morphed into full-blown dread.

"What?"

"My phone. They took mine. We assumed Porter tossed it somewhere in the woods or along the road. What if they didn't?"

"Why wouldn't they discard it? They didn't recognize or peg you for a cop. Not wearing your colorful camouflage. And they already had

Keiki."

"I had pictures of her on it."

"As any boyfriend would..."

"But not with speed dials to the station and other cops. Shit."

"It's not like you do online banking over your phone, right?"

"True, but I don't erase text messages right away..."

"We'll sort this out in a few minutes. It's show time."

The undercover officer pulled her cap lower and brushed her long, blonde hair over her shoulder. Tucker rubbed her back and smiled.

"Things never go as scheduled," his partner's rumbled warning filled the space between them. "Stay focused."

"This is the only way to keep Keiki out of the limelight. The captain is pissed it took so long to get that video from her."

Voice match to recordings from their present op would identify Porter as the killer. If he pled guilty, that video would never be a source of contention.

"When Porter turns on his boss, we'll have them all." Coyote turned the binocular's focusing thumbwheel and pursed his lips. "I think our undercover officer is a bit nervous."

"Huh. Tucker can loosen her up. I don't see any loopholes. You?" Nolan hadn't been present in the latest debriefing, his priorities lay elsewhere knowing his partner would catch him up to speed.

"Nope. We've got this dead to rights, airtight. Which means your gut shouldn't be setting you in a fit. Unless it's Keiki herself? Or maybe the possible combination of Keiki and Tucker?"

"Fuck off. We're finally gonna put this shit behind us." Nolan exhaled as a communication received over his earpiece advised of a vehicle's approach in turning off the highway.

"Showtime." Coyote handed off the binoculars and picked up his rifle to follow the incoming vehicles through the scope. "I see Porter and a passenger. Can't see passengers in the back due to window tint."

Acknowledgment came in a murmured confirmation from another team across the meadow, also facing upwind.

"Leave it to the gator hunter to be a sharpshooter," Nolan muttered.

"Hey, if you don't hit 'em just right, the smaller shot bounces off their skull. The larger stuff makes a mess."

Below, Tucker and the doppelganger straightened but stayed together while Porter's sedan skidded to a stop twenty yards away.

The two used as bait remained out in the open, leaning against the pickup. College kids wouldn't have the tactical training or experience to take cover.

Porter stepped out of his vehicle, followed by three others. As expected, he'd come with backup.

At the same time, Tucker raised his head and took a stance in front of the undercover officer. "Afternoon, boys. Shall we wait for Harock to join us?" His hidden body camera offered a bird's eye view of the car's approach along with clear audio. The recorded conversation would be the evidence they needed.

"Who the fuck are you?" Porter's anger carried through the open space.

"Think of me as her manager or business partner if you want to make a deal."

"My deal is with Harock. We don't need you." Porter palmed his gun, as did his subordinates.

"Aw, don't be like that. Of course you do. You might have the list of our contacts, but you don't have their trust. If we disappear or die like the girls, no one's gonna deal with you."

Two of Porter's men pivoted to cover Harock's entrance, his Mercedes rolling to a stop a short distance away. The man was smart enough to park in a position offering cover and distance between himself and intended partner.

"Harock's on my side. I've got sights on him." Coyote's tone embodied the concentration of a tiger ready to pounce.

When Harock opened his door, he glared at Porter. "I don't think we need guns to negotiate, do you?" His posture stiffened as if in preparation to move. "You need the tech of Harock Industries, both the drones *and* our ability to track our devices. Those two kids are part of the deal."

"All right. But if you don't keep them in line, I'll take care of them the same way as the others. We aim to make money and expand our distribution with a safer drug." With everyone present, Porter and his minions lowered their weapons but didn't holster them.

Harock gritted his teeth in assessing his opponents, the need for revenge saturating his aura. One way or another, he wanted retribution against the monster who'd killed his little girl.

Nolan didn't need a close up of the CEO to read his intent. "Fuck. Head's up on Harock."

When Porter turned his attention to the PI, Harock pulled a pistol from his suit pocket and raised his arm.

Before the CEO mogul could pull the trigger, the report of Coyote's rifle filled the silence. Harock dropped his pistol and crumpled to the ground beside his vehicle.

"Harock's down but not out," Coyote murmured into his mic. "Repeat. Harock is down, and I no longer have a visual."

Through his mic, Nolan heard another agent, located closer to the meadow's entrance. "He's holding pressure to his shoulder and trying to get back in his car."

Simultaneously, the female officer and Tucker took up a shooter's stance as the PI stepped aside.

Coyote fired another shot close enough to Porter's thugs in warning.

At the same time, the SWAT leader announced their presence via megaphone from the tree line on the meadow's other side.

Both Porter and his men froze in assessing their options. The underlings dropped their weapons and raised their hands first, each glaring their hatred as they condemned Tucker and the undercover officer to a slow and painful death.

Once the cuffs had clicked in place, rights were read, and suspects seated behind cages of patrol cars, congratulations and a few back slaps dispersed much of the tension. Harock was transported via ambulance to the hospital with an officer in attendance.

The operation had gone off without a hitch, yet Nolan's gut churned. In counterpoint to his expectation, no one died.

Operations rarely go this smooth. "I'm gonna call Keiki."

Coyote snickered. "See if she has some new fashion statement ready to go. I liked the multicolor, but maybe something a little tamer would better suit your complexion."

"Jesus. I'm never gonna live it down."

"Never." Tucker picked that moment to join them in conversation.

"Not a word, man. Not a word." Nolan turned away in hopes of a more private talk. To his dismay, both Tucker and Coyote followed, their comments and chuckles filling his mind with promises of revenge.

"Aw, hell. She's not answering her phone. I know she's been glued to it since we left." Nolan disconnected and checked the app. "Damn it. It shows her still at the apartment at Carolyn's. Do you think she found your tracker, Nick?"

"Possible, but I doubt she'd be searching for anything now, not while waiting for news," Tucker replied then checked his own cell's screen.

"Doesn't feel right," Coyote murmured. "Let's go check."

"Tell them where we're going, Tucker." Anxiety pinched Nolan's throat and tightened his chest as he turned to rush through the woods to Coyote's truck. His partner remained tight on his heels.

"Maybe she's taking a shower or something."

Platitudes didn't disperse rising tension. "She'd answer if she could. Keys, I'll drive. You call and leave a message. She won't consider your voicemail an intrusion."

Coyote flipped the keys across the hood and tucked his rifle back in its case before dropping into his seat.

Nolan drummed his fingers on the console. "You're getting slow in your advanced age, gator man."

"And your itch for a young lady is making you cranky."

While the jibe hit home, Nolan didn't flinch as he gunned the engine and slewed on the dirt road's sharp turn. When he reached the highway, he stomped the accelerator.

"Try her phone again, Coyote. See if she answers." Fifteen minutes separated them from settling his nerves. He needed to see her in one piece, studying one of her devices or playing with Horace in the backyard.

"Still no answer. Maybe she went to see Carolyn and forgot her phone. The tracking device isn't that specific."

Nolan shook his head, telling his partner to shut up without uttering a word. "Call Tucker."

Silence during the drive served up a number of possibilities, all farfetched, yet deadly nonetheless.

When the truck skidded to a stop in a small nook seventy-five yards from Carolyn's driveway, nothing looked amiss in passing. "There's another access to the apartment through the home's second story, but it's hidden in a closet."

"You take that. I'll go up the stairs around back." Coyote suggested as he slid out of the vehicle and bolted into the woods.

The smallest clicks of the door's closing reverberated in Nolan's mind. A foghorn would sound quieter.

She wouldn't leave her phone behind. It didn't seem possible Porter's boss could associate Keiki with the current address in so short a time. It would've taken too much digging since there were no legal connections between himself and Carolyn.

Each step on leaf litter or small branch blared proof of his passing. Walking through woodland areas without making a sound was a myth perpetrated by daydreamers and Hollywood directors.

At the edge of the tree line, he approached the home from the bedroom side. His key unlocked the back door while the porch kept him hidden from view if anyone stood at Keiki's window. No squeak or rasp gave away his presence.

Inside, Carolyn startled at his sudden appearance. Nolan held his finger up in a cautioning motion.

Carolyn whispered. "I heard Horace barking a few minutes ago, but he stopped, so I didn't go over. She'd said she wanted to lie down and wait for your call."

The murmured words sent another chill down his spine. Pointing to her small parlor, he sent her on quiet steps to relative safety, miming her locking the door.

He took a deep breath.

Padding up the stairs, he headed to the spare bedroom and blind entrance to the apartment. Common sense dictated two exits. Now more than ever, he was glad this one was relatively hidden.

The barrel of his gun trembled until determination shored up his reserve with knowledge of her innate strength. Slight intermittent floorboard groans had given away his presence, so he shoved the door wide then stepped in and to the left.

In one glance, he surveyed her entire space. The bedroom was empty, as was the living room and kitchen. Pieces of a broken lamp lay in front of the couch. Coyote entered the kitchen.

His partner's look of disgust indicated another problem.

Nolan stepped forward to see his dog on the kitchen floor, lying flat out.

Coyote crouched to touch Horace's chest. The dog didn't stir with light pressure applied to his shoulder. His silent and still nature remained a mystery with no visual evidence of injury, until he used his handkerchief to remove a dart from the underside of the dog's neck.

"Damn. They came prepared. He's been tranqed. I'm guessing Keiki let him outside when he barked. They shot him then carried him up after snatching her." "Porter's boss has her now." Nolan looked around. "How'd he find her?"

"Maybe with this." Coyote picked up Nolan's cell phone off the floor, which had been taken after thugs knocked him unconscious and dumped in the woods. "How many times have you called Carolyn?"

"Damn. Probably once a week. They've been running down my contacts until they found her."

"Which is why it took them a while. Don't beat yourself up over it, Nolan."

"That doesn't tell us where she is now or *why* they took her. They've got to know we have Porter." Nolan nodded toward the broken lamp. "She put up a fight."

"Porter's boss is probably counting on him keeping his mouth shut, or providing a permanent solution before we can get a statement. Think about it. Without Keiki's testimony or Porter's admission, tying him to the drug ring will be difficult at best."

"He's protecting Porter. It was his backup plan." Nolan prayed they hadn't found the device and disabled it. For once, he was glad the apartment remained a little chilly. "I don't see her jacket. The tracker is in the lining. Check your app while I call Tucker."

Coyote retrieved his cell and pulled up the app. "Her tracker's active." Studying his cell's screen, he elaborated, "She's heading south on Route 23. We didn't miss them by much."

"Let's move it."

Coyote's flicked his glance to the dog, stalling him before pushing to his feet.

"Carolyn will call a friend to take him to the vet." En route to the truck, Nolan updated Tucker and Coyote reported the situation to their captain. From there, information would be coordinated.

"Call vice. See what Bitner can find out about the cartel's county holdings, if there are any known. Maybe they're going to Philly."

The flicker of light filtering through overhanging branches failed to keep pace with Nolan's escalating heart rate. He'd been the one to tuck Keiki away in the countryside. Having her taken from him once again was unbearable. *No wonder she has little faith in cops.*

"Hey, she's stationary. They're not going far and not taking her to the city." Coyote tapped his screen. "I've got coordinates."

Nolan glanced at the phone. "It looks like they're stopping in the middle of nowhere. Fuck!"

"They won't kill her until they figure out what she knows." Coyote reasoned then relayed information to their chief.

"They won't know we're following." Nolan thought of all the crime scenes he'd witnessed. Not many homicides took place in their remote locale, but they'd all been through the same training, all seen the after effects of torture during their classes. "If they'd wanted her dead, they wouldn't have taken her away."

His partner had enough sense to remain quiet for the drive despite Nolan's intermittent interjection of profanity or possible outcomes. Neither of them could guarantee Keiki still drew breath. "If they drugged her too, she may not be awake yet, and therefore unable to answer questions."

She might be buried alive if they want her to suffer.

Chapter Twenty-Eight

"How'd Tucker get here before us?" Nolan pulled in beside the PI's pickup. Desolate country roads driven didn't bode well for his girl.

She's not my girl. Yet.

"Likely, he was already on her trail while we were sneaking through the woods," Coyote murmured.

The PI leaned against his tailgate, maneuvering some kind of controller. He'd seen their approach and nodded.

"He's got a drone doing surveillance." His partner slipped out and sidled up to watch the screen over Tucker's shoulder.

"Back up will be here within fifteen. Glad you two could make it." Tucker concentrated on the screen.

Nolan edged closer to see. "Head count?"

"Four inside and two on perimeter checks. They haven't made a full sweep yet, so I don't know their timing." A gentle manipulation of the controls offered a different view sweeping the countryside. "She's unconscious. I think they drugged her."

The drone hovered lower over the treetops to disappear behind a thick trunk when a black-clad gunman passed. "Don't worry, this machine's real quiet, compliments of our girl."

"What's the inside look like?" Nolan ignored the PI's comment of familiarity.

Intricate maneuvering of the device existed outside his bailiwick. In her apartment, he'd noticed her controller far exceeded anything he'd seen on the open market.

"As best as I can tell—clear span. One room is walled off and has a window. It's closed and too high for me to gain access." Tucker tilted his head to the side. "Coyote, get the other drone off the front seat. I have a plan."

"O—kay." Coyote looked to Nolan, who merely nodded.

"Listen, guys, if we wait till the Calvary arrives, she's dead. You know it as well as I do."

"Coyote and I can remove the two perimeter guards, then go in."

"Good. There's one man, who I assume is their boss, in the room with her now. If you can take down the guards, I'll provide a distraction when the time comes."

"How?" Nolan wasn't sure he wanted to know.

"With Keiki's other drone. It's bigger." Coyote smiled as he held up the other device. It should be heavy enough to break glass, or at least get their attention."

The drone appeared similar, except for the barrel underneath with what appeared to be a receptacle capable of holding a small payload.

"I heard one of them call their boss Theo. We'll let him think this is loaded with the same drug used to kill Shelly. He might suspect one of his men of pulling a double cross. At the very least, it'll cause confusion, a distraction." Tucker settled the larger drone on the tailgate.

"There's nothing in that thing, right?" Nolan pointed to where the machine could hold cargo.

"No. Of course not. But they won't know that. I suggest you get going. You both still have your coms?"

"Yeah." Since they hadn't made it back to the station, both detectives were prepared.

"Let me finish showing you the lay of the land. I'll keep in touch with both, but I will only have eyes on one." Tucker looked to Nolan, who pointed to Coyote.

"I'll take the south side, the land is flatter. Coyote, you'll need advance warning before taking your man on the north." Nolan wouldn't admit it, but his approach would take less time and put him in position sooner.

Both detectives palmed their guns and headed out.

Each tick of time projected another scenario where Nolan failed to protect his witness. In his heart, he recognized she was so much more.

As promised, the PI kept them informed of the guards' positions while making their way around the perimeter.

Nolan ducked down to let the first sentry pass unscathed. Coyote wasn't yet in position.

It'd be the one free pass given today.

The building squatted in the center of a small clearing with a twenty-yard buffer of unkempt grass.

According to the PI, the next guard's approach would occur in less than five minutes. It was the longest wait of his life, filled with missed opportunities and accusing silences.

A small deer trail leading around a pine tree provided cover and would offer the shortest approach to the personnel door. He gauged the timing and judged his distance, controlling his breathing when again hearing the scuffle of boots through weeds.

The second man.

Instead of rimming the edge of the woods, the guard strolled too far out for a quick approach. A shot would alert his comrades inside; hence, options were limited without getting closer. Waiting for the next pass for a better position wasn't going to happen.

Low hanging branches of a pine tree offered visual obscurity but no cover from rifle shots. He still wore his vest, which wouldn't protect his head or the rest of his body.

Instead of offering his enemy a target, he pulled back the slide of his gun, the sound distinctive enough in the still morning air. The bastard halted in his tracks.

"Drop the weapon or die. Your choice." Nolan waited, praying for some good karma to come his way.

The guard stood ten feet away.

A rifle slid from his grasp before he held his hands up. The handle of a Glock 19 peeked above the rig attached to his belt.

"Face the building and forget the pistol." Nolan closed the distance and with his left hand, retrieved his handcuffs. He had no tape to silence the guard or keep him from sending up an alarm. A piece of torn cloth would have to do.

Time was precious. Through his mic, he received updates on Coyote's position and the remaining guard.

"Hands behind your back. Now." Perspiration dotted his forehead and slid down his neck. An update on Coyote acknowledged success in subduing the second perimeter guard.

Stepping within striking distance, Nolan slapped the first cuff on with more force than necessary, anticipating a reaction.

Experience taught him to be prepared for his prisoner to twist around.

The following maneuver wasn't taught in training but had saved more than one officer's life. Instead of hanging onto the attached cuff, Nolan let it go and reared back with his gun hand, still holding the weapon.

The bastard wheeled around but crumpled with a solid whack to his head. Turnabout was fair play.

Handy in any situation.

After cuffing and dragging his prisoner into the woods, he scooped up the rifle and spare pistol. Using the gunman's own belt, Nolan secured him to a sturdy poplar. Removing his jacket provided material to bind his feet, at least long enough to rescue Keiki. Dirty socks stuffed in his mouth with a strip of shirt holding it secure made for a nice quiet touch.

In the meantime, Tucker advised of Coyote's success in subduing the other guard adding, "There's one entrance, guys. I've got the puffer drone in position, so as soon as you engage the ones inside, I'll hover it in sight and get the last one's attention."

"Anything for cover?" Nolan asked.

"There are tables both left and right once you enter, but I can't tell if they are fiber board or metal. Sorry. Choices are slim and pot luck today."

Nolan tapped his com and bolted for the personnel door. Once there, he whispered his question while waiting for Coyote to round the far corner of the structure. "Is she still out?"

The quiet murmur didn't conceal the PI's escalating anger. "She's waking up. He's slapping her face."

In the distance, the sound of multiple engines coming to a halt announced the impending arrival of backup.

Tucker's warning supplied motivation. "Lots of company. I suggest you two move your slowpoke asses."

The first sign of uncertainty furrowed Coyote's brow after reaching the opposite side of the door. He huffed several quiet breaths and gripped the handle then after he mouthed the words, *"One, two, three,"* he yanked the door wide.

Light spilled into the darkened interior.

Wasting no time, Nolan burst inside and dove left. Coyote barreled right. Each had their weapons up and had taken down one adversary before the other two engaged.

Unfortunately, those two had flipped a table on its side for cover. They were metal.

Nolan and Coyote did the same.

Chapter Twenty-Nine

Keiki blinked to clear the fog from her mind and concentrate on the mouth yelling foul obscenities inches from her nose. Pain narrowed her concentration to internal sensations, agony exploding in her head.

The strike of an open palm caused less pain than a fist would have, but judging by the escalating force behind each impact, the latter would soon occur.

She expected to see Porter's face, not the stranger with a scar running from the corner of his eye to his temple.

Someone had bound her wrists in front of her with duct tape. A shorter piece lay stuck to her jacket flap, accounting for the pain in her lips.

Brief assessment put her on a thin cot in a small block room. Light streaming in through a narrow window and visible treetops suggested the location an outbuilding, but not Harock's hideaway. The angle was wrong and air too fresh.

"You will not be my downfall, *puta*. I've invested everything in this!" Her captor leaned closer to deliver the full force of his rage.

Judging by his position, he wasn't much taller, but carried a solid hundred and fifty pounds more than her slight frame. His weight alone could crush her if she couldn't finagle her hands free.

Tucker had taught her the trick of ripping tape from a standing position—holding one's hands overhead and swinging them down with all the force possible.

"Tell me where that flash drive is. Did your police friends find it?" Spittle flew from his mouth.

Shouted words made no sense until her mind layered in the familiar accent; a different voice but the same underlying dialect. Details of her abduction came crashing through her thoughts.

When he raised his hand high, she tried to tuck her chin to chest and roll her shoulders forward.

The strike would include a closed fist.

Hesitating, the bastard gritted his teeth after looking over his shoulder. Sudden successive pops from outside the door diverted his attention.

Gunfire. Nolan found me.

Her mind couldn't work out the logistics since she didn't know how long she'd been unconscious. She needed a minute to clear her thoughts.

"You're still looking for the formula? Gabby didn't give it to you?" The thought of her friend trying to do the right thing near the end burned the back of Keiki's eyes.

"No. Even after Porter tied her hands, the bitch found a way to defeat him in the end. She lunged forward onto the knife he held at her throat."

The agonizing punch twisted Keiki's head to the side. Her vision blurred. Vestiges of drugs preventing her from focusing also produced nausea which threatened to eject burning acid.

"The cops have the flash drive." She spit the words out seconds before another impact left pain graying the periphery of her vision.

Maniacal glee overtook his mien in an instant. "Well then, I have no use for you."

His hands spanned the circumference of her neck and squeezed.

Her thoughts went to Nolan, Coyote, and her departed friends, the latter, she wasn't ready to join. Even Horace wagged his tail at her from the corners of her mind.

Wrapping one hand over the other fist with knuckles pointing out, she formed a reinforced wedge shape to jam at his throat. Her position and weakened state produced little more than an irritant.

He smiled, and in that study of evil, she saw her own death minutes before help could arrive.

A crash from above and the tinkle of glass snapped her attacker's attention to the window, now broken. He straightened to decipher the interruption.

The distraction gained her the time to curl her legs into a ball. When he twisted back to face her, she kicked out and shoved him back.

A few feet gained, allowed her to stand upright and perform Tucker's maneuver to free her hands. She expected him to pull out a gun, or at least a knife, so was surprised when he strode to the object which interrupted his current undertaking like she were a helpless babe and no threat.

"Damn. Interrupted by a drone."

His grin dictated he judged her intelligent enough to not open the door while the firefight outside continued.

At least in here I have a fighting chance.

Collecting the device now lying useless on the cement, he snapped off each of the motors then tossed it back to the floor. His booted foot stomped the metal body and reduced her work to pieces.

"Now, where were we? Oh, yes, eliminating evidence against my men."

"You don't have the formula." The flash drive equaled the ultimate bargaining chip in her mind. He was playing with her and would continue to do so as long as the guns signaled the fight in progress.

"Ah, but you know how it is. Evidence in lock-up goes missing all the time. At least I know its location. That's all I needed. I'll even waltz out of the holding cell with it sitting in my pocket."

"You'll spend time in jail for kidnapping."

"My men will have me out and on a plane before they know I'm missing." He rolled his shoulders and stretched his neck as if preparing for a much-anticipated event.

Keiki's gaze flicked around the small room but found no suitable weapon other than the remains of her smashed drone.

His grin widened when he kicked several pieces to the side. "I do love it when they struggle. Please, don't hesitate."

She didn't know many self-defense moves. She was a college kid geared toward other pursuits.

His leer broadcast intent to kill, with as much suffering as time allowed. When he rushed forward, she dove to the side and snatched up a broken metal arm. It was one she'd put together, six inches in length and a quarter inch round.

Shuffling steps announced his approach from behind. With no time to stand, Keiki rolled to her back.

When he reached for her throat again, she had a feeble plan, and prayed it could save her life.

* * * *

It'd been at least four minutes since he and Coyote had rushed inside and engaged in a firefight. Lack of planning could cost Keiki her life.

The exterior door banged open, and reinforcements rushed in to take cover.

The last combatant lowered his weapon and raised his hands at the same time his cohort dropped to the ground. "I'm done. I give."

Crimson bloomed on the downed man's chest and froth bubbled from his mouth. His eyes closed on a cough then opened to stare into oblivion.

Instead of cuffing the last gunman, Nolan nodded at his partner, leaving him to deal with the prisoner.

"I'll be there in a sec." Coyote moved forward and gestured for the officers to secure the area.

It was too quiet. From beyond the door, the shouting had stopped. Nolan darted toward the room and tested the knob.

Locked.

A murmur through his earbuds advised the drone had been destroyed, hence no visual access to give him a clue as to what currently transpired inside. Nolan took a deep breath, rammed a new magazine in his Glock after ejecting the old.

The interior door was aluminum, sitting in a frame which wouldn't withstand more than a few solid kicks.

It only took one.

Breaching the room granted a view that froze him mid-step, a smile spreading across his face.

Keiki stood over her kneeling captor, her hatred locked onto her opponent, her frame tight. In her hand, she held a sharp piece of metal less than an inch from the prick's left eye.

Taking stock of her condition, he evaluated the bruises forming on her cheeks and the rips in her shirt. The possibility of them raping her hadn't occurred to him until that exact second.

Rage flooded his mind. If he didn't get a grip on his emotions, they would feed her own and goad her into an action affecting the rest of her life.

"Don't do it, Keiki." He didn't step forward and didn't make a sound as the air left his lungs in a *whoosh*. "If there's a need, I'll see to it." Those words, spoken with casual restraint, committed his soul to a path he hadn't determined with rational thought but meant just the same.

"He killed Gabby and Shelly, and probably many more," she seethed.

Nolan holstered his weapon but remained at the door, blocking the entrance for other officers. The hand tapping his shoulder signaled his partner standing at his back. Coyote wouldn't allow anyone to interfere.

In prior circumstances, when stressed, her brain flicked a switch to flippancy. If her mind went there, and he couldn't provide a redirect, he wouldn't succeed in talking her off the emotional ledge.

Nolan had dealt with hostile victims before, but never to one who owned a piece of his heart. The right words now failed him when he needed them most.

"You don't want this on your conscience. Trust me, Keiki," Coyote's voice rang clear, and dipped into the realm of southern gent.

"How do you know what I want?"

Nolan's mouth dried, his fear for her an emotional wood chipper grinding his gut. If she killed this man, it would destroy her.

Coyote was the one to delve through the murky waters of revenge. "Keiki, I was in the military. I don't talk about it much, because it eats away at me every waking moment. I wake up nearly every night to screams and the sound of a single shot, then fall asleep hours later dreading their return. You don't want that. I know. Please. Drop the weapon."

"He said he's gonna walk out of his cell with the formula in his pocket." Her hand shifted closer.

"No, Keiki. He's not." Nolan's thoughts stuttered at his partner's confession. He'd known Coyote had enlisted out of high school and served overseas. That was the extent of his knowledge.

It was difficult to witness the slight twitch of the dirtball's mouth and hard glint in his eyes. The nonverbal proclamation declared the war just beginning with a pledge to even the score.

"My new best friend here claims to be the local kingpin. Says he can do whatever he wants to anyone and get away with it. I think it's time for him to experience a little of what he's given." Keiki patted the leader's hairless dome. The grin sliding into place equaled a ball-shriveler and revealed cracks in her reality. "He needs a little convincing."

"He's full of shit." Nolan soft-stepped sideways so she had full view of the thug and the exit where Coyote stood guard.

Keiki's gaze slammed into him long enough for him to recognize the war waging within.

"If I let him live, he's gonna kill us. Maybe I deserve it, but you and Coyote don't."

"I call bullshit on that one, kiddo." Coyote shook his head at someone in the main room. He wouldn't budge until his partner gave him the all clear.

"Keiki, we've gone over the evidence. We've proven you had nothing to do with, and no knowledge of, the mess entangling your friends. You're clear."

"Maybe I shouldn't be. If not for my drones, Shelly wouldn't be dead. Her father wanted a sideline empire."

Sweat marbled Theo's bald pate. Pure hatred emanated from every pore. "You're a dead man, pig. Along with your little whore."

Her muscles bunched.

"Keiki, don't." Panic produced a thin film of sweat on Nolan's brow. "Keiki?"

His heart beat harshly in his ears, the sound a death toll. If she carried out her threat, a part of her innocence would also die. "We have unfinished business, you and I. I've even marked your graduation date on my calendar. When that time comes, I don't want the specter of this asshole between us."

Keiki's concentration broke for a split second.

"Your man's right, ya know. Not to mention—that'll be hard to work out if bars stand between you two," Coyote added.

Nolan glared at his partner.

"He wanted to humiliate me. I think I'll strip him naked, take a picture with a close up of his shriveled nards, and post it on social media. What d'ya think, handsome? Will folks need a magnifier to find anything interesting?"

Red infused her captor's face with spit seeping from the corner of his mouth. "You're dead. You just don't know it yet."

"Maybe I'll take a video of you doing jumping jacks and post it on a 'Where's Waldo' site." Keiki managed a humorless giggle and lasered a look on her captive. "Where you're going, they'll be dicks swinging everywhere."

"She's heading for deep water, man. Reel her in," Coyote murmured low.

Her shoulders dipped a little, contradicting the energy and resolve coiled deep inside; a cobra preparing to strike.

Another smooth step put Nolan in position to deal with Theo if he attempted to make a move.

"I've got plastic cuffs here. I'm going to apply them while we decide what to do with this piece of shit, okay?" Without waiting, Nolan retrieved the restraints and zipped them around her prisoner.

"Ooh, I hear in jail, some get real cozy with all kinds of inventive and kinky restraints. Shall I tell you what I've heard? It'll give you something new to contemplate." Something maniacal twinkled in her eyes.

"Nolan..." Coyote warned.

"Okay. He's secure now, Keiki. See? He's not going anywhere."

Preference dictated she relinquish the weapon of her own free will. Wild glints infiltrating her eyes mandated that time quickly passing.

Her body tensed further when Nolan inched forward to get close enough to snatch the makeshift weapon.

Anger and pain clouded her judgement at a time she needed clarity. In her heart, she'd know the right thing to do—if her inner demons didn't goad her to draw blood and take a life.

"She's right. I will be free, and when I am, I'll be coming for you both." The prick smirked when he glanced over his shoulder.

"The only thing that's gonna be free is your ass, dickweed." Her grin widened. "I'd even be willing to visit wherever you're going. I'll spread the word and make sure your future boyfriends don't use lube."

Coyote cringed and rubbed his chin. "Damn. Nolan, your girl sure has a charmingly brutal side to her. I like it."

Nolan sneered. "He's done either way. The how doesn't matter to me. He'll be kept busy."

In hopes of nudging the situation to conclusion, Nolan shoved the prisoner to his side and away from Keiki's temptation, then watched as she shifted position to hover with her weapon ready.

"C'mon, Keiki. Give me the shiv," Nolan cajoled.

"Hey, kid. It's time to go home." Coyote's tone slid deeper into his down-home dialect as if he were sitting at a backyard barbeque.

"Keiki, listen to me, and I swear no one will pass this threshold until we're finished talking." Coyote glared a warning over his shoulder. "I've been in your shoes, and took a wrong turn. Overseas, my buddy and I'd just cleared a building and walked out the back door. It was late and we were damned tired."

Several rapid blinks cleared Coyote's eyes. "The shot came out of nowhere and threw Luke back against the building. I was so fucking stunned. I fired in the direction the shot came from and got lucky. I knew I'd hit the bastard when he screamed."

A second passed before Coyote continued. "Turns out, the guy was about my age. I'd hit him in the leg. He'd dropped his gun and just stared at me. Waiting."

"What happened?" It was Nolan who murmured the question.

"I remember looking back at Luke, the way his eyes stared up into... nothing. We were coming home in a week and had made so many plans." Coyote willed Keiki to understand.

"I heard a shot and ducked thinking the bastard wasn't alone. I thought I was gonna die. I waited. When nothing happened, I looked down again. The kid had a bullet hole right between the eyes. I don't recall pulling the trigger, but no one else was around. I've relived that scene every day since."

Silence engulfed them all with the admission.

"I can't tell you how many times I've woken up in a sweat and wished I could go back in time. I'd find a way to not pull that trigger. I swear on my brother's life, I would."

"You were at war. This is different, more complicated."

One hand kept her weapon close enough that the arrogant thug couldn't move and survive With the other, she rubbed his smooth head. "I wonder if douche bag here can still get a hairline fracture.

Shall we test that theory?"

Coyote picked up the gauntlet. "He won't be able to play volleyball in the prison yard 'cuz inmates will swing at his head."

"Lame, partner. And not helping." *She needs to engage, not a push further out in looney land.*

Coyote's voice dropped further. "No, Keiki. It's not complicated. It's very simple. It's about taking a life and having one moment haunt your every waking and sleeping moment. It would define the rest of your days. If my enemy's weapon had been pointed at me, I wouldn't endure sleepless nights and personal demons that won't let go. But he didn't. He had dropped his gun."

Background noise from the outer room came into focus and consisted of officers reading Miranda rights and shuffling steps over concrete.

"C'mon, Keiki We've got to work things out. In my mind's eye, I've already cleared out the other half of my garage for your car."

Her hesitation gave him hope in continuing. "We don't want this hanging over our heads and coming between us. This isn't the way." He'd reached the point of using any advantage to help reboot her emotional state, but also realized he meant every word.

A long, low growl erupted from her chest, the sound of ultimate pain. Her emotions had run the gauntlet, draining her energy and leaving animal instinct in its wake.

Nolan was close enough to see the shiver of fear in her prisoner's eyes along with the perspiration in the cleft of his chin. Alternating expressions included hatred and fear.

An internal sigh of relief remained trapped when he viewed a tear trailing down her cheek. It was the break for which he'd waited and prayed to see.

In a silent bid for her to yield, he held out his hand.

A lifetime of possibilities flashed through his thoughts while he waited.

Her fingers tightened on the metal, and she crouched to get closer to her prey. "I should do it. I really should. But this is me, being better than you, asshole." She stood and tossed the metal aside.

In the next instant, Nolan urged her close and wrapped his arms around her, not caring if others saw and judged him.

"Well, guys," Coyote's words paused on a dramatic sigh, "I guess we all know where Tinkerbell's heart lies."

Smothered chuckles erupted from those entering, Nolan's fierce scowl be damned.

"Give it up, Knotty. You're stuck with it," Keiki teased then snuggled closer and buried her face against his chest.

"Seriously? I think I prefer Tink." The warmth of her body seeping into his frame settled some deep and primitive need for the connection he'd fought since their first meeting.

She may not believe it now, but one day, he'd stake his claim and not let go unless she walked away. First, she needed time to grieve, to grow, and to figure out her life.

In the meantime, he'd be there to listen and help.

Of their own accord, his fingers smoothed the tangles in her hair, softer than anything he'd ever imagined. Minutes passed in wordless silence, their quiet interaction a testament to mutual need.

When her eyes fluttered closed, he rested his chin on the crown of her head and sighed his relief. It was homecoming for his heart, his mind, and his soul.

Where's—" she began.

"We got them. We got 'em all, Keiki." If he could envelop her in bubble wrap to keep her safe, he would. They both knew the score, though. No matter what measures were taken, the chance existed for Theo to escape and make good on his threats. Someday.

Coyote's southern rumble lacked his usual unreserved undertone. "She okay? EMS is outside waiting for an all clear to enter. I'll give you another few minutes if you need it."

When Theo grunted, Nolan nodded toward the prisoner. "How about getting this piece of shit out of here?"

"He said he was going to kill me, real slow, and make you and your partner watch." Keiki rubbed her nose while uniformed officers hoisted the prisoner to his feet and thrust him out the door.

"Only in his dreams." Nolan inched back, needing to separate before he lost the ability to let her go. She clutched him tighter.

"You still don't understand, do you?" Quiet words meant for his ears and no one else's.

Her look held more awareness than he could fathom.

Underestimating her wouldn't just cost him his heart, but perhaps hers, too. He was a patient man. He could wait.

The lightest stroke of her fingers across his nape closed the distance between them.

Her lips, so light and warm, breezed across his own with a contact that scorched him to core level. Understanding came with the caress along his jaw and down his chest. It was a claiming, as firm as any commitment he'd ever imagined, one that declared she owned him body and soul.

When she pulled back, he almost clutched her tighter, needing the contact, the affirmation. Yet the look in her eyes expressed everything he needed to hear, without words, without touch, simply understanding.

"You can't argue that we're too different. You know that, don't you?"

"Jesus. Our worlds *are* so far apart." Despite his weak attempt to justify his position, in reality, he'd already conceded, in spirit if not physically. From the corner of his eye, he saw the PI evaluating the situation.

"No. You've just spent too much time alone. Sometimes that makes people... eccentric."

"You mean squirrely, don't you?" His sigh ushered out the last of his resistance. "You need to finish school first, and get a job."

"I have a, oh, I guess I don't anymore."

"Sounds like you're gonna branch out on your own, kid. I can help with that." Tucker snickered under Nolan's glare.

"I have an idea."

Her look spoke of mischievous pranks and embarrassing consequences, and he groaned with the thought of his colleagues attaching an even more embarrassing moniker. "As long as it doesn't involve glitter, okay?"

"I also have a calendar. I'll mark graduation day as D day."

Her smile held none of the innocence he knew existed in her heart.

Epilogue

"This isn't exactly what I had in mind when I suggested a relaxing evening." Nolan sat on his patio, waiting for the rest of his family to arrive.

Tucker and Keiki sat on one side of the picnic bench while Coyote fiddled with his cell on the other. Three bags of chips surrounded a bowl of dip at the table's center.

"Hey. I need a job. I don't graduate until May."

"No. You don't *need* a job. You may *want* one, but you don't need one. Carolyn cut your rent until *after* you graduate and are gainfully employed. I'll cover utility bills and anything else you need."

"She is employed, Garnett. She's working part-time for me." Tucker took a swig of his coke and nabbed a few more chips, tossing them on his plate before spooning up guacamole.

"She needs to concentrate on her schoolwork, not peep through keyholes and risk her neck on one foolhardy venture or another." Seeing Tucker and Keiki side by side, poring over a map and discussing surveillance options, raised the hair on his arms.

"You can't fly a drone over the middle of a hundred acre piece of private property to take photos." Coyote shook his head as if realizing keeping the two out of trouble was going to be a full-time effort.

"Well, not if you want to take said photos into court." Tucker used his index finger to draw a circle around his target's property.

"You've got to learn the laws if you want to avoid complications," Nolan declared and flipped the last of the steaks on the grill.

"He's right." Tucker grinned then waggled his brows. "Monitoring someone in the middle of a forest entails a different set of rules than if you're on a city street. Even then, you get into gray areas such as, does the homeowner have a solid fence which would suggest a desire for privacy. Is the house one story or two? How far is it from a public road?" Tucker tapped the map again. "Many variables. However, we are responsible for knowing whose land we're on or flying over when obtaining confirmation of infidelity, insurance fraud, or whatever."

"You guys put a tracker on me without my knowledge." Keiki tilted her head side to side then added, "Not like I'm going to complain since it saved my life. I still don't understand how Theo and his goons found me."

"They got Nolan's work phone. We'd figured since it was registered to the department and not in his name, they wouldn't track you. They had to have traced and monitored all the contacts. One, of course, was Carolyn." Nolan hated reminding her of the ordeal, but fear for her safety was still too close to the surface.

"Then I'll learn. I'll get better. Maybe I'll decide to become a private investigator." Hiking up her eyebrows signaled her insincerity.

"You don't have three years of law enforcement experience," Coyote reminded her.

"No, but I work for Tucker."

"You have to be at least twenty-five to get a license, and you won't be twenty-one for a few more weeks," Nolan added. "Oh, and for the record, I think you've lost your marbles."

"Maybe there's a hole in the bag and I've lost a few, but I still do okay." She smiled at his darkening scowl, obviously remembering his promise and their unconsummated commitment.

They weren't idle words she'd spoken. He'd witnessed the determination in every line of her body, but it would not wear down his resistance. His assertion she needed time to let the dust settle hadn't sat well with her. No, she'd narrowed her eyes and smiled.

He'd sweat bullets, knowing her power over him entitled her to liberties he'd never granted another soul.

The southerner grinned then stood to snag his ringing cell from his pocket. "Glad that focus isn't lasered on me. It'd make me a bit nervous." Turning away, he answered the phone while ambling out into the backyard.

Nolan groaned, but inside, his heart swelled. He'd endure cold showers and sleepless nights for a few months, but realized she was well worth the wait.

Coyote returned, his face pale and murmured words unintelligible. His sitting at the picnic bench equated to gravity's pull more than conscious control.

"Hey, partner. What's up?" Nolan had never seen his frame so tense or the vacant look in his gaze.

A silent minute followed when his partner held a finger up, collecting himself. His other hand tightened on his phone until a cracking sound broke the stillness. "I need to take a leave of absence."

The End

Thank you for picking up your copy of A Critical Tangent. If you've enjoyed it, please consider leaving a short review.

Turn the page for an excerpt from *Pivotal Decisions,* book two in the Moonlight and Murder Series.

Join Reily's newsletter to catch the first glimpse of the next book and know when it goes live. Plus, get exclusive content for free. Reilygarrett.com

Pivotal Decisions
Moonlight and Murder
Book Two

Pain flashed through his entire lower leg, followed by a soothing calm and warmth flooding his brain. Confusion over conflicting sensations diminished with the tingling warmth spreading throughout his chest.

His mind fought to remember what he'd intended to do. He recalled walking to the kitchen, then... sitting on the side of his bed. His feet weren't chilled from the cool tile floor, nor did he recognize the scene from the window.

He lived in a modest contemporary rancher, surrounded by two acres of St. Augustine Grass. The closest neighbor enjoyed a Spanish Revival house with a low-pitched tile roof, half round arched doors and windows with adobe brick.

He saw none of it.

Instead, miles of beautiful flowerbeds with blooms that shouldn't appear in December sprawled over lush hills. Rolling hills, another thing absent from southern Florida. Despite the conflict, he couldn't muster the energy to look away. Inability to turn his head lost meaning in the wake of the scents wafting through the open window.

He experienced the soft, sweet taste of each blossom despite not tasting them. Bird song encouraged him to linger and ignore any unpleasant sensation. No obvious reason to move or feel concern existed.

A slight tug at his head reminded him he hadn't picked up his glasses, yet he could see each flower petal in the distance with crystal clarity. The pad of each fingertip tingled with their softness.

Every cell of his body felt cocooned in a warm fuzzy blanket.

His mind flashed to a different scene. Before him, the soft ocean surf lapped at his feet, the sand warm under his toes. Pungent scents of salt and something undefinable filled his nostrils and he briefly held his breath until it passed. Calm, balmy breezes whispered through nearby feathery palms and whisked them away.

If he died and was lucky enough to pass through the pearly gates, this is where he wanted to stay. Life's concerns drifted away on a sea of contented bliss.

He briefly closed his eyes in ecstasy then found himself standing on the deck of a large ship. The rolling motion forced him to grab the railing on either side of him and clutch tight. Knowledge that there should only be one in front of him didn't prevent his grasp for dear life.

Something tugged against his lower leg and back, he thought to rub it, then decided it wasn't necessary as his spirit drifted above the beauty before him.

Nirvana was confirmed in the next flash.

He'd never witnessed the beauty of a gentle snowfall. Silent flakes floated to the ground covered in a white blanket.

A peculiar numbness infiltrated his lower legs, followed by a lightheadedness not overcome by the pleasant tingling at the base of his skull.

Perhaps he'd take a nap and let the strange sensations pass.

Reily's Books

Romantic Thrillers
McAllister Justice Series
Tender Echoes
Digital Velocity
Bound By Shadows
Inconclusive Evidence
Carbon Replacements
Shattered Reflections
Remnants of Evil

Moonlight and Murder Series
A Critical Tangent
Pivotal Decisions

Erotic Romance
Carnal Series
Carnal Beginnings
Carnal Innocence
Bending Fate
Carnal Whispers: Mind Stalker
Carnal Obsession: His Heart's Prisoner

Paranormal Romance
Immortal Lovers Series
Unholy Alliance
Blood Union

Standalone paranormal romance
Tiago

About Reily

Reily is a West Coast girl transplanted to the opposite shore. When she's not working with her dogs, you can find her curled up with a book or writing her next story. Past employment as an ICU nurse, private investigator, and work in the military police has given her countless experiences in a host of different environments to add a real world feel to her fiction.

Over time, and several careers, many incidents have flavored the plots of her stories. Man's cruelty and ingenuity for torment and torture is boundless, not contained by an infinite imagination. Witnessing the after effects of a teenager mugged at knifepoint for a pair of tennis shoes, or an elderly woman stabbed repeatedly with a screwdriver for no apparent reason, left an indelible impression that will forever haunt her subconscious. In counterpoint, she has observed a woman stop her vehicle in severe, snowy weather to offer her *own* winter coat to a stranger, a teenager wearing a threadbare hoodie. Life's diversities are endless.

Though her kids are her life, writing is Reily's life after. The one enjoyed after the kids are in bed or after they're in school and the house is quiet. This is the time she kicks back with laptop and lapdog to give her imagination free rein.

In reading, take pleasure in a mental pause as you root for your favorite hero/heroine and bask in their accomplishments, then share your opinions of them over a coffee with your best friend (even if he's four-legged). Life is short. Cherish your time.